She most definitely would not be his wife.

"You are going home, Miss Parker."

She lifted her chin, determination etching her brow. "That isn't an option, Mr. Garrett. And until you are my husband, you have no authority over me." Her eyes turned softer. "Besides, Oak Grove seems a nice town."

With that look, she tugged on heartstrings he'd believed severed long ago. He needed a good night's rest. And he needed to treat her like a double-headed moccasin and stay far away.

"Even some men do not have the fortitude to survive here." And not with the passel of misbehaved children he wrangled.

"Then it is providence that I am not a man." She picked up her pace. "So how soon before we are married?"

He gritted his teeth. "There will be no marriage, Miss Parker."

He jerked to a halt with the force of her boots digging into the mud.

"You're not understanding me, Mr. Garrett. I came here to be a wife, and a wife I will be." She poked his chest. "Your wife."

Christina Rich lives in northeast Kansas. Her passion for stories comes from a rich past of reading and digging through odd historical tidbits, where she finds a treasure trove of inspiration. She loves photography, art, ancestry research and, of course, writing happy-ever-afters.

Books by Christina Rich

Love Inspired Historical

The Guardian's Promise
The Warrior's Vow
Captive on the High Seas
The Negotiated Marriage
The Marshal's Unexpected Bride

Visit the Author Profile page at LoveInspired.com.

The Marshal's Unexpected Bride

CHRISTINA RICH

LOVE INSPIRED
INSPIRATIONAL ROMANCE

LOVE INSPIRED®
INSPIRATIONAL ROMANCE

Recycling programs
for this product may
not exist in your area.

ISBN-13: 978-1-335-47475-9

The Marshal's Unexpected Bride

Copyright © 2021 by Christina Rich

This edition published by arrangement with Harlequin Books S.A.

For questions and comments about the quality of this book, please contact us
at CustomerService@Harlequin.com.

Love Inspired
22 Adelaide St. West, 40th Floor
Toronto, Ontario M5H 4E3, Canada
www.LoveInspired.com

Printed in U.S.A.

My little children, let us not love in word,
neither in tongue; but in deed and in truth.
—*1 John* 3:18

Carolyn Bolen, thank you for sharing your beautiful Flint Hills with me, for the back road adventures and precarious stops along the way so I could take photos. Much love to you and Popeye.

Brian, there is not enough space to write what deserves to be said about your preciousness. Thank you for your isms and scumptions, for the country drives, hand-holding, Shedi time, front room two-stepping and snuggles while watching romances. Thank you for encouraging me to be myself and to chase my dreams. Thank you for cooking and doing dishes while I write and do homework. Thank you for filling my heart with laughter and, most of all, love.

Chapter One

Oak Grove, Kansas
1868

Penelope Parker sank her fingers into Harvey's long golden fur and scratched the top of his head as she marveled at the subtle change of scenery. Favorable weather had finally met with her plans. Favorable enough for the coach to finally depart Topeka, nearly a month later than expected. However, that had been days ago. Long days of bumping into her travelling companions' elbows and wide girths. The constant jostling had rattled her teeth and left her with head pain a tincture had completely failed to dissolve. The momentary discomfort would be worth it if her destination meant she'd finally have a family of her own, not one ready-made or one that promised to end poorly. Most likely with her buried in the church graveyard next to her predecessors. Swollen, impassable waterways, thanks to torrential rainstorms, gave way to a winding, narrow path coated with dust and surrounded by craggy hills topped with lush green rugs. She stretched her toes. The emerald softness called to her aching feet, encapsulated by hard leather shoes and for hours on end. She rubbed Harvey's soft ears between her fingers, willing him to sense her apologies for being bounced around, without even a moment's halt to relieve himself.

The poor little fellow had given up his anxious panting shortly after their departure and had lain limp on her lap for most of the journey. However, if she were to be truthful, she'd have to admit that her continuous petting was more to bring her comfort than him. Since the moment she'd decided to rebel against her father's wishes, she'd had a terrible knot in her stomach. Well, most of the time. There had been small moments of peace and equanimity. Such as when she'd taken her morning tea and drawn in air unmolested by refuse and pollution. Her father might have a king's ransom at his disposal, but he preferred living amid the hustle and bustle to further his business transactions and fill his coffers.

She leaned into the upholstery and sighed. Her travels may have abused her body, but she no longer carried the stiffness of keeping her posture in perfect societal form, as had been expected from the time she'd entered a schoolroom.

Memories of those painful lessons sent gooseflesh over her skin. She'd perfected the slight tilt of her head, a posture purely acceptable in social circles. However, she'd learned quickly if the angle tilted too much, the books balanced on her head would tumble to the floor, smashing her toes. Soon the switch would find the backs of her legs, and she'd be forced to try again.

If it hadn't been for Mrs. Blackwell's authoritarian

lessons, Penelope would have never survived the many balls and dinners forced upon her. The facade she'd been forced to display had served her well in the face of adversity and even more so in the midst of vicious gossip. Mrs. Blackwell had taught her to always hold her head high and shoulders back, even when ambushed with raw eggs. The training quickly taught her that one misstep would be met with punishment. Which was why, since her first social outing, Penelope armored herself with aloofness when necessary, kept to the shadows when possible, and looked forward to the refuge of her bedroom and the downy pillow that muffled her sobs.

She blinked and reviewed the days since she'd run away from home. Not once had she cried or fretted over her posture. Not once had she cared whether or not anyone disapproved of her.

Would that change once she arrived at her destination? Would her future husband find her lacking and be a hard man like her father and Mr. Wallace? Nervous excitement had been her companion since they'd departed Topeka, a slight intermission between her life in St. Louis and Oak Grove. She knew what she'd left behind, but she had no idea what to expect going forward.

The coach had been engulfed by a red cloud of dirt for the past two hours, and as they drew closer to Oak Grove, she was beginning to wonder about the rash decision she'd made to leave St. Louis. She'd left the familiarity of civilization and home to be bathed in several layers of filth. The perspiration sliding down her neck and pooling in the crook of her elbow no doubt had turned the dust to muddy rivulets.

She glanced at the other occupants of the coach.

They all seemed unbothered and quite accustomed to the conditions. Penelope and Harvey had no such experience, as they'd never traveled outside St. Louis. She had absolutely no idea how to remove the dust layering the inside of her cheeks and lodging in her throat.

As if he understood her dilemma, the portly gentleman sitting across from her held out a silver flask. Unable to speak, she shook her head and silently pleaded for the man's understanding. She'd choke on dust before she sipped the poison her father kept close to his heart, just on the inside of his coat pocket. Always patting the object like a beloved pet. He hadn't always been deep in his cups, and she had seriously doubted that in his right mind he'd be willing to sell his only child to the highest bidder once he decided she was too long in the tooth to receive any acceptable offers of marriage. However, that is exactly what he'd done.

She harrumphed. Who said twenty and six was long in the tooth? Who said she needed to marry at all? And to a lecherous widower with a horde of unruly children? Penelope remained amazed by the rebellious act she'd committed when she'd walked out of the small church, leaving behind her groom-to-be and their tightly knit group of acquaintances. No doubt she'd caused a tremendous uproar among their set and she could quite imagine her picture front and center in the paper.

She smiled to herself. What she wouldn't have done to see Mr. Wallace's face when he'd discovered her disappearance and realized he'd been thrown over by a mere mousy chit of a girl who should be utterly grateful to him for rescuing her from the distasteful state of spinsterhood.

If it hadn't been for Wren's tenacious desire to learn reading, Penelope would have paid no heed to the ads in the paper. It was pure happenstance that her maid had been reading a mail-order-bride ad as Penelope prepared herself at the church. Curiosity piqued, Penelope had snagged the paper and skimmed the lines.

A hardworking, kind and gentle man seeks a bride willing to move to Kansas and care for a simple home with a white picket fence.

Salvation! Was it possible? Had the good Lord seen fit to answer her prayers? Even now, Penelope could hardly believe it. She'd read the ad many times over, waiting for the words to disappear.

They had not. The bold wording remained, tempting her to lay claim to the offer. And who would blame her? Besides her father and Mr. Wallace, of course.

Everyone who knew anyone in St. Louis was aware Penelope's marriage would shortly end in her demise. As it had with each of Mr. Wallace's previous wives. Gossips whispered his vows had been purely for their inheritances to keep him in his fine coats and carriages.

Who was to think plain, mousy Penelope Parker would be any different? After all, she held no great beauty to incite a man's undying love. The lightly spoken words in the dark shadows of the Creighton's library still smarted. She was too socially awkward, too gangly, too pale, her hair too dark and unruly, her eyes too blue. Even her father's riches hadn't been able to produce an acceptable marriage offer for her, or any offer for that matter.

The audacity that her father would stoop so low as to marry her off to a man such as Mr. Wallace shocked her even now. Twice her age and with a bulbous nose, the man cared more for his riches, his drink and gullet than he had for any of his former wives, all of who'd left him with hefty inheritances and a passel of children.

Penelope leaned back into the hard and cracked upholstery. Still, she couldn't help but feel pity for Papa. After Mama had fallen ill and moved on to Glory, Papa had lost all sense of proper form. At least that's what she'd been told. She'd been only five when her mother passed. Memories of a sober and playful Papa had faded long ago, much like the memories of her mother. She still caught images of him laughing as he tossed her onto his shoulders. However, she suspected those mental pictures were nothing more than dreams conjured by the wishful thinking of a young girl in desperate need of attention.

Harvey stretched his little legs, shook out his fur, turned a few circles and resumed his former position. At least Papa had humored her with a pet. It was something.

The cloud of dust thickened inside the coach and Penelope held her silk handkerchief over her face, covering her nose and mouth. Her venture had failed to maintain the excitement she'd clung to since sneaking from the church in the middle of broad daylight with one trunk and several carpetbags. Fear owned her, and not from the stories of thieves she'd heard about while taking a meal in Topeka. Rather, fear of what Oak Grove held for her. Fear of what her new husband was like. Would he be as abominable as Mr. Wallace?

She slipped the ad and the responding letter from her reticule and read over the bold type. She worried her bottom lip. What sort of man had she agreed to marry? Was he old, like Mr. Wallace with three wives in the ground, or was he young, robust and handsome?

"Two miles!" The driver hollered from outside the coach.

Penelope folded the papers and tucked them back into her reticule. Two miles before the coach reached her destination, and her nerves rattled more than they had when she'd struck out on this adventure. Only Wren had been privy to her plans and the reasons she was running from home. She'd hadn't had time to say farewell to Cook or reason with her father. Upon reading the ad and mulling over the possibility of a new life, a life without fear of death, she'd departed the church, taking the carriage and her belongings to the train station. Staying would have meant only impending death, after Mr. Wallace received her inheritance and tired of her. His previous marriage had lasted all of three months. Poor Allison Juxton hadn't even seen her twentieth birthday. Too young to die from apoplexy. Penelope would much rather take chances with a stranger. Most assuredly he'd be an improvement over her father's choice of husband for her.

She lifted Harvey and sank her nose into his fur. She prayed her future groom was handsome of face and kind enough to allow Harvey a place in their home. Kinder than Karl Wallace and preferably absent of children. She didn't know the first thing about them, other than what she'd seen of the Wallace brood, and they were enough to send her to the asylum for a spell. Still, the romance stories she'd read had stirred a longing for a family of her own.

"What brings you to Oak Grove?" the matronly lady across from her asked. The cloying scent wafting from the woman tickled Penelope's nose.

Etiquette dictated she respond politely. However, proper etiquette dictated that one did not inquire into a stranger's business. Besides, Penelope's tongue continued to cleave to the roof of her mouth, making it nearly impossible to speak. She attempted a proper response only to be met with a croak.

"Oh, dear, do not bother with words. A simple nod will suffice. Are you the new schoolteacher?"

Penelope shook her head.

"A pity. We've been waiting for a new one to arrive for quite some time. Hayes's seamstress?"

Penelope shook her head again.

The older lady looked at her from head to toe. Clapping her hands together, she said, "Ohhhh! You must be here for the Garretts."

Penelope swallowed. *Garretts?* As in Beau Garrett *Garretts*? She'd memorized his name, she'd dipped her pen in ink and written it down, and then she'd written *Penelope Prudence Garrett*, practicing her new name for when she signed the church registry after their marriage,

The coach slowed and then rolled to a halt. Penelope waited for her turn to exit. By the time she stepped out, her luggage was on the ground and the driver had already climbed back onto his seat. Not a hint of her groom, or anyone rushing to meet her. She didn't need to reread the missive stating he would greet her upon arrival. She'd memorized it by heart.

She clutched Harvey to her chest and her purse to her stomach. She glanced up and down the street. A handful of simple wooden buildings in various colors of paint lined the wide carriageway, a sharp contrast to the various sizes and shapes of St. Louis's brick-and-mortar shops. The overhangs covering these boardwalks were much lower, not much higher than a man's head. A small limestone structure blocked the end of the street, as if to stand in rebellion to the rest of the town.

She spun around on her heels. She had no idea which direction to go to find her groom. A drop of rain landed against her cheek. She tucked Harvey into her coat and climbed onto the walkway to plaster herself against the side of the depot. The poor mite must be sick of rain. After all, she was for certain.

The downpour chased her. She tried the door to the depot only to find it barred. She peered through the window, but not a single lamp winked at her in the darkness. And exhausted, she felt tears press against her lashes and rain soak through her coat. Her hair clung to her nape. She shivered.

What was she to do? Had Mr. Garrett forgotten his promise to meet her? She was several weeks late. Still, would he not watch for her arrival? Had he given up on her and found another bride, even though she'd explained the delay and promised to be there as soon as circumstances allowed? Her shoulders sagged beneath the weight of her worries. Her lip quivered. She drew in a breath and released it with irritating slowness. *Now, now, Penelope Parker, you mustn't give up.*

She hadn't traveled all this way to be left out in the cold rain. If Beau Garrett had found another bride, she'd just demand he find her another groom and before Mr. Wallace discovered her whereabouts and demanded restitution, or worse. Of course, she didn't think Mr. Wallace would imagine her in a place as unsophisticated as Oak Grove.

Snapping her shoulders back and lifting her chin, she left her luggage and trekked through the muck toward the closest establishment. Raising her chin a little higher, she pushed through the swinging doors. The eyes of every person turned toward her. The room was divided into two, and a tall, thin gray-haired man sat behind a podium in the center, a gavel in his hand. A lady in the front row turned, tears rolling down her cheeks. A man in homespun, holey britches held up by suspenders, snickered.

Penelope gulped. Had she interrupted a court proceeding? She dipped her head in apology. "I—" she croaked and then made another attempt at clearing her throat. "I am sorry. I do not mean to interrupt. I've just arrived, and I am in need of Beau Garrett's direction, if you please?"

Laughter erupted. Her cheeks burned hot.

"I'm Beau Garrett."

She snapped her gaze to a shadowed corner. She could not see much, but she saw enough to cause her a fit of vapors. Hands cuffed and teeth rotted, a man grinned at her. He sat by a tall, imposing man with a shiny badge.

Harvey growled, and she snuggled him closer.

The lawman nudged the criminal with his elbow. "Shut yer, trap, Jessup."

The room spun before her.

"No, ma'am." The man wearing suspenders lifted his bound hands and said, "I'm Garrett."

The lady gasped. More tears rolled. The woman glanced at the judge. "He does not even hide his willingness to sway from our vows, Your Honor."

"It does not give me just cause to dissolve the marriage, Susan. As I recall, you knew good and well the sort of man you were marrying when you said 'I do' to Calvin, here. I believe I even counseled you to run as far as you could."

Penelope bit her bottom lip as trepidation threatened to overwhelm her. She knew Mr. Wallace, had known him for years. That is why she'd sought refuge in a want ad. This woman knew her husband. Penelope did not know Beau Garrett. What had she done? Was it too late to change her mind?

"But, Pa!" The lady stomped her foot on the floor.

Pa? The judge was this lady's father? And yet he still would not dissolve the marriage? Were all women subject to the whims of the men in their lives? Even the lower classes? That piqued her curiosity since she had always believed only wealthy daughters were bound by an unwritten rule to honor their fathers' wishes when it came to marriage. Usually those wishes were swayed by finances or a good name. What could the judge have gained by allowing his lovely daughter to marry such a rotter?

The judge shook his head at the lady and then glanced at Penelope. "Nice to meet you, Miss—"

"Parker," she filled in with burning cheeks as everyone's attention seemed to be focused on her.

"I'm Judge Greg Winter. Last I saw, Beau was at the jailhouse."

"Oh, my!" Penelope's hand fluttered to her chest. She'd obviously made a mistake. What sort of man had she agreed to marry? Although she'd given her word, she wasn't bound to him yet. Was she? "Very well. Thank you."

She turned to leave. Her heavy, soaked skirts twisted around her legs, and she fell against the swinging doors and straight onto her backside on the muddied, plank walkway. Harvey landed on her chest. Another round of laughter erupted.

"I pity Garrett when he gets a look at her."

More laughter.

"Good thing she's here for the children and not for marrying."

With the blood pounding between her ears, she didn't quite trust what she'd heard. She rolled to her knees, picked herself up and shook out her skirts. She hadn't become a spinster without having a bit of a backbone and aloofness. Social gatherings in St. Louis had been her nemesis, potted plants her best friends as she'd watched the courtship of her peers. Their advantageous marriages, their children. From her first ball, it had been apparent that she wasn't cut from the same cloth as her fellows.

As she walked toward the jailhouse, she hugged Harvey. "I'm sorry, boy. I don't always have the grandest of ideas. I must admit though I thought we'd fare much better here than in Mr. Wallace's household. Perhaps I was wrong."

When she'd read the mail-order-bride ad, she'd not only been hopeful to escape an awful marriage but hopeful that she'd finally find a place she belonged. Given her encounter here in Oak Grove, her hope waned. Drastically.

She knew she was far from the fairest beauty, with her slender, tall frame, black-as-night hair and blue eyes. Men, eligible proper men, seemed to prefer short ladies with curves and golden-honey locks. Garrett hadn't mentioned what sort of wife he wanted in looks. Perhaps because he did not care, especially if he spent most of his time in jail. She squeezed her eyes shut as she adjusted Harvey in her arms and reached for the door handle.

Once she crossed the threshold, would there be any way to turn back? The door eased open, and two little blond heads turned her way. She had no experience with children, but an acquaintance back home had a four-year-old that seemed to be about the same age as the youngest of the pair. She reasoned the other to be about eight. The duo had blond hair hanging over their eyes, the young one with curls dancing around his jawline. Their faces were smudged with dirt. She swiped her knuckles over her own cheek. At least theirs were dry, which was more than she could say for herself.

"Hello," one of the children said as he shoved his hair from his brow, revealing bright blue eyes.

Harvey wriggled until she deposited him on the floor. The traitor quickly greeted the children with nose kisses and the happy wagging of his tail. Penel-

ope glanced around the small room as her eyes adjusted
to the dim interior. A chair and a small desk occupied
one corner; a set of bars closed off another. A man, with
thick waves the color of wheat springing out from beneath his hat, stretched out on a cot. Two smaller children with matching locks to the other children curled
around him, their little bodies rising and falling with
each of his even breaths. A toddler and an infant. For
a moment, her own breath stilled for fear of disturbing
them. No wonder the young boy had whispered when
she'd walked into the jail. Something stirred inside her,
a need to watch the trio a little longer than what was appropriate. A longing to want what she'd never allowed
herself to want. A family. A child of her own. A husband. Not a man to further her father's business. Not a
man who would save her from spinsterhood in exchange
for her servitude as an obedient wife until she took her
last breath once his greedy hands clutched her inheritance. No, an honest-to-goodness, genuine husband.
A husband who would care for her and protect her.
A husband to hold her in his strong and capable arms
when the world went awry, just as this man seemed to
do with these children.

The infant stirred and Penelope recalled where she
stood, and that the man—her prospective groom—was
behind bars! What sort of man was he to bring his children to jail with him? To lock them up like criminals,
too?

One she most assuredly did not wish to be associ-
ated with, let alone marry. Perhaps she should take the
urchins and care for them until a proper family mem-
ber could be found. Maybe even clean them up a bit.

A tug on her skirt pulled her attention away from the snoring man. She peered down at a dirty imp with grubby hands and a wide toothless smile. So young and innocent. He deserved more than what this man offered. They all did. Maybe she would inquire the help of a resident in town. Someone more suitable to the caring of filthy boys.

"Are you our new mama?"

Harvcy yipped and stood up on his back legs.

"Wh-what?" she sputtered, and quickly decided the unladylike sound was due to the dust plaguing her throat and not her nerves.

"You here to marry our pa?" Another child crawled from beneath the desk. His small voice was quiet and hesitant.

"Oh! How many of you are there?" She searched the shadows for more and even ducked to look beneath the desk. Her last count was five. Three outside the cell, two in with their father. She needed to sit for a spell. However, the only seating seemed just as covered with filth as the rest of the countryside. What had she'd gotten herself into? Whatever was she to do? She couldn't very well return to St. Louis. The scandal she'd caused had no doubt angered Mr. Wallace beyond reason. If she returned, he'd make her pay dearly for causing him such embarrassment. No, she must remain here and find a husband. Crawling back to her father and Mr. Wallace was not an option. She drew in a slow breath and was just about to speak when she was interrupted.

"Don't be silly," the oldest child chastised. "We're getting a lady. Not her. Least that's what Mrs. Bobby Jean said."

* * *

Beau jerked his eyelids open beneath his Stetson. His surroundings had changed. There was a change in the atmosphere. He sniffed. A distinctive smell of wet dog. He wrinkled his nose and mentally sought the weight of the young'uns on his chest. Esther lifted her little head, the spot instantly feeling barren and cool. He still couldn't believe how quickly the urchins had wriggled their way into his heart. Even the older boys, with their propensity for trouble. Like locking him in when he chased Esther and John into the jail cell. The two had giggled as they ran. He hadn't been quick enough to capture them before Luke slammed the door shut. Beau had hollered for a time, and recalling most of Oak Grove had crowded into the saloon for the week's court proceedings, he settled on the cot hoping Miller Gannon, his deputy marshal, would arrive after court.

Beau should have been at court, too, but after chasing Jessup all night and finally capturing the scoundrel, he needed a bit of shut-eye. He still hadn't gotten used to being a father and the sleepless nights that came right along with that duty, just like the sleepless nights that came with being a marshal. For some reason, he'd thought the marshaling would be a lot smoother than it had. But thanks to Jessup Davis, his job had been anything but smooth, and he couldn't quite figure out why. The man had always been a burr in his saddle, but in the last several weeks, his petty crimes had escalated up to robbing folks. Which didn't seem like the scoundrel. Perhaps if he moseyed on over to court, he'd get an explanation. Esther snuggled into his neck and Beau drifted back to sleep. Explanations could wait.

Mark's quiet voice made him flinch. Pa? The boys had taken to calling him Pa a few weeks back, which was nice even though it disturbed him more than a little. It still caught him off guard. Beau didn't have any idea how to be a pa, and he couldn't replace his brother.

Wait!

Hold on a mighty minute. What was this about marrying? Who was getting married? He adjusted Esther and slid out from beneath John's little body. Righting his hat, he sat on the edge of the cot and blinked the heaviness of sleep from his thoughts.

"Boys," he rumbled. "What's going on?"

Matthew grinned. Mark slunk beneath the desk, and Beau regretted the gruffness in his voice.

Luke looked him straight in the eye. "Hey there, Pa. We got us a new ma and a dog. You said we could get us a dog, and now we've got one." Luke pointed over his shoulder with his thumb. "She's here to hitch up with you."

Beau grimaced. "Nobody is here to hitch up with me, Luke."

The lady shifted from her statuesque pose. The toes of her delicate boots peeked from beneath her mud-encrusted skirts. Skirts that seemed to once have been a pale pink. The fabric molded to her legs and slender hips. Her bead-embellished coat dripped on the floorboards. He'd noted the place had been in desperate need of a good swabbing anyway after the urchins had had a tussle involving their lunch. He shouldn't get too upset at the mud pooling under her feet.

A long, creamy, slender neck stretched from the collar of her clothing. Her cheeks burned bright red beneath mud splatters. Long curling black hair plastered in parts down her back while the rest remained pinned.

"Is, too." Matthew's blue eyes sparked with mischief. "She's gonna be your wife and our ma."

"Wife? Mother? She doesn't look like she knows the first thing about being a mother to mischievous little boys." Not to mention she seemed a little too old to be seeking out a husband. Most ladies her age were married by now. "How old are you?"

Her pert little nose lifted into the air. "Twenty-six."

He scrubbed his hand over his prickly chin. "A widow?"

She flinched. "No. I haven't had an acceptable offer."

Once again, he eyed her from head to toe. What was wrong with her if she hadn't had a proposal from her own class? Was she daft or too particular about her options? "If you make it a habit of presenting yourself in such a state of uncleanliness, I can see why."

She gasped.

Beau immediately regretted his words. He needed coffee to keep his tongue from running away from him.

"I mean no offense." He held up his hand to keep her from speaking. "Obviously, travel has taken its toll. That being said, you seem more suited for pouring tea for well-to-do guests born with silver spoons in their mouths. These boys have never seen a silver spoon, nor have they acquired the taste for tea."

"I assure you I'm fully capable. Besides, we have an agreement."

"Agreement?"

"Yes, an agreement of marriage."

Beau choked on his own breath.

"I beg your pardon. You must be mistaken. Even if I was in want of a wife, she wouldn't be like you."

Her clothing and graceful posture, even disheveled, told the facts of her upbringing. He'd seen enough high society ladies to know a few truths about them. They were haughty and dangerous when they set their minds on an objective. Mainly unsuspecting gentlemen out to rescue damsels in distress. Unfortunately for Beau, he'd sniffed out the lies too late, at the cost of a few of his men. His brother, Zach, had been caught by the wily schemes of a fortune-hunting beauty, who knew how to bat her lashes to get what she wanted, and ended up disowned by their father.

He also knew ladies of her ilk did not know how to survive without a throng of servants at their beck and call. How could this woman care for these boys and little Esther when their own ma had failed to survive the wilds of Kansas? How could this lady mother these children when she'd been unable to defend herself against his churlish behavior? She didn't have the fire needed to take the boys in hand. She was too much like Mary Ella. Pampered. Spoiled. Calculating. "Given your appearance, I have doubts you can survive in Oak Grove without a maid and a bevy of servants."

Her sharp intake of breath rattled in his ears.

"I mean no disrespect, ma'am," Beau grunted. "But I don't recall requesting a wife."

Her chin rose, a flicker of determination sparking in her eyes and making him doubt his previous assumptions about her. Perhaps she did have the character to care for the urchins. It just needed to be coaxed and challenged to come to the surface.

She slipped something from the purse clutched to her chest. "Mr. Garrett? Mr. Beau Garrett?"

He narrowed his eyes. The hair at the base of his neck stood on end, but he couldn't deny who he was. He nodded. "Yes."

"I'm here to inform you that you did exactly request a wife. This ad and our correspondence proves as much." Her lips twisted, and then she lowered her voice to a whisper as she leaned forward. "However, you did fail to mention you had children."

She glided toward the iron bars and he found himself impressed with her ability to walk like a lady, even with clumps of mud clinging to her skirts.

He unfolded himself from the cot as she slid her slender arm through the bars. She held an envelope between the tips of her thumb and index finger as if she feared he would bite her or soil her further. He snatched the envelope and grunted as she jumped back and nearly tumbled to the floor. He pulled out two sheets of paper and scanned the lines. His mouth flattened as he slid his gaze to Matthew. He'd tasked the boy with posting an ad for a nanny, even paid him a nice coin for the chore. "What'd you do?"

"Nothing, Pa. Sent the ad like you asked."

"This isn't exactly my ad." Beau cleared his throat. "As I recall I requested a caretaker. A nanny. A nursemaid. Not a wife."

"Mrs. Bobby Jean helped."

Beau rolled his eyes. Leave it to his cousin to interfere.

The soaking-wet beauty flushed beneath the mud

stains. Her ice-blue eyes flamed in challenge as she tugged her shoulders back.

"Get me out of here," he commanded.

Luke jumped to his feet, his golden locks falling over his eyes as he fished the key from his front pants pocket, and Beau made a mental note to take the boys to the barber. Luke approached the cell and glanced up at the lady. "'Cuse me."

"You—you can't let him out," the lady sputtered.

A muscle twitched at Beau's temple. "Why not?"

She inched toward the door and placed her hand on the handle as if to run. "You—you're a criminal."

"Is not," Luke argued as he turned the key in the lock.

The door swung open. The lady jumped. Beau chuckled. "The only criminals here are the scamps who locked me and the babies in that there cell." He stuck out his hand. "Oak Grove's city marshal, Beau Garrett."

"P-Penelope Parker." She lifted a shaking hand covered in once-white gloves, now dingy and brown and coated in strands of dog hair. He was thankful when she jerked her hand back and dropped it to her side. She snapped to attention like a soldier. Shoulders straight, chin up. "I hope you intend to keep your word, Marsh—Mr. Garrett."

The tick at his temple increased. He needed strong black coffee and more than twenty minutes of sleep. "My word? I don't recollect giving my word to anything more than room and board and a monthly stipend to care for the children."

"As I said, our correspondence says otherwise." She shook a finger at the papers in his hand.

He smiled. "Correspondence I had hide nor hair to do with, Miss Parker." To which he would make his displeasure with Bobby Jean known. She might be kin, but she had no right to interfere. The tears illuminating Miss Parker's blue eyes pressed onto her lashes, and he grunted as he looked from one boy to the next. "Very well, from the looks of it you must be exhausted from your travels. After a spell of rest, I expect you'll see to reason and see the misunderstanding."

She drew in a deep breath as if to speak, and he held up his hand as he shook his pounding head. "Miss Parker, not now. Children, let's take Miss Parker home."

He had half a mind to deposit her on Bobby Jean's doorstep, but Judge had a day full of court and shouldn't be bothered with the antics of his wife.

"So she ain't gonna be our new mama like Mrs. Bobby Jean promised?" Mark asked, climbing from under the desk.

"Mrs. Bobby Jean has no business making promises, Mark." Beau squeezed the boy's shoulder. "Not on my behalf."

"Not fair." Mark shook off the touch, dusted off his breeches, and then walked over to Matthew and punched him in the arm.

Miss Parker gasped.

"Boys! Best behavior in front of the lady."

"Ow," Matthew whined. "What was that for?"

"Ya lied, Matty. You always lie." Mark pushed past the lady and ran outside.

"Yeah, Matty!" Luke sneaked in a punch and ran after Mark.

"It wasn't me, Pa. It was Bobby Jean. She said we'd have a new ma."

Miss Parker looked bewildered, as she should. Even if she were here for only the job, Beau would still send her packing. She didn't have the spine to handle the boys. He adjusted Esther in his arm and stepped back into the cell. He tapped John's shoulder. Sleepy eyes looked up at him. "Hey there, little guy, it's time to go home."

John stretched his arms up as he slid off the cot. Beau knelt and wrapped his free arm around the child's legs. He rose and nodded to the wide-eyed lady. "Well, are you ready, Miss Parker?"

Chapter Two

Beau dropped his chin to his chest and grunted. He was tired from the last few days chasing after Jessup, and he couldn't believe Bobby Jean had taken advantage of his situation. Actually, he could believe it, though he wished he couldn't. He drew in a breath and scrubbed his palm over his scruffy jaw.

How had his good intentions gone awry? He needed help with the children, good help, while he enforced the law in Oak Grove. He didn't need a wife. And he certainly didn't need a spoiled high society lady with no experience. However, he couldn't keep leaving the children unattended or with the widowed Mrs. Wheelwright, like he'd done the last two days while he trailed Jessup Davis.

Bobby Jean and Judge had offered to keep them for a spell, but he couldn't impose on their generosity when they had their own troubles. He eyed the well-to-do lady and shook his head. The last thing he needed was another delicate, tender soul to worry over as he rested his head on a bedroll beneath the starry night, listening for the wayward snap of a twig.

And he'd worry. Worry if he could rescue her from her own foolishness. Worry about what sort of scheme she was conniving. Worry whether or not she was for him or against him. Just as he should have done with Mary Ella. If he'd taken a moment to give her a thought, maybe she wouldn't have gotten involved with the enemy. He'd forgiven her, but the scars of her actions remained, and he'd never easily trust another woman again, not with his heart, and if he wasn't so desperate for help with the young'uns, he wouldn't trust a lady with them either.

He pressed the tip of his fingers to his temple. The thumping in his head increased, and he pulled the heavy, humid air into his lungs. Things hadn't just gone a little awry, this was a downright runaway coach in the middle of a torrential rainstorm, veering over the edge of a cliff. He wasn't looking for a wife. He didn't need a wife. And he sure did not want one. However, it seemed one was attempting to hitch to his wagon.

Wondering why he wasn't hearing her slopping in the mud behind him, he turned back. She stood there, one hand clinging to the wooden post, the other clutching the poor pooch to her chest. The door to the jail remained wide open. He scratched at his sideburn. Had she expected a servant to come behind her and close it for her? Well, she wouldn't find one in these parts, not unless she brought one with her, and from the looks of it, she hadn't. One foot jutted forward and hung in the air. She teetered and then settled her foot back on the porch. Worry, and a mite of fear, creased her brow. Once again, he roamed his gaze over her from boots to head. She looked like a handful of withered rose petals after an encounter with hailstones.

She eyed the mud with trepidation. No doubt she'd had her share of it today. He bit his tongue on the slew of words better left unsaid.

Mary Ella, another damsel he'd believed in need of rescue, had left his heart cold and black when she'd used him. The information she'd obtained had given the Confederates the upper hand. Her actions had caused the death of good men, and when she'd been caught she had accused him of taking her virtue. That action had left a rift between him and his father when he'd refused to make right the wrong she'd accused him of, a wrong he hadn't committed.

Fresh wounds, raw with grief, still stung over her deception. If it hadn't been for her lies and her schemes, good men would still be alive. He was certain his brother would be alive, too, if he'd been allowed to remain in the pampered life he'd been accustomed to rather than toiling the hard earth with very few comforts, a punishment doled out by their father to rectify the situation when Beau had refused to.

If not for the mercy and compassion of his commanding officer, Beau would have received a just and deserving punishment. He hadn't been deemed a traitor to his country, but he still carried the deaths of his fellow soldiers. He'd been guilty of trusting a long-standing childhood friend, a woman he'd thought he loved and had hoped to marry.

At least he'd discovered her intentions before he'd been vowed to her for life. If only his brother had had the courage to stand up to their father. If he had, then Zach wouldn't have been blackballed when he'd taken Mary Ella as his second wife after the death of his first. Beau had nearly been disowned by his father because he'd refused to participate in Mary Ella's lies, when she'd accused him of forcing her into ruin. Her deception had twisted them all up in a big tangle. He'd rather spend an eternity in Andersonville prison camp than relive the trial and the testimonies. And he'd rather relive the trial and testimonies than see the disappointment and rage on his father's face, which was why he hadn't been home since.

What was the Good Lord doing bringing him another woman who seemed too similar to Mary Ella? Testing Beau's patience and perseverance, no doubt. Maybe even testing him to see if he'd actually forgiven her for all the damage she'd caused. Whatever it was, Beau knew better than to drag his feet too long and hard over trying to figure it out, which meant he should listen to his gut instinct. Miss Parker was pure trouble. Plain and simple.

He wanted to hold her responsible for Mary Ella's crimes. However, he figured he should give her the benefit of the doubt. After all, she was probably a victim of Bobby Jean's good intentions, too. Still, he'd do well to see her on a conveyance back to where she'd come from, and until then, he'd keep his eyes wide open and his senses alert. And, while he was at the waiting, maybe he should act the gentleman and treat her like the lady she portrayed instead of like the two-bit, mangy, thieving raccoon he suspected she was.

"S'pose we should help the lady," he said to the silent duo in his arms. He plopped John to his feet and took hold of his small hand. He hefted Esther higher in his arm and cradled her against his chest. The little mite laid her head on his shoulder as he strode back to the jail. Miss Parker stepped off the walkway and wobbled. He lengthened his stride as she teetered. She leaned forward, one arm swung out and then upward like a windmill. The dog yipped in her tightened grip. Beau stretched out his hand and snagged her arm, catching her to his side just as her feet began to slip out from beneath her. The dog's pink tongue darted against his hand in gratitude.

However, it was the gratitude reflected in Penelope's sky blue eyes that captivated him. Her heart thundered against the side of his chest, reminding him how long it'd been since he'd held a woman this close—shortly before the war had ended, at a ball thrown by his father to announce Beau's engagement to Mary Ella. He'd nearly forgotten the sensation of attraction and the thrill of the dance. But he would not forget the dangers of such attraction. Penelope dropped her gaze. Dark lashes fell against her cheek, and he quickly remembered why he'd kept his distance from feminine beauty. Especially women with an agenda and willing to use artifice to get what they wanted. Holding on to her upper arm, he placed some distance between them.

"You're going to need serviceable shoes, and a serviceable, simple dress until arrangements can be made for you to go back home."

"This is my home, Mr. Garrett."

He stole a glance at her. The determined set of her chin sparked his competitive nature. She'd challenged him, and for some strange reason, he didn't feel weakened or tired by it like he had when Jessup stole a pie and then some minor trinkets from the general store. He felt awake, alive. He felt encouraged, refreshed and renewed. And he almost agreed to allow her to stay, to see how well she would survive all Oak Grove had to toss at her. He cleared his throat and paused as he thought about his next words. He gave her a hard gaze. "You are going home, Miss Parker."

Again, she lifted her chin. The determination etching her brow and pursing her pink rosebud lips rocked her shoulders back. The act was too quick to be a facade. Was it possible this woman was straightforward and held no artifice?

"That isn't an option, Mr. Garrett," she said with a great deal of firmness and finality. "And until you are my husband, you have no authority over my comings and goings."

"It's a grand thing I'm not your husband, Miss Parker, or you'd find yourself tossed over my knee and a switch to your hide for your impertinence."

She flinched with a gasp. Her soiled, gloved hand hovered in front of her lips. If it wasn't for the genuine fear in her wide eyes, he'd chalk it up to an act. He shook off the notion this lady might know the sting of a thin branch.

"I see my humor has failed to ease your mood."

Some of the tension left her, but the solid attention worthy of any soldier in the presence of his commanding officer remained in place. "I fail to see the humor in beating one's wife, Mr. Garrett."

"Marshal Garrett, if you please. Mr. Garrett was my

father." His mouth pressed into a flat line and he tugged her forward, leading her toward the buckboard wagon he'd left at the livery two nights before. "My apologies for my insensitivity. I've never had a wife and, therefore, have no experience in the matter. However, my father was fond of the switch whenever my brothers and I gave him cause."

Although he'd been sparked by her challenging nature, he was still too tired to argue, and he decided to take a step back and relent for the moment. "We'll look at your options and consider them before final decisions are made. One thing is for certain, Miss Parker, you can't remain in Oak Grove."

And definitely not as his wife.

"Whyever not, Mr. Garrett? It seems like a nice enough town. Much quieter than where I come from."

Again, with innocent wide eyes, she tugged on heartstrings that he'd believed were severed long ago. He needed a good night's rest. Several good nights' rest without a shooting, a robbery or a crying child. And he needed to treat her like a double-headed moccasin and stay as far from her as possible, and with haste.

"Although Oak Grove is somewhat tame, Miss Parker, it is not a place for a lady of your upbringing." He exhaled. "You do not have the fortitude to survive here."

Just like Mary Ella hadn't had the fortitude to survive the life she'd forged for herself and his brother with her misdeeds. He'd once felt guilt over her death. Seemed he still did, given the panic stirring in his chest at the thought of Miss Parker remaining in Oak Grove. He would not make the same mistake, which was why he would send Miss Parker back to where she belonged. Posthaste.

"I beg your pardon, but we've only just met. I do not believe you've known me long enough to ascertain what sort of fortitude I may or may not have."

He held back harsh laughter. "I would not make a good city marshal if I did not have a quick judgment of character."

"I'll reserve my thoughts as to whether or not you're a good lawman as it seems to me a *good*—" she elongated the vowels in *good* "—or even a fairly adequate lawman would not be apprehended by a posse of children."

He gave in to laughter. It rumbled from his gut and burst forth. Something he'd been on the verge of doing since the children had entered his life after the death of his brother. However, he'd been unable to laugh due to weariness and grief. Until now. This woman had sass, and he oddly found it an appealing trait.

He quickly sobered and hardened his jaw. Perhaps he had misjudged the lady, he thought again. Maybe she had the backbone it took to tame the boys. Except he did not wish to find out, especially since the disheveled woman with black hair and bright eyes caught his attention when his attention should not be caught.

He grunted.

"Are you in agreement, Mr. Garrett?"

He tensed. Her lyrical tones struck a chord, somehow making the burdens he'd carried since the war seem lighter. The sun broke through the stormy gray clouds. Even nature seemed to respond to her.

"That posse of children, as you call them, can outwit the most intelligent of men."

"Then, perhaps, Mr. Garrett, it is Providence that I am not a man."

Amusement once again began to boil to laughter, but he simmered it down before it made itself known. He kept the smile hidden beneath his gruff exterior. He smoothed his fingers over his mustache in need of a trim. One misstep for the day was enough, and he attributed it to his lack of sleep, lack of coffee and his need for a shave.

"How soon before the deed is done?" she asked. "Before we are to become married?"

"There will be no marriage, Miss Parker." Her zealousness to become his wife set his teeth on edge. Why was she set on marrying him, and quickly? "As soon as arrangements can be made, you'll be returned home."

He jerked to a halt when her boots dug into the mud. He glanced over his shoulder as she yanked her arm from his grip.

"I do not know if it is your inability to comprehend the English language or if you are too thick-skulled, but you're not understanding me, Mr. Garrett. You are my only option. I came here to be a wife, and a wife I will be." She poked a finger at him. "Your wife."

His teeth ground together as he considered her for a moment. If she wanted to be a helpmate, perhaps it'd be easier if he found her another husband here in Oak Grove. His mind raced with all the eligible men in the area. The only suitable ones were the banker, Reverend Scott and the Gannon brothers. He'd heard from Mrs. Wheelwright that the ladies of the First Congregational Church had sent inquiries for a proper wife for Scott. Perhaps he could save them all the trouble and introduce Miss Parker to the committee. He smiled to himself, pleased with the solution and ready to act. Tomorrow, after he'd had sleep, black coffee and a hearty, edible meal.

He moved closer and pressed his face near hers. She shoved a black curl behind her ear and lifted the pert heart-shaped chin of hers. She was standing her ground. Good, so was he.

"You do realize, that as my wife, you'll become mother to five children. Children who need to be fed, bathed, guided with a strong yet gentle hand." He took small delight when the determined glint in her eyes wavered and her shoulders sagged a hair. He pressed on. "Children full of vigor and mischief. Children capable of fooling a *distinguished* lawman, a decorated soldier, and locking him in his own jail." He arched his brow. "You do know how to cook, don't you, Miss Parker?"

She blinked and attempted a step back, to which she stumbled. Beau wrapped his free arm around her, steadying her footing, and waited for her to tell the truth, to tell him she knew how to make only a poor man's winter soup and tea. That small moment stretched into several. He flexed his hand against the small of her back. The curve perfectly matched his palm.

"O-of course I do."

He snorted. "We shall see about that. You'll need to prove yourself, Miss Parker, if you intend on being my wife."

He immediately clamped his jaw, disbelieving he'd tossed out the words. He didn't want a wife, and he wouldn't have one either. He released his hold on her and gripped her elbow before she fell. He may not want a wife, but he would not allow her to tumble and flail around in the mud. He wasn't a complete scoundrel. He'd just have to make sure she failed in her attempts, which shouldn't be a problem, given the lady didn't seem to know the right end of a hairbrush. Something he'd have to show her if he was going to introduce her to Reverend Scott and the Community Church ladies. At least the dog was well-groomed. Did Scott like mutts?

He loosened his hold on her, formed Little John's chubby fingers around his pants leg and then held out his arm to Miss Parker. "Shall we?"

Her long, dainty fingers gently wrapped his biceps, and he wondered if the panic welling in his chest was akin to how his prisoners felt when he fettered their wrists. He choked down the knot lodged in his throat and shook off the warm sensation cloaking him like his duster in the middle of a winter snowstorm. It had taken a mere few days for the urchins to warm their way into his heart. He'd need to rid himself of Miss Parker before she had a chance to do the same.

"Where does one purchase serviceable shoes and gowns in Oak Grove?"

He evaded her question, determined that she'd leave before she settled long enough to need such items. "Have you experience with children?"

She worried her bottom lip. "Not exactly."

That was a truth he believed.

Little John tugged on his britches. "I'm hungry."

Beau glanced down at the child and smiled. "As you should be, John. You tossed your lunch on the floor.

However, Miss Parker assures me she can cook and will see to your stomach as soon as we reach home."

"Wh-what would the little boy find pleasing to eat?" The hand around his arm tensed. "So as to not toss his meal on the floor?"

Beau held his laughter in check. To be honest, he'd tossed his own meal, due to it being burnt black as charred wood. Before the urchins arrived, when it was just him, he'd taken his meals at Moore's House, but he wasn't certain Oak Grove was prepared for the children's antics and ill manners. If he let the boys loose on Oak Grove, he'd be forced to move, and not just out of the area but out of the entire state. "Honestly, I do not know."

She sucked in a tiny breath. Her gaze darted between him and the youngest of his wards. "How could a father not know the likes and dislikes of his children?"

Beau rolled his eyes. How indeed? He hadn't seen his brother since before John had been born, and he felt a great deal of guilt over the matter. He should have been around. Should have known his nephews. Been there for his brother after the death of his first wife and after the death of Mary Ella. He should have known the urchins' names before they arrived in Oak Grove with notes pinned to their coats. He shouldn't have allowed his father to dictate their relationship. He shouldn't have allowed his father to keep them apart. "Well, Miss Parker, it's fairly simple. They're not my children, and up until a couple months ago, I didn't even know the names of the youngest two."

"They're not yours?"

He couldn't tell if she was shocked or hopeful.

"Before you get ideas in your head, they're mine. They just haven't always been mine. I inherited them from my brother after he fell off his horse and suffered a deadly head injury." Another deed to lay at his feet. If he'd been there during Zach's grief, he could have been the one to ride out in the storm, looking for Mark.

"Oh, dear," she said as she pressed a curled fist to her mouth. "Their mother?"

"I imagine my brother buried them in the family cemetery."

"Them?"

Beau halted his stride. He searched her eyes for malice and deception, but he'd learned to not trust his instincts where ladies were concerned, especially beautiful damsels in distress. And he should take greater caution with this one, hidden beneath layers of mud. At least this one didn't seem to understand her state of dishevelment and maintained her grace. Still, he pierced her with a hard gaze and spoke through gritted teeth. "The children do not have the same mothers," he said, grimacing. Matthew, Mark and Luke were carbon copies of Zach's first wife, the younger two the spitting image of Mary Ella. She'd grown ill with melancholy after birthing Esther, at least according to Zach's letter. Beau felt a measure of guilt over her death, although he had tried to warn his brother. She'd been too self-absorbed to care for children and meet the expectations of motherhood without the benefit of servants.

He eyed Miss Parker. The lady before him was cut from the same cloth. A few hours and she'd leave. A week at the most. She didn't have what it took to attend to young'uns.

"I hope you do not find yourself with any grand ideas of winning the children over. They've had quite enough loss in their young lives. They don't need attachments to folks who are bound to run away when they become too difficult."

Penelope absentmindedly dug the tips of her fingers into Harvey's fur. She wasn't certain how to think or what to say. Having lost her own mother at a young age, she understood. Since her father hadn't been himself since her mother's passing, she understood the loss of a father, too. Although he continued to breathe, he hadn't made himself available, often keeping from her presence. She'd hoped one day he'd see to reason and realize he had a daughter, not a pawn.

These orphans didn't have that hope. They needed something to make them feel better—or perhaps someone. Harvey knew how to cheer her whenever she felt a hint of self-pity. Perhaps she could entice the children to take over some of his demanding need to be held and petted. However, what she sensed each really needed was a hug. Her heart went out to them. She wanted to wrap her arms around them and cuddle their hurts away, but the concept was foreign to her. She'd read about such embraces in her books and had sighed with longing and wonderment. She had somehow convinced Father to allow her a pet because very few people came close to her, and none were willing to offer her the comfort of their arms. After witnessing hugs in action a few times between mothers and their children, while strolling in the park, she knew Harvey couldn't bear the responsibility alone. She'd resigned herself for the isolation and loneliness of spinsterhood.

Tongue lolling out, Harvey licked her hand and she warmed. Occasionally he greeted her with what she'd hoped was a smile and a furious tail wagging, but it was nothing compared to the warm, genuine smiles that seemed to enrapture the participants in the park. She'd always wondered why the action of arms circling another human coerced such…joy. She couldn't recall ever being held. How did one form a personal connection to receive that sort of affection? Was there a secret that she had yet to ascertain? Or was there something wrong with her?

She cleared the travel dust still coating the inside of her throat and steeled herself. "Forming attachments won't be a problem, Mr. Garrett."

"Good."

"However, you should know that I can be very persuasive when I set my mind to something."

He squinted. "And what have you set your mind to, Miss Parker?"

To not be sent back home and become the fifth Mrs. Wallace. Or was it the tenth? Whatever it was, she intended not to be it. "I have a mind to honor the agreement, which we've both agreed to, Mr. Garrett. Even if you did not disclose the fullness of the situation. I dare say, you should have included information about the children." Her next words lodged in her throat. She was already running, running to Beau Garrett and the protection he didn't realize he offered. She had nowhere else to go, except to a pine box in the church graveyard. "I—I will not flee from you, or them."

His mouth twitched ever so slightly, but it seemed to her that movement, as slight as it had been, showed a great deal of irritation. She almost smiled over the matter. She'd irritated her father until his cheeks blistered red, but usually due to her ineptness at serving tea for his guests or a missed note when she was called on to sing. She'd certainly irritated Mr. Wallace with her attempts at dodging his unwanted attentions, so much so that their last encounter had ended with threats of beating her with his cane once he had authority to do so. The threat had been a promise, one she was overly grateful to render void by her absence. Mr. Garrett's irritation was mild, almost nonexistent. Not bordering a fit of rage. It pleased her greatly, and she made up her mind Beau Garrett would not harm a fly, let alone a hair on her head. She had no fear that he would make good on his threat of throwing her over his knee.

She thought he might say something. Anything. However, he tugged on her arm and pulled her alongside him. Thick mud clawed at the heels of her boots, sucking her into the earth. The hem of her skirts dragged and snagged like cloth in the midst of rose bushes. The little girl remained locked against Beau's chest, her lips smiling around her tiny thumb. Wide blue eyes blinking, watching Harvey. Penelope smiled. Perhaps Harvey would ease their troubles after all.

They walked, serenaded by the musical tones of her heels slurping and popping in and out of the mud. The most unladylike sounds to be certain, which served to reinforce the knowledge that she never would have survived as Mr. Wallace's wife. He forever criticized her about various things, even before their engagement, and he seemed to take delight in ambushing her with his high opinions of her disgrace when there was an audience. Her cheeks burned at the horrid memories of being deprecated. She always continued to hold her head high, just as a lady should, just as Mrs. Blackwell had instilled in her, at least until her bedroom door clicked closed and she collapsed on her bed in a fit of tears. She'd maintain her dignity now, too. However, she took care to not appear prideful. All of which, Beau seemed completely unaware of. How was she to win him over with her charm if he paid her little heed?

"Hello, Marshal," an older man greeted Beau when they stepped into the livery. "The boys said you'd be along."

Warmth chased the chill from her skin at Beau's smile toward the liveryman.

"I thank you," Beau said as he released her arm and deposited the little girl into the back of a wagon and then swooped up John and sat him next to his sister. "And where have the scamps gone off to?"

"Toward home I s'pect."

"As they should," Beau said.

"They's excited about their new ma." The man tipped his hat. "This must be the lucky lady."

"Penelope Parker," she said as she held out her hand. Before the man could act like a gentleman and kindly introduce himself, strong fingers gripped her waist and lifted her and Harvey onto the seat. She harrumphed.

Actually harrumphed. Cook harrumphed. Wren harrumphed. Her father harrumphed. Penelope had made it a point to never harrumph. Ever. Bewildered over the sound that had emitted from her, she blinked and gaped like one of those fish kept in the clear glass bowls used as centerpieces at one of the Donahues' fancy soirees. Beau had not only dismissed her but forced the kindly gentleman to dismiss her, as well.

Beau climbed in beside her. His muscled thigh brushed against hers and she sucked in a sharp breath. She shifted away from him and harrumphed again. Harvey tilted his sweet little head. His eyebrows danced up and down like butterfly wings. Her poor pet thought she'd lost her wits and perhaps she had, dragging him to Oak Grove through torrential rains and dust clouds.

"Much obliged, Tom." Beau clicked his tongue, and the wagon lurched, throwing Penelope back against the hard seat.

She righted herself and tried not to think about his rudeness when he stopped the liveryman from properly greeting her. Had Beau not heard the man? Did her future husband suffer from deafness? The wagon creaked with the turn of the wheels. John mumbled from the back. His little sister made *la-la* sounds, and Penelope tried not to worry over Beau's gruffness and focused on her surroundings, committing to memory the main thoroughfare. The businesses, the houses with white picket fences. Satisfaction sank into her heart. The homes were nothing like the massive structure she'd shared with her father, but they were appealing to the eye and inviting. Excitement infused her. Which house was to be hers? The one with blue shutters or the one with the wraparound porch? She could see herself milling about on the porch and taking her morning tea or looking out the small window with white lace coverings.

"Are we far from home?"

Beau tilted his head in her direction. For the first time she noticed the dark shadow outlining his jaw. Somehow the lack of a razor upon his face only made him that much more handsome. The dark circles below his eyes made him look vulnerable. Weary. Perhaps his crass demeanor was due to exhaustion. Maybe she should excuse his rudeness with the holster and grant him a reprieve. She wouldn't press the matter of their marriage until after she had rested and allowed him the sleep he looked in desperate need of.

"Not too far." He turned the wagon down a narrow lane. The houses became smaller and farther apart. Some of the excitement at seeing her new home vanished as the ground lost the green grass and gave way to the muted brown of mud. She scratched the spot between Harvey's ears as she chewed the inside of her cheek.

A few minutes later, Beau stopped them in front of a small, crude cabin, no bigger than the gardener's shed at her father's house. From the moment she'd decided to respond to the mail-order-bride ad she'd never once considered what sort of roof would hang over her head. She'd cared only about living beyond her next birthday. She never thought the roof would be nothing more than thatch. But she had envisioned one thing, ever since she'd read the ad. The white picket fence. But as she looked around, she realized that mental picture had been very wrong. These fence posts stood at odd angles, as if they'd given in to the sway of the wind. Not white, not straight. She shivered. From her soaked clothing or from fear of the unknown, she did not know. Harvey licked her hand. The poor boy was scared, too. What had she done?

Up ahead, two of the children dueled with sticks. They moved back and forth in a dance, tapping their sticks together. The third, the middle child, the one who'd been hiding under the desk at the jail, sat on the rickety, sloping porch. The wagon rocked as Beau jumped to the ground. He snagged the youngest of the boys from the back of the wagon, and then the little girl. He carried them into the yard.

"Matthew, start the fire."

"Yes, sir." The oldest boy dropped his stick.

Beau turned toward her. "If you're determined on staying in Oak Grove, I dare say you'll need to learn how to exit the buckboard without assistance."

Her cheeks burned with embarrassment. She had never considered herself pampered or spoiled. After all, she had had only Wren to tend to her needs, and then on just the rare occasion. Penelope had found her, or she should say Harvey had found her, huddled in an alley in a fit of tears. The young lady, no more than a child, had lost her parents and her home. With no place to go, Penelope had brought her home, much to Papa's displeasure. However, there had always been a servant or gentleman to offer her a hand down whenever she chanced to be in a conveyance.

She peered over the edge and then looked back at the house. Beau and the children disappeared inside. Harvey dug his sharp tiny nails into her arm. "It's all right, boy."

The wagon dipped when she shifted her weight. She gripped the back of the seat and scooted to the edge until the toe of her shoe touched the step. The sight of her soiled clothing made her cringe. No wonder Beau had not been impressed with her attire. It was ruined, and she'd chosen her finest to meet her future husband for the first time. She should have planned better, perhaps changed at their last stop in Onion City instead of travelling in the same gown for days. She sighed. No matter. What was done was done. There was no use in risking frown wrinkles over something she could not change.

She gripped the side tighter and took a breath and imagined descending the next few feet was nothing more than descending marble stairs in a ball gown or, rather, a walk in the park. A muddy, treacherous park. She stretched her foot toward the ground. Harvey shook and whined. She startled when Beau appeared directly in front of her and snatched her pet from her arms. "You'll frighten him to death if you're not careful."

She tugged the inside of her cheek between her teeth to keep the hurt stinging her chest from making her cry. Beau's strong, warm hands curved around her waist and he lifted her down. Still smarting from his gruff words, and angry that she'd been weak and easily moved by his tartness, she whispered, "Thank you."

She must be more exhausted than she thought to be so easily overcome with emotion. She'd been schooled by her father's terseness. She'd learned to not show emotion, especially the weakness of tears, lest it brought on more humiliation. She needed to remain aloof no matter the occurrence. According to her father, it was what any prospective husband would expect. She simply needed rest to return to the reserve she'd learned to perfect.

Beau released her but grabbed hold of her elbow and kept her steady. "I feared the children would perish from starvation if I waited for your success."

She gulped. They were back to that, were they?

He escorted her into the small home. She folded her arms around her waist to ward off the chill permeating her bones now that the sun no longer touched her. What's more, she schooled her features and tried not to show shock or disappointment over the meager furnishings inside the dim little hovel. Sparse light filtered in through the west window, illuminating a small table and two spindle-backed chairs. There was a ladder leading to a loft. It looked as though it had been newly installed as it wasn't the same dark wood as the rest of the home. A frayed and worn homemade quilt, which had certainly seen better days, hung on a rope dividing the room nearly in half. Another, just as tattered, covered a doorway she hoped led to another room. Perhaps a washroom, but given the pitcher and bowl on a small table beneath the window, her hopes faltered.

No parlor.

No sofa.

No ballroom.

No kitchen.

No white lace curtains to look out of while she drank her afternoon tea.

Not even a chandelier hanging from the rafters. Rather, just a lone oil lamp on the table. One of the boys worked to light a fire in the fireplace, where pots and pans hung from a crude mantel.

"Since you've assured me you can cook, I'll leave you to it." He turned to leave.

Panic gripped her. "Wait! I can't—"

One dark eyebrow inched upward. "You can't what, Miss Parker?"

She glanced from him to each of the children. She'd heard Mr. Wallace and her father tell her she couldn't so many times, she'd believed she wasn't capable of much of anything, not even simply walking without causing a problem, which was why she'd often kept to the shadows and out of sight. Their constant disapproval had weighed on her shoulders. For once, she wanted to do something, like respond to a mail-order-bride ad. Like travel to the wilds on her own. To choose her own husband. If she could do those things, certainly she could find the means to feed these children.

She risked a glance at Beau. His look dared her to speak the truth. The boys looked at her with hopeful expressions, as if she was the answer to their prayers.

And what of her prayers? Her prayers of a life free from Mr. Wallace?

She tugged her bottom lip between her teeth, which was becoming quite the most annoying habit. Beau was correct. She didn't know the first thing about cooking or mothering anything other than Harvey.

He was easy.

He slept, walked and ate.

Mostly he begged for treats.

A moment of doubt slammed against her chest. Perhaps she should return home and beg her father's forgiveness and face Mr. Wallace's wrath. No! She could not. He'd already buried several wives. Gossip whispered in every ballroom told her what she knew in her heart. Mr. Wallace was either one poor soul at choosing brides, or he knew how to get rid of them. She would be his next victim if she walked down the aisle. That thought alone made her dig in her heels. She snapped her shoulders back.

"I have no idea where the supplies are."

He narrowed his gaze. "You're stubborn, I see." Then he nodded. "The boys will show you."

She shook her head.

His eyebrow inched higher, and then quickly settled back into position. The harsh lines creasing the corners of his eyes softened. For a moment, he seemed hopeful, as if she were about to wave a white flag and surrender. But she'd never surrender, lest she find herself returning to St. Louis on the next wagon out of town.

"I don't know their names."

"Do you know your Bible? The four Gospels?"

"Yes, of course." Her father wasn't the best of men, but he insisted on Sunday service, mostly to further his business contacts.

"Matthew, Mark, Luke and John," he said, counting on his fingers, and then pointed at the little girl with wild blond curls. "Queen Esther."

"Oh."

"I know it isn't much but try not to burn down my home while I'm gone." He twisted his hat in his hand, and color rose high in his cheeks as if he was ashamed of his own home. "I'll be staying at the jail until other arrangements can be made for you, Miss Parker."

He shut the door. Gone. Leaving her alone with children. Children she didn't know.

She smiled at each of them. "Very well, then, what shall we have for dinner?"

"Biscuits," the littlest boy said.

"John, is it?"

The child nodded.

"Would you like to help me?"

"He don't know how. He's too little," Matthew said. "He's only three."

"Then how about you?"

Matthew eyed her. "You don't know how to cook, do you?"

"Of course I do. All I need are some turnips and carrots." She rose and pulled her shoulders back, and then they quickly sank at the boys' crestfallen expressions. It was obvious there were no turnips or carrots available. "However, given the day of travel and being left waiting in the rain, perhaps I'll treat you to dinner at that café in town. Moore's House, is it? I saw it when I was looking for your pa."

They whooped and clapped their hands.

"First you must clean your faces and comb your hair."

"You gonna clean your face, too?" The middle child asked.

"If I am to be presentable, I must." And then she needed to find something dry to wear and preferably clean, which posed a problem given all her belongings remained where the driver had left them.

Chapter Three

Penelope snipped a loose thread from her tidy knot, slipped her feet into the pant legs and then wrapped the marshal's black tie around her waist. She formed a pretty bow and rotated it so it hung down her back. She glanced down the length of her body and took delight in her created fashion. She may not know how to cook, care for children or dismount a wagon on her own, but she knew how to make fashionable clothing out of meager supplies.

She pulled aside the blanket dividing the bedroom from the rest of Beau's home. The boys waited in a line, oldest to youngest, their eyes wide. Queen Esther sat on a threadbare rug, playing with blocks. Penelope fished a comb from the borrowed vest pocket and dipped it into the bowl of water. "Come along. Let's see you tidy."

"What'd you go and do with Pa's things?" Matthew asked as he leaned back from the comb.

"Pardon?" she asked as she grasped the boy's chin, tugged him closer and pulled the comb through his thick white-blond curls. She leaned in and sniffed. "Now, don't you smell handsome and clean? If you wish to eat a good meal, you'll look like a gentleman, not a waif having weltered in the mud."

The boy's eyes grew as round as saucers.

"But those be Pa's church clothes," the middle child protested.

Luke, was it? "Are. Those *are* Pa's church clothes, and I've done nothing that can't be undone. They'll be right as new come Sunday."

Mark shook his head, his mouth turned downward.

Kneeling in front of the shy boy, she held his gaze while she combed his hair. "I promise. Your pa won't even know I've worn his clothes."

She motioned for Luke to stand in front of her. "I couldn't very well go out to dinner wearing a soiled gown with such handsome young men, could I?"

"S'pect not. But don't say we didn't warn ya when Pa gets right blister'n mad," he said, finishing with a toothless grin.

Penelope had seen blistering mad, and she had a difficult time believing Beau was capable of such emotion. There had been enough going on this afternoon for a man to lose his mind, and he hadn't. She doubted he'd do so when—*if*—he discovered she'd altered his clothes. "All will be well, you'll see. Right as rain."

She finished taming the mad curls of the children the best she could and scrubbed down their cheeks before opening the door for some much-needed fresh air. She'd expected shuffling feet to be racing for the door and turned to find the boys motionless. "Well, are you coming along?"

Matthew shrugged his shoulders. "You're forgetting Esther."

"And what about your dog? He can't stay here by himself," Luke said as he scooped Harvey into his arms.

Penelope blinked. Harvey panted his happy little pant, like he did whenever they went on their walks, walks which consisted of him being carried. Her pet deserved a part in a drama, especially when he held his poor little paw up as if in discomfort as soon as they hit the cobblestones back home. "Harvey will be content staying behind for a while. He needs his rest after all his travels."

Satisfied, Luke crouched and placed Harvey on the floor, to which she received a raised brow from the spoiled pet. She turned her attention to the infant. Esther drooled. Her chin glistened with wetness. The front of her little shirt was soaked. Penelope tried to recall how Beau had taken Esther in his arms. However, she'd been so preoccupied with all that she'd heard and seen since her arrival in Oak Grove that she hadn't paid any heed. She'd expected her future groom to greet her upon her arrival. She hadn't expected to find him locked in jail with a passel of children. She certainly had not expected his objections to their marriage. Her plans, albeit made in haste, were quickly falling apart, and she needed to do everything possible to keep them together—which included picking up the baby. She bent down to scoop the child off the floor.

"No!" Matthew shouted, drawing her attention. The boy smirked. "Her flannel needs changing."

"Her flannel?" Penelope's eyebrows knitted together.

"Her napkin. It's wet."

Penelope had never heard of an infant's shirt called a flannel or a napkin before. She had never had the occasion to consider what an infant needed.

Luke rolled his eyes and pointed to the baby's bum.

"Even I know what a flannel is. I'm only five." Luke giggled. "What sort of ma did you get us, Matty?"

"I didn't do it. Mrs. Bobby Jean did," Matthew argued.

Penelope bent forward, and then tilted her head as if to see beneath the baby. "The sort that has not had the chance to encounter a child."

"You best learn if you want to be our ma." Matthew grabbed a cloth from the back of a spindled chair and then knelt on the floor in front of Esther. He laid the baby on her back and instructed Penelope on how to change the soiled nappy.

"Thank you," she said as she patted Matthew's shoulder. "I did not expect to be a mother when I answered the ad to be your pa's wife."

"You don't want to be my ma?" Mark's soft whisper held fear.

"It's not that I don't want to be your mother, Mark. I am surprised, and I fear I do not know how to be one."

What if she failed?

She'd meant what she'd told Beau, about not forming attachments to the children. Bonds were something she did not understand, except to Cook, Wren and Harvey. Cook had been a part of her life since she could remember. Wren and Harvey were desperate creatures with no homes to call their own. To her surprise, she'd quickly discovered she'd needed them more than they'd needed a roof over their heads. She could not need these children. No matter how much she wanted to need them.

Mark's small hand slipped around hers, and before she knew what she was doing, her fingers curled around his. The warmth seeped into her heart. She knew in that moment maintaining her aloofness with them would be impossible. She could not keep her heart distant from these young ones, so obviously in need of what she'd secretly longed to give for longer than she could remember. She would have to break her word to Beau. Certainly, he would understand. "I give you my promise. I'll do all I can to learn, if you boys can be on your best behavior and be patient with me."

Matthew stuck out his hand. "You have my word, ma—ma'am."

"Mine, too," Luke said as he held out his little hand.

Mark wrapped his arms around her, and burying his face into her neck, he hugged her. Penelope froze. The air in her lungs caught. She sputtered and coughed. The boy stepped behind Matthew and blinked at her.

"I am sorry," she said, clutching her neck. "I fear I have captured a good deal of travel dust in my throat and it has yet to vacate."

As if he understood, Mark slipped out from his hiding place behind his older brother.

Penelope drew in a breath and clapped her hands together. "Very well," she said as she scooped up the baby. She settled Esther on her hip and circled her fingers around John's wrist. "Now, shall we eat?"

The boys whooped and hollered as they raced out the door. Following behind them, she stepped onto the porch and let the late afternoon sun warm her. Her bones still shook with a chill after her time in the spring rain. She turned to bid the shack she was about to call home goodbye and realized it didn't seem as in disrepair as she'd first thought. Still, it was small, especially for a family of seven. It was a shame she hadn't had the notion to beg Father for an increase in her allowance while she'd been in St. Louis. Then perhaps she'd have saved enough to acquire a home more suitable to her needs and to the children's needs.

The door clicked behind them. A high-pitched whine turned to an insistent yip. The pitiful noises clawed at her resolve to leave Harvey in a strange place by himself. However, she could not risk the commotion her well-mannered pup might cause if anyone objected to his presence. "Harvey, stay and be a good boy. We'll bring you some tasty morsels."

"Morsels?" Matthew asked. "What's that?"

"A bit of food."

Matthew fisted his hands on his hips. "Do I have to? We never been to an eating place before."

"Of course not." Penelope shook her head. "I would not ask you to give up food from your plate, but you can if you'd like."

"I want to feed Harvey. Does he bite?" Luke jumped up and down in front of her. "I don't want to get bitten."

"He only bites naughty little fellows, so you best be on good behavior," she teased. "Now, what has happened to the wagon?" she asked, fully expecting the conveyance to be where it had been left.

"Pa must've taken it back to town."

Penelope stomped her foot. Why would he leave her alone with the children and with no wagon to get around? She thought back to her failed attempt to exit the conveyance earlier and had her answer. She did not know how to get in the thing. She did not know how to hook up the horse or make it move. She smiled. It was quite grand Beau had not left the wagon. He'd saved her from more embarrassment. Still, the convenience to ride to Moore's would have been a blessing. It would have been a greater blessing had Beau remained and escorted them to dinner. After all, the day had been long. The weeks had been even longer. She was cold, hungry and frustrated. Suddenly her hope of a new beginning seemed tenuous. Failure began to jeer in her mind, like her peers had whenever she'd attended a social gathering at her father's insistence. She'd milled in the shadows, keeping her gaze guarded and her chin high, her words kind and few whenever she'd been approached. Not once had she wavered in her determination to show strength and grace. However, in this new place, a place she believed to be her new home, with a new husband, she trembled and her back ached from keeping her upright. She feared she would crumble.

"It's not far. We can walk," Luke offered.

Her toes stretched and curled in her boots. The tiny blisters forming on her flesh smarted. The stockings she refused to hang out to dry by the fire remained wet. Traversing the mud with Beau's support had been difficult. Carrying Esther and holding John's hand, it would be impossible. "I don't think we should. Perhaps I can make biscuits."

Disappointment painted the boys' faces. The crestfallen looks were enough to sting her eyes.

Matthew took Esther from her arms. "Luke, take John's hand. Mark hold Ma's hand."

Mark's eyes widened.

Her heart lurched at being called *ma*. She'd become accustomed to being called many things, *wallflower*, *plain*, *simple*, *lanky*, a *social disgrace*, *spinster*. Never had she imagined she'd be called *ma*. It had a nice sound, but it wasn't a name she'd earned or deserved. Allowing its use would be a facade she'd have to give up once the curtains closed the stage. It seemed dishonest to encourage the word. "Miss Parker is fine, if you please."

She did not like the disappointed frowns on their faces. She didn't want to hurt their feelings any further. However, she was not their mother.

"Yes, ma'am, Miss Parker." Matthew wrinkled his nose.

She stepped off the porch and onto the muddy ground. Her heels sank.

Mark tugged on her wrist, drawing her attention. "If you walk with your toes, you won't get stuck so much."

She doubted he spoke the truth, but her way wasn't efficient. She offered him a smile. "Thank you."

The boy was right. Walking on the tips of her cold toes helped her navigate the slippery mud. The restaurant wasn't far, and with Matthew's shortcut it didn't take them long to reach the main street. He seemed aware of her dilemma and tried his best to find her patches of grass for her to use until they reached the boardwalk. She'd seen more courteous behavior from an eight-year-old orphan than she'd seen from most gentlemen of her social class. Someone had instilled good manners in the children, which nearly brought a torrential downpour of tears from her eyes. Whoever had taught them, taught them well.

She brought her fingers to her mouth. Would she ruin them? She certainly hoped not, but the thought was enough to send her back to St. Louis. If it had been an option, which it was not.

Once they were in front of Moore's House, Penelope drew in the aroma of warm fresh bread, roast chicken and vegetables. Her stomach grumbled and she prayed for an edible, tasty meal and fortitude to face the dining patrons. She hoped for grace and etiquette, something she most assuredly lacked when it came to being in the public's view. She'd hoped to leave a good impression on the folks of Oak Grove, but thus far, she'd done nothing but make a fool out of herself when she'd fallen in front of Judge Winter and his court. And now she was about to enter an eating establishment where, no doubt, fine, reputable people enjoyed their meals. She hoped she didn't twist an ankle and tumble, spill her water, or worse yet, drop Esther once Matthew handed her back.

"Achoo!" Oh, dear, or sneeze. At least she'd left Harvey at home and didn't have to worry over his sweet, spoiled little entreaties for scraps.

Beau sank onto the cot, settled his hat over his eyes and crossed his legs at his ankles. Even if he hadn't been bone exhausted from the last few days trailing Jessup, wrangling Miss Parker's luggage would have done the deed. How she'd managed to procure passage for her luggage was beyond him. The trunk was large enough to hold his entire household belongings, and it had to weigh just as much as Brian Gannon's ox. Her carpetbags weren't much lighter, considering they were soaked from the afternoon rainstorm.

The deed was done, and the children were being supervised. Now maybe he could find some much-needed sleep. His stomach growled in protest, reminding him that he'd forgotten to grab a bite to eat from Moore's before rescuing Miss Parker's belongings from the curious doves milling on Main Street. He adjusted his hat to block the light. His lids felt heavy as sleep beckoned him.

Quick, heavy footfalls clambered on the porch. Beau ground his teeth. The door to the jail burst open.

"Marshal." Miller Gannon's calm tones belied the nature of his visit. Especially since Beau had threatened to hang his underling if he allowed anyone to disturb him.

"Oak Grove best be on fire, Gannon," Beau growled.

"No, Marshal. It'd be better if that were the case."

Beau righted his hat as he swung his feet to the floor and glared at his friend. "Invasion?"

"Not the sort you're conjuring. Ya best make your way to Moore's."

"Jessup?" Beau pulled his eyebrows together and then looked at the occupied cell next to him. Jessup curled on the cot, snoring like a train. The outlaw had taken a shine to Moore's eldest daughter, and everyone in town knew it was only a matter of time before he tried to snatch the young lady. Beau sighed, thankful Jessup Davis was behind bars for the time being. Exhausted as he was, he'd nearly forgotten they'd captured him early this morning. "Never mind. A twister?"

"Worse," Gannon said. A lesser man would have

twisted his hat in knots. Miller was the epitome of calm, with a steely-eyed gaze that made most criminals hold up their hands before his pistols left his holsters. He wasn't one to get nervous at Beau's displeasure.

"What could be worse than a tornado ripping through town?" Beau jumped to his feet and slowly shook his head. "No. The boys?"

Miller didn't budge a muscle. He didn't blink. He held Beau's gaze.

"I left them with their nanny."

Miller's Adam's apple bobbed, and Beau knew he was in trouble, given Miller never showed signs of distress.

"I've never known you to be lost for words. Spit it out."

"Well, I saw it with my own eyes while taking a meal with Brian and my nephew, Ben." Miller paused. His fingers bit into the rim of his hat.

Good gravy, what had happened that had made his deputy marshal fit to be tied?

"Miller Gannon, I'll lock you up this instant if you don't get the words out of your gullet."

"Seems your, uh, wife is leading the charge."

"My wife? I don't have a wife." Beau pushed past Miller and strode across the road. "The stubborn woman. I told her I wasn't itching to marry. I wasn't going to marry. I. Am. Not. Going. To. Marry. Not her, not anyone."

"Seems to me she didn't understand your intentions, Marshal," Miller chuckled.

Beau turned on his friend and poked him in the chest.

"This isn't funny, Gannon. Not funny at all. You want a wife?"

Miller sobered. "I don't have need of one. Not like you do, Beau."

Beau thrust his hands on his hips. "What about your brother? Brian has a whelp in need of a ma."

"And you have five." Miller smiled.

Beau flinched as if he'd been punched in the gut. He turned on his heel and stomped up the stairs to Moore's establishment.

"Beau?"

"What?" He turned on his deputy marshal.

"There's more."

Beau narrowed his gaze. "Go on."

"There's a dog."

"Gravy and biscuits, she didn't."

"Fear she did. Well, kind of. Seems the pooch broke free of his jail and followed your family."

A growl emitted deep from Beau's throat. "Family? What family?" Up until two months ago he'd been on the outs with his kin. Hadn't spoken to his brother in years, and then he up and crossed the pearly gates without so much as a farewell, leaving five orphans with mouths and stomachs and little minds of their own. Now Beau was surrounded by more chaos than he'd ever imagined possible.

The door swung open before he was able to grip the handle. Savory scents of roasted meat and baked bread assaulted him, forcing his stomach to release a loud grumble.

"Marshal," Mr. Moore greeted him.

"I've come to collect my children and my—"

"Your wife?" Mr. Moore interrupted. A gray bushy brow snapped at him. "We had not heard you were looking for a wife or else I would have suggested my daughter. It would have put Jessup off her trail in a hurry."

"I am not married, Mr. Moore," Beau said, and then added, at Mr. Moore's smile, "nor am I looking to be. I hope the youngsters haven't made too much of a disturbance."

"No, Marshal. It's your wife—er, the lady with the children."

"Pardon? What of the dog?"

"The dog is well-mannered and welcomed among my patrons, especially by Mrs. Moore, much to my displeasure. Once Mrs. Moore caught sight of the furry beast, she took him up on her lap and allowed him to eat straight from her plate. The audacity! Thanks to you and your wife—er, the lady with the children, I'll be pestered into purchasing a four-legged companion. As for the lady, Moore's might not be a big-city eating establishment," Mr. Moore said as his cheeks reddened, "but I dare say we have a dress code. The lady refuses to leave."

Beau closed his eyes and drew in a mighty slow breath. What sort of mess had the children gotten him into? "You're telling me the boys are behaving themselves?"

"Right thing, Marshal."

"And the lady?"

"Not so right."

"I see." No, he didn't see. Excepting maybe she still looked like she'd taken a swim down the Neosho River and lay out to dry on the muddy banks. And what on earth was she doing here when he'd left her and the children at his home? And why had she not taken the dog back when the mutt had first arrived? He'd never hear the end of Mr. Moore's complaint. Never. However, that was something that could be dealt with once the Moores acquired their pet. For now, he had other pressing issues. "I will take care of the matter, Mr. Moore."

"Thank you. Dressed as she is, no wonder she's shivering, sneezing and sniffling." Mr. Moore dropped his chin. "After all we've endured last year, we can't have sickness burning through Oak Grove again."

The hair on Beau's nape stood on end. Had Penelope fallen ill? The familiar gnaw of guilt nibbled at him. He shouldn't have left her in a state of disarray and without making certain she knew to sit in front of the fire to warm herself. He assumed she would have been drawn to the heat once Matthew had the flames going. Obviously, she was more pampered than he'd first believed. Had her servants told her when to warm herself? He drew his hand over his eyes. What a selfish fool he'd been, concerned about his own well-being. Beau tugged his vest down.

"Oh, and, Marshal, Mrs. Moore and I'd appreciate it if you didn't make any more of a scene than what's already been done."

"Yes, sir." Beau approached the dining area as if he were walking into a den of rattlesnakes, all the while wondering what sort of fit Penelope had thrown. No need to ask, since he'd hear about it soon enough or read it in the Oak Grove's *Daily Record*.

"Pa!" Two of the boys rushed toward him, nearly tackling him to the ground, but he focused on the pale slender neck thinly veiled by strands of lustrous black hair. He stared at the spiral curls teasing her collar and racing down her back. "Matthew, Luke."

"Ma—er, Miss Parker—bought us dinner," Matthew said.

Beau flinched in tandem with Miss Parker. She turned in her seat. The soft curve of her cheek grew pink in the glow of the lamplight. Her blue eyes caught his and held him prisoner for several long seconds. He shifted his weight to shake the increase of his pulse.

"Yeah, roasted potatoes and biscuits," Luke said, drawing Beau's attention. The boy swiped a crumb from the corner of his mouth. "Best fixin's I ever ate."

"Is that so?" Beau returned his attention to Miss Parker. "I thought you were making the children supper."

Dark lashes brushed against the high curve of her cheekbones. She angled her head, forcing a curl to waltz. The motion captivated him until it halted against her neck.

"After a strenuous journey and the day's events, I did not think it would hurt matters overly much as to how I provided a meal for the children."

"When I am disturbed from my sleep in order to fetch my wards, it matters, Miss Parker." He cleared the gruffness from his voice and then smiled. "Now, do tell me, what it is you've done to stir up Mr. Moore's hornet's nest."

"Besides Harvey making an excited entrance?" She scooted from the table and rose.

It took Beau longer than it should have to realize what was amiss. "Are you wearing britches?"

She nodded.

Narrowing his gaze, he peered closer. Although his necktie cinched them at her waist and they were gathered up the sides to fit her length into neat ruffles, he was certain she wore his britches. "Are those *my* britches? My vest and shirt?"

She blushed, then dropped her chin to her chest before meeting his gaze.

"Told ya Pa'd get blistering mad," Luke said as he left Beau's side and climbed back onto his seat.

Miss Parker held his gaze for a moment, then she began to twist her fingers together. The stubborn determination she'd carried like a pistol on her hip seemed to shrivel beneath his scrutiny. He recalled the damp gown she'd worn earlier and the luggage he recently placed in the back of the wagon. He'd acted like the worst of scoundrels since her arrival. He should have suggested dinner after her long travels and her ordeal in the rain instead of expecting her to immediately care for children she didn't even know.

He couldn't fault her for her ingenuity and practicality. Admiration for her ability to adapt sparked in him. And that was a skill his wards could use in life. He expanded his chest in pride. She wasn't his wife, and she wasn't even the hired nanny he'd sought, but he was proud to have her sitting at a table with his children.

A quick glance around at the turned-up noses and pursed lips of the other diners told him they didn't feel quite the same as he did. It was obvious the majority of Moore's patrons disapproved of Miss Parker and her attire. One lady even had the audacity to nod her approval with a raised brow toward Beau, as if to grant him permission to take Penelope in hand. As if he would ever abuse a lady in such a way. He gave the woman a hard look, and then glanced at each diner until they returned to their own business and their meals.

The irritation at having been pulled from his cot due to the ruckus she'd caused quickly dissipated in the face of the derision she'd received from these folks. Empathy and anger on her behalf burned his ears. He knew what it was like to be the focus of gossip, but he'd had the anger of betrayal at the hands of a woman he'd loved to shield him. What shielded Miss Parker, that she could remain in a dining room full of uppity ladies and gentlemen? He scrubbed his hand over his scruffy chin.

"I'm not mad, Luke." Beau ruffled John's neatly combed hair and lifted him from his chair. He settled the tot on his lap, and then scooped a bite of potatoes into his mouth. He spoke around the mouthful and received several glares. "Are you going to sit, Miss Parker?"

The perfect little bow tied at her back shuddered. She lengthened her spine. Her shoulders inched back. Good, she was posturing, hopefully back to her cool reserve.

"Miss Parker?"

He broke off a piece of biscuit and fed a bite to Harvey, who now perched his front paws on Beau's leg. He tore off another tidbit and gave it to John and then shoved a bite into his mouth to keep from smiling when she took her chair. She kept her hands in her lap as she stared at her plate.

"Thank you, Miss Parker."

She lifted her eyes. "Pardon me?"

"Thank you for cleaning up my children and combing their hair."

"Yes, of course. I couldn't very well bring them here with dirt smudged on their faces."

Beau dipped his napkin in his glass of water and leaned forward.

She leaned back.

"Yet you've a good deal of mud on yours."

"Oh." Wide blue eyes held his. He had the odd desire to knuckle his breastbone. Having gone the day without a meal must have stirred up a bit of indigestion. He ignored the sensation and pressed the cloth against her soft pink cheek.

Her lids fell over her eyes. Her chin dipped again. "I can cook, Mr. Garrett," she whispered. "But you had no turnips or carrots."

"We'll discuss it tomorrow. For now, let's enjoy our meal." The fact that she even knew about those items impressed him. Perhaps he'd further misjudged her.

She looked at him, hope in her eyes, and he wondered what it was he'd just done. For now, it didn't matter. All that mattered was the sense of peace that settled around him. Maybe it was the satisfaction of silencing the gnawing of his gut. Maybe it was because he was eating with his children without food being thrown.

Or maybe it was her, Miss Penelope Parker.

Chapter Four

Penelope ran her hands down the front of her skirts and smiled. All she'd thought about the last couple of nights was how relieved she'd been that Beau hadn't chastised her for wearing his britches to Moore's House. She'd waited on pins and needles the following morning for him to reprimand her for her behavior. Instead, he'd invited her and the children to dinner. He'd even arrived and escorted them. And last night, he'd even sat beside her. Hope welled in her chest. Perhaps he'd had a change of heart. Perhaps he'd marry her, and sooner than she'd thought possible, given their first encounter upon her arrival. Then she could breathe and quit looking over her shoulder for her father and Mr. Wallace. Once she was married, once she was Mrs. Garrett, Mr. Wallace could not lay claim to her or her inheritance. Not that she cared about her father's wealth.

She waltzed outside, lighter on her feet than she had moved since leaving St. Louis. Easing the door open to the henhouse, she peeked inside. An awful stench assaulted her nose. Her mouth watered and she gripped

her stomach. Why would anyone keep such fowl creatures in a small, confined space? She didn't recall the
mourning doves she'd fed during her afternoon walks
smelling so bad, but then Harvey had kept them at a
distance with his overly excited yipping. It was a good
thing she'd made sure he was shut up in the house. A
bribing promise that they would attempt another meal
at Moore's House later today hopefully ensured the children's cooperation at leaving her obnoxious pet inside
until she completed this morning's frightening task.

After several days in Oak Grove, she figured it was
time to attempt the chores expected of Beau's wife, if
she was going to prove to him she was capable.

She tilted her chin to better see around the door.
Rising sunlight streamed in, and she caught a glimpse
of one little beady eye. The hen shook her feathers
and Penelope slammed the door closed. The mourning doves she'd come to call by the names she'd given
them weren't nearly as big. And they most certainly did
not have claws as long or sharp.

"Are you certain we must gather eggs every morning?" She drew in a long breath, which was most certainly a mistake she regretted once she caught another
whiff of *chicken*. Harvey had never smelled so bad,
not even after his back-scratching roll in a pile of refuse on one of his escapes from home. That stench had
been so horribly horrendous that Papa had threatened
to send Harvey away. Fortunately, Cook had her remedies. Remedies Penelope had failed to learn. However,
she doubted such solutions would work on foul-smelling
birds. She took one last glance around the yard, focus-
ing on the hitching post, hoping to see Beau.

"Go on. Whatcha waiting for?" Luke propped his hands on his hips, a gesture she'd seen Beau do. They may not be his children by blood, but they sure mimicked him. "You're not afraid of a little chicken, are you?"

Penelope wrinkled her nose. If she was going to convince Beau their marriage was advantageous, she had to win the children over, whether he liked it or not. Besides, she was already growing fond of them. "It stinks."

"You ain't ever smelled chickens before?" Matthew questioned.

"*Haven't* you ever smelled chickens before," she corrected. "And of course I have." Although it was usually after Cook served one for dinner, right along with roasted vegetables and warm, buttery bread straight out of the oven. Her stomach grumbled in response. Her lids fell over her eyes, and for a moment, she was sitting at the large glossy dining table and inhaling—she gagged—*chicken*. Live chickens, not the roasted sort coated in spices and herbs.

"She looks ill," Luke said.

"Nah, just a little green." Matthew clutched his throat and made over-exaggerated gagging noises until he collapsed on the ground. He laughed and then jumped to his feet. "She'll be good if she wants to marry our pa."

This statement was directed at her. "I—I suppose you're correct, Matthew. Now, will you quit funning around?"

If only she could have packed Cook and Wren in one of her bags and brought them along to Kansas, then she would not find herself in such a precarious position. Cook would have girded up her loins and barged right into the beady-eyed birds' domain, and without any hint of fear. It was a shame that Papa hadn't appreciated Cook's efforts, always complaining she never used enough salt or that the juicy meats weren't tender enough. Penelope sensed her father was happiest when he was complaining.

And poor Wren had never been anything but a nuisance to him, even though she kept to the shadows and quiet as a mouse whenever Papa was in residence. No doubt, Papa believed she was a waste of her monthly allowance. Since it was Penelope's to do with as she pleased, she pleased to hire Wren. More for companionship to stave off the loneliness than anything. Still, she'd been a great deal of help, fetching afternoon tea on the occasion. A stab of guilt poked at her conscience. Although she'd left an envelope for Wren, she couldn't be certain her father hadn't intervened and taken it from her. Especially if he'd discovered her maid had had anything to do with Penelope running from marriage to Mr. Wallace.

"You ain't gonna make a good wife if you can't gather eggs for breakfast." Matthew elbowed his younger brother. "Ain't that right, Luke?"

She sighed. Sending for Wren and Cook would sure make her life in Oak Grove easier and meals more tolerable. And she'd have friends. Having Cook around would also go a long way to winning over Beau. However, if she sent word for Cook and Wren, she risked revealing her whereabouts to Papa and also Mr. Wallace. Without the protection of Beau's name, she wasn't ready to tell her father what she'd done.

"Yes'm. Everyone knows how to get eggs," Luke said with a huge grin, revealing missing teeth.

Everyone except her.

"And Pa likes his eggs, too. Every morning. Fries them right up over the fire."

She knew this, had seen it the last few mornings as she exited the bedroom. She'd been surprised to find Beau had returned from spending the night at the jail, crouched before the fire, frying up breakfast for the children and for her.

Matthew pressed the basket into her hand as his lips formed a firm line. She couldn't tell if he was teasing her or being serious.

Well, there was nothing to do but gird up her own loins and perform the deed herself. She white-knuckled the basket. It hung low with the drop of her shoulders. Eggs meant marriage. No eggs meant no marriage. No Beau. No protection. It meant going home and apologizing to the widower Mr. Wallace for running off and leaving him standing at the altar in front of his friends and family and then facing his wrath behind closed doors. If she couldn't gather up the courage, how could she gather eggs? She might as well return home and become Mrs. Wallace. She could see the epitaph: Penelope Prudence Parker Wallace. The Fourth or was it the Tenth Mrs. Wallace. Long in the Tooth. Childless and Chicken. Never Knew the Kindness of a Gentleman.

She sniffed and swiped an imaginary tear from her eye. Not all of it was true. Beau had shown her some kindness, even though he'd been slightly surly. She certainly couldn't blame him. After all, he'd thought he was getting a nursemaid for his children, not a wife.

Especially not a wife with nothing to recommend her. No domestic skills. No beauty. And certainly not one single egg.

"So?" Matthew prodded.

"Very well, I will try."

Matthew hitched up his britches, and she noted to herself to see about finding him a belt or suspenders at the general store.

"You can't just try, Miss Penelope. You must conquer." Matthew puffed out his chest. She couldn't help wondering where the child had learned this persistent tactic.

Her brow dipped and she knew it had to be the most unladylike furrow. "The hens?"

Luke snickered.

"No, you goose, the eggs." Matthew laughed.

"Yes. Yes, you are correct. The eggs." If she could snatch one egg, then she could snatch two, maybe even three. First, one. A single egg would prove to herself that she could capture anything she set her mind to, including Oak Grove's Marshal Beau Garrett.

She snapped her shoulders back. Penelope Prudence Parker, stubborn as Cook's bread dough, could do whatever she set her mind to do. Why, hadn't she traveled to the wilds of Kansas alone, without a companion to accompany her? She could face the mean-looking hen with the sharp beak, if it meant gaining Beau's approval and the protection of his name.

"Very well," she said and yanked open the door. She planted her feet inside the smelly coop and dared not breathe.

"Go on, they won't getcha," Luke teased.

The beady-eyed hen cocked her head.

"Hello, Mrs. Hen," she said in a soft whisper.

Cluck.

Penelope jumped. The bird ruffled her feathers, but then she settled down and Penelope relaxed. This wasn't so bad. She was just a bird, as the rest of them were. They weren't as big as she'd imagined. If only removing an egg from beneath the hen's belly was as easy as tossing breadcrumbs to the mourning doves.

"Hmm." She tilted her chin. What if she fed the chickens? Would they abandon their eggs for biscuit crumbs? There had been a few left over from dinner last night that the boys had saved for Harvey.

"Boys," she said. "Can you get a biscuit from the table?"

Silence met her ears. She turned just in time to helplessly watch as the door closed. Followed by a distinct click. "Boys?"

Penelope shoved against it. It didn't budge.

"Matthew," she called. "Please open the door."

A small yip and a yap sent dread through her. One of the children released Harvey. Could things get worse?

"Did you get the eggs?" Luke's little voice filtered through the cracks.

"Open the door, Luke." Her tone must have reached a level of panic that alarmed the hens. Before she knew what was happening, the creatures jumped from their nests and began clucking and squawking. Brown ovals, illuminated by streams of sunlight through the slats, gleamed at her from each nest. She reached for one, and then another, and another. Three eggs! Not enough to feed five children and Beau. Still, she'd accomplished her goal. Now to surpass her own expectations. She reached in for a fourth. The birds became louder. One screeched. Penelope spun around. The beady-eyed hen attacked the smallest bird. The other hens joined in.

"No, shoo, shoo," she said as she waved the basket at them. Then they turned on her.

Beau led Dusty down the lane in front of the house and noted the walls remained intact. After a decent night's sleep and a fresh shave, he was proving tolerable. At least that's what Gannon had said when he woke him this morning with a strong brew of coffee.

Of course, apprehending Jessup Davis had gone a long way in making him much more tolerable. The thief had been a spur in his saddle ever since Beau had taken on the position of Oak Grove's marshal. Nevertheless, after a few good nights' sleep and a satisfying draw of coffee, his headache had disappeared and he could think a mite clearer. With clarity, he'd about come to a simple solution, even though it went against every grain in his body. He needed a caretaker for his children, and he was downright desperate since he couldn't continue with Mrs. Wheelwright's charity. She was too crass for his liking, and often berated the children for the smallest things, which was the last thing they needed. The last thing he wanted for them.

However, was he desperate enough to marry Penelope?

She was just as good as any woman, he supposed. Excepting maybe she was a bit soft on the eyes. He speared his fingers beneath his hat and scratched his head. Their meal together at Moore's House had been delightful and interesting. Fun, even when the patrons realized he wasn't going to bring his "wife" to heel. He laughed. Their evening had been the talk of the county, and no doubt would be for some time to come. What was more surprising, his teeth hadn't set to grinding once while enjoying the savory meal. The best meal he'd enjoyed in two months. No wonder the children seemed happier than he'd ever seen them. Who knew how long it'd been since they'd eaten anything as good as Moore's fare, if ever. Or had seen a dog eat right off a lady's fork. Beau still couldn't quite believe how Harvey had bamboozled Mrs. Moore into feeding him.

Then there was Penelope herself. Snubbing her nose at convention. A well-to-do lady tampering with his Sunday best. Wearing britches in an establishment as fancy as Moore's House. She'd been even prettier than when he'd first laid eyes on her, not that he'd tell her that and give her grand ideas of rushing him to the altar. Of course, she'd looked like a mutt that'd been out for a swim in the swollen, raging Neosho. Still she'd been the most comely thing he'd seen in a long while. Clothes dripping wet, hair plastered to her alabaster skin, face covered in mud.

He smiled to himself and then froze. He'd grown soft and warm, like Moore's fresh buttery biscuits straight out of the fire. That was no good. No sirree! The turn of his thoughts needed to veer off that treacherous course and head right back to *no, thank you*! He didn't need a wife and he certainly didn't want one, which was why his desperation would stop with needing a nanny. Not a wife!

Although…

She sure had spiffed up the boys a bit. Their hair had been combed, their faces washed, and they'd been like that each morning he'd come home to fix breakfast, which was more than he could have said about her. She might have been wearing his best Sunday getup at Moore's, but her face and hair had been a horrible mess. No wonder Mr. Moore had thrown a fit. To be honest, he was glad she'd given Moore a conniption, and the man should be grateful for the increased business her indiscretion had brought his establishment. Beau sure had been grateful. The talk of the town had quit revolving around Jessup and spun around Penelope, which had been a nice change. Gravy, he'd been half tempted to beg her to wear his britches to Moore's last night, too, just to see the shocked and bewildered looks.

He slowed Dusty to the memory of Penelope sitting with the boys, treating them with kindness, Esther on her lap. Not a harsh line etched her brow, as if irritated with the children for being children, like he'd seen on Mrs. Wheelwright's when he'd arrived to gather them after a long day chasing Jessup. He should have turned around and left the moment he'd seen all was well at the café. He should have left when curiosity stirred in his chest.

He twisted his lips. He should have left the moment he'd seen her. The moment he'd realized the patrons of Moore's House hadn't bothered her one bit with their condescending behavior over her britches. Her posture, hunched and uncertain, had straightened. Shoulders back, head high. She'd puzzled him from the beginning. One moment, she accepted his uncalled-for surliness, the next she used her tongue like a bayonet in battle.

Sometimes, she seemed shy and hesitant. Others, she had confidence, as if she were entertaining majors and generals at a ball. He didn't know if he needed to protect her from wagging tongues or allow her to defend herself. Which left him confused. She wasn't fully assured of herself like most ladies of her ilk, not like Mary Ella had been. Penelope didn't always have backbone, but she seemed to snap it in place when it counted.

As much as he'd heard about Penelope being a bad influence on the children if he allowed her to remain in Oak Grove, he couldn't deny the strength of character and fortitude she displayed when it counted, not to mention her practicality was exactly what the boys needed. However, guiding them and feeding them were two different things, and he suspected she didn't know one whit about cooking. How could she guide young ones if they were wasting away from starvation?

He jumped from Dusty as he halted in front of the hitching post and leaned his elbow against the rough wood. He certainly shouldn't have joined her and the children for dinner the last two nights. It was becoming a habit.

A soft coo reached his ears. His brows dipped as he focused on the porch. Esther sat on the planks, Harvey beside her, panting with his little tongue lolling out the side. Esther's little finger poked the mutt in the ear, but he didn't flinch. What a good dog.

The adorable, picturesque scene gave him pause. His stomach churned. Where was everyone else? Why was Esther being watched by a four-pound furry mutt? Beau's hackles rose. He scanned the yard. Little John sat beneath the shade of their lone tree, tossing a handful of dust into the air. The boy squeezed his eyes shut as dirt splattered his face. The white-blond locks dangling below his brow no longer held a silvery shine but rather a coat of dust.

Beau narrowed his gaze. Had Miss Parker had her fill? Had she skipped out of town already? He swept his hat from his head and smacked it against his thigh. "I should have known better than to trust a woman."

Not just a woman, a lady. A spoiled lady from the finer side of society. A lady who could ascertain between fake jewels and real ones before she had grown her first tooth. Heat crept up his neck. The daring of the woman. She had so easily turned her nose up at him when she believed him a criminal locked in a cell, yet she willingly left small children unattended to fend for themselves.

The audacity! He seethed. He didn't think he'd ever been this angry over another person's selfish deed, not even when Mary Ella had betrayed him to a Confederate soldier, which had caused the death of several of his men. He'd been angry, but he'd also felt a great deal of pity for her. She'd been a mere victim herself. A victim of vanity and greed.

"John, come along." Beau motioned with his hand. He didn't wait to see if the boy complied. Beau stomped across the yard, up the stairs and swept Queen Esther into his arms. Her chubby hands patted his cheeks as she giggled. His anger fueled further. "What have you been doing, little lady? Entertaining yourself, I see. Now, where has Miss Parker taken off to?"

He stepped over the threshold through the wide-open front door and glanced around. No sign of bright blue eyes and waist-length curly hair. His anger bordered near rage. She could have at least given him the courtesy of waiting until he arrived before she hightailed it out of town. "Miss Parker?"

He dipped his head into the curtained-off bedroom. Some of her belongings remained, which cooled his temper. A thump hit his boot, accompanied by a high-pitched yip. Beau dropped his gaze to the panting pooch. Harvey. Penelope wouldn't have left her pet behind, no matter how desperate she might have been to get away from the children, which meant she was the most incapable lady to have ever set foot in Oak Grove for leaving the children unattended. Either that or— No. Could it be? Suspicion coiled his gut. He spun around to look for the older boys.

What had they done? Had they taken to locking her up, the way they had him? Visions of Miss Parker tied to a pole left at the mercy of the Kansas wind screamed into his mind.

"Miss Parker?" he hollered as he avoided trampling Harvey underfoot. He swept back into the main cabin area. It was then he noticed the back door ajar. He lengthened his stride and then jumped over the two stairs leading outside. Mark was there, drawing circles in the dirt with a stick. Childlike giggles wafted from behind the chicken coop. The hens squawked up a storm. He heard pounding on wood and muffled pleas aimed at Matthew and Luke. Harvey raced in front of him. He pawed at the chicken-coop door, yipping and jumping, his tail wagging furiously.

"Boys!"

Mark jumped. The giggles quieted. Luke's small

blond head peeked from behind the henhouse. Beau cupped his palm over Esther's ear as he pressed her head onto his shoulder to shield her from his shout. "Penelope!"

"Beau?" Penelope's frightened voice cut through him, and yet at the same time, relief washed over him like a downpour in the middle of a drought. She was safe. "Is that you?"

"I'm here." He swung Esther to his hip and unlatched the coop. He was met by Penelope's bright blue, tear-filled eyes. She quickly swiped the wetness away.

"Are you all right?"

She nodded.

Beau handed the baby to her and turned on the boys. He thrust his hands on his hips. "Matthew, Luke, start explaining."

"She was fetching eggs." Luke blinked up at him.

Beau narrowed his gaze on Matthew. "Is that so?"

Penelope's small fingers touched his shoulder. "Yes, Beau. They didn't mean me harm. The door swung shut behind me."

He shifted his gaze from her to the boys and back again. "I've never known that door to just close. And it certainly did not latch on its own, which means it had help. This time your shenanigans have gone too far."

"I'm fine, Beau, really." She was calm, which un-nerved him.

"Be that as it may, this is twice in a week. First—" he counted as he held up a finger, the muscle in his jaw ticking furiously "—they locked me in the cell with the babies. What if there had been a robbery, a shoot-ing? I was indisposed because of their behavior. It was fortunate Deputy Gannon was in town. And now," he added as he held up a second finger, "they took the only responsible adult around here and locked her inside the henhouse." He turned on the boys. "Do you realize what could have happened? Your sister was left alone, crawling on the front porch. She could have fallen and gotten hurt. John was by himself by the tree. Far from any of you." He held up his hand to keep Matthew from arguing. "Snakes, Matthew! I have warned you about snakes in the coop. Did you care to inform Miss Parker of the dangers?"

Penelope gasped. Matthew paled. Luke stared at his shuffling feet.

"Did you warn her about them? Did you tell her to be careful? What if she'd been bitten? What if I hadn't arrived? How long would you have left her in there?"

Matthew's eyes welled with tears. Luke, too young to fully understand the consequences of his actions, continued to look unashamed.

He swung on Penelope. His heart pounded against his chest. Fear for what could have happened shook him to his core. He shouldn't have left her alone, not without informing her of the dangers slithering around these parts. "Do you have snakes where you come from, Miss Parker? Poisonous snakes? Are you still interested in remaining in Oak Grove?"

Her hand squeezed his arm as she pleaded for understanding. "Beau, there was no harm. I am fine."

"You could have been harmed."

"But I wasn't." She walked to Matthew and handed Esther to him, then said, "Take your sister and your brothers inside. We'll be in to discuss your punishment in a moment."

Beau dipped his brow and scowled.

"Come on." Matthew motioned to his brothers and led the way inside.

Their obedience to her command somehow deflated his anger. He didn't move a muscle. He'd never seen the boys listen to him the first time he gave them an order. She single-handedly managed the children. And him. And he didn't like it. He drew his palm over his face and grunted. "What did you do that for?"

She blinked up at him. "Do what?"

"Naysay me in front of my children. You had no right interfering." He huffed. What was it with the women around him interfering? First, Bobby Jean and now Miss Parker. "They deserve to be punished."

Dark curls danced around her shoulders and down her back. "I do not disagree, Beau. However, your anger should cool before doing anything too serious. I simply removed the objects of your ire from your presence so you could think rationally. Calmly. Before devising an appropriate punishment suitable to the deed."

He propped his hands on his hips and drew in a deep breath to argue. He let it out in a huff. She'd done just that. When she'd removed the children, his anger had dissolved. He shook his head. "What experience do you have with schooling youngsters?"

"I was a child once, weren't you?" She laughed. "I quickly learned to leave my father's presence whenever I displeased him. The distance proved to be to my advantage. The longer I stayed clear, the better. Seemed time often made him forget why he'd been angry to begin with." She gazed off in the distance. A shadow crossed her eyes as if painful memories haunted her. "I also understand their loss. I lost my mother at a young age."

He wanted to reach for her hand and offer her comfort. Instead, he froze. Speechless, he did not know what to say. Sympathies seemed too late. What comfort could he offer her for something that had happened so long ago?

"From what I understand," she continued, "they've lost three parents in a short amount of time. They're bound to misbehave, and understandably. I did."

"I'm sorry." This time he couldn't stop his sympathetic response.

"Don't be. I was five, and I turned Cook's hair gray, and according to her, I curled her toes, too."

"Where was your father?" It was a question that flew off the tip of his tongue. He had a feeling he didn't want to know the answer, especially since she'd chosen to become a mail-order bride to a stranger in an unfamiliar place. What was she running from? Her father?

She shrugged and then turned toward the henhouse, ignoring his question when she finally spoke. "Before you dole out punishment, consider the reasons they might be misbehaving." One dark eyebrow arched upward. "Is there anything you can do to change your behavior?"

"Ha!" He guffawed. "My behavior? What have I done that needs changing?"

He'd been a single, lone man chasing criminals. Now he was a guardian to five orphans and, it seemed, to a woman on the verge of spinsterhood.

"Did you see how happy they were when you joined us for dinner at Moore's the other night and how relieved they were when you arrived last night?" She smiled. "Of course, you hadn't seen them beforehand. They were quiet and nearly fearful of making a misstep. The clink of silverware on the china nearby had them jumping out of their skin. I tried my best to reassure them, but my efforts failed."

"They weren't ready to be out."

"They did not cause a flurry of scandal," she said.

"No," Beau chuckled, feeling exhilarated at the release. He was surprised that she admitted creating a stir. "You did that."

A small smile curved her cupid's-bow lips. "I did. However, you made them at ease. They are proud to call you Pa. All they want is your love and attention."

Her words stung. He was doing the best he knew how to do, and he was fed up with Oak Grove's ladies telling him how to do it right and turning their noses up at his efforts. He'd never been a father before two months ago. "Excuse me, Miss Parker, may I remind you that you've been in Oak Grove only a few days. You have no business instructing me on how to be a father to my children, especially when you have none of your own."

"Excuse me."

At the intrusion, Beau turned on his heel. Three ladies from the Oak Grove's First Congregational Church smiled. Reverend Bradford Scott peered at them through his spectacles. The well-tailored black suit and claret silk vest placed the man in a category of *debonair.* The man's mode of dress with his black top hat and bouquet of flowers in his hand made Beau uncomfortable, and he wasn't certain he liked it. He should be the one bringing gifts to his nanny, not this minister. Beau settled his hand at the small of Penelope's back and took delight at her sharp inhale.

"Miss Parker, may I introduce you to Mrs. Donnell, Mrs. Travis and Mrs. Wheelwright."

The pasted-on smiles beneath their turned-up noses and steely eyes told Beau the ladies had come to investigate the newcomer. He was on to their hidden agenda. They'd been itching to marry off Reverend Scott since the day he'd arrived, and Penelope was their target. Of course, her little stunt at Moore's House could have changed their minds, and he wasn't certain if he should be pleased about that matter or not.

Without thought, he shifted closer to Penelope. Close enough to feel the warmth of her skin from her forearm. Close enough for his left boot to disappear beneath her wide skirts.

Penelope smiled at each lady. "It is a pleasure."

"And this is Reverend Scott, Oak Grove's First Congregational preacher."

Penelope politely nodded, with another smile. Reverend Scott took three long strides toward them, and the scent of cloves and mint enfolded them. Beau stopped himself from leaning forward to get a better whiff. Taking Penelope's hand in his, Reverend Scott lifted it to his mouth. Beau felt as if he'd been strung up by his toes and punched in the gut. A most uncomfortable feeling, to be sure. He cleared his throat and refrained from snatching her hand from the preacher's.

"Oh, yes, Miss Parker," Reverend Scott said as he rose to his full height. "My dear, these are for you. They are a welcoming gift from the Oak Grove's First Congregational Committee."

"Humph," Beau grunted.

Penelope ground her foot onto the toe of his boot as she buried her nose into the bright bouquet. "They are lovely."

Beau gritted his teeth. Did his nanny like gifts? Perhaps he should stop at Taylor's General Store and see what sort of trinkets might be suitable for a high society lady like her. By his recollection, not much. He snorted. When had he thought of her as his *nanny*? Not once had he come to that conclusion. And when had he thought of her as *his*? Why, if he recollected, it was only two days before that he'd considered introducing her to Reverend Scott. What had changed?

"I expect we'll be seeing you at service tomorrow," Reverend Scott addressed Penelope.

What had he been thinking, introducing Penelope and the reverend? She couldn't marry a preacher. Not this preacher. At least he couldn't take the blame for the meeting, as that was all Mrs. Wheelwright and the ladies' doing. However, as much as he disliked the thought of the preacher spending any more time with Penelope than necessary, he couldn't very well skip church when he hadn't missed a Sunday since the building had been completed. "Yes, of course. Miss Parker, the children and I will be in attendance. Together."

"I look forward to tomorrow then." Scott lifted his hat and smiled.

The smile directed at Penelope burned in Beau's gut. His fingers flexed against the small of her back, and then he dropped his hand to his side faster than dropping a hot coal. One thing for certain, he needed to find Miss Parker a suitable husband before he changed his mind, and Reverend Scott, the first on his list of possibilities, had just been nixed.

Chapter Five

"Ow," Penelope cried as she jerked her hand from the washboard. A red rivulet slid down her finger and onto the small white undergarment. She sat back on her haunches and stared at the disaster. A small tear pressed at the corner of her eye, and she swiped it away with the back of her wet hand. The soap burned, and she gathered the corner of her apron to press against the spot. The burning subsided, but there was no stopping the weeping.

At least her pride was saved by Beau's absence. She would never live down the shame of him seeing her cry, never be able to hold her head high. Not when she was such an abysmal failure.

Whatever had she been thinking? That she could up and leave her home and become a wife to an unknown man. A man who had expectations of domestic experience. She couldn't even be a proper wife to a man of her class with a bevy of servants. Come to think of it, none of the women Mr. Wallace had married had been a proper wife in his eyes until after they'd given up their inheritance and were swiftly buried in the church graveyard. Only then had he displayed mourning and touted their virtues.

She'd been thinking of living beyond her twenty-seventh birthday, many years beyond. She'd been thinking that maybe she might have a chance to have a child of her own to hold. Still, if she couldn't grasp the cleaning of a tiny cloth and the cooking of a simple meal, her efforts at survival would be for naught. If she couldn't succeed in gaining Beau's name and protection, she'd perish at the hands of Mr. Wallace. If he found her. She'd seen her father's business partner angered, but he'd never struck out at her. However, she'd seen him hit a servant, and he had threatened her. She feared it wouldn't take much for him to act out toward a wife, if he felt just cause.

More tears streamed down her cheeks. She fell back onto her bottom. She feared what waited for her if she returned to St Louis, and staying here was seeming less likely, especially if she couldn't complete as simple a task as washing clothes.

"Lord, what am I to do?" She sniffled. "Most assuredly, You will not hold it against me for disobeying my father's wishes. I couldn't have married Mr. Wallace. It would have meant my death."

"Are you mad?"

At the sound of a deep voice, Penelope spun. "Beau!" She jumped to her feet and dropped her apron back into place. Her cheeks burned hot. How many times had she heard that question asked by her father? She stilled herself for the tirade that usually followed, right along with the accusations that she was just like her mother, who suffered of the same. Nothing came. Pure silence from the man standing inside the doorway. "You're home."

"It appears that way." He slapped his hat against his thigh and shoved a box wrapped in brown paper into her hand. "Do you make it a habit of talking to yourself?"

Penelope turned the package over and inspected each side. She wasn't certain what it was or what she was to do with it. She thought to ask him, but something more distressing occupied her mind. How much had Beau heard of her one-sided conversation? She deposited the box onto the table, next to the wilting bouquet of flowers shoved into a tin cup of water and looked at Beau. "Occasionally. Having been an only child, I had very few companions to speak with besides Cook, so I took to talking to myself."

Beau glanced at the box with a glare. He looked as if he was about to say something but instead wrinkled his nose and then sniffed. "What's that smell?"

Penelope snapped her gaze toward the fireplace. She rushed over and reached for the lid but found Beau snagging her hand back.

"It's hot. You'll burn yourself." He grabbed a towel and used it to pull off the lid. Smoke filled the house and he took the pan outside.

Penelope glanced around his shoulder to look inside the pan at biscuits. "My! What happened to them? They're black."

Beau cocked an eyebrow. "They're burnt. Overcooked."

"Oh!"

"Yes, *oh*. Dare I hope your cook taught you anything?"

Penelope's jaw fell open, but nothing came out. She couldn't keep denying her inabilities. Eventually he'd know the truth of the matter anyway. She shook her head. "Not much. She didn't like children underfoot while she made her recipes, and as I became older, she told me it wasn't a business for ladies."

"I see, so you lied?"

"Not exactly, Beau. I just didn't tell the entire truth. I can make a winter soup."

"Winter soup? Never mind," he said as he held up his hand. "I do not wish to know, as I'm certain it is neither filling nor reasonable for children to sustain their activities. Do take care not to carry on a one-sided conversation lest the children take on your habit."

"Oh, Beau, there is no worry there. They have each other. Besides, I have no need to talk to myself when they fill every fiber of air with chatter."

"That they do." Beau laughed, and then glanced around. "Where are the urchins?"

"John and Esther are napping." She pointed toward the blanketed-off room. "The older boys are out back."

"And you?" he said as he grasped her chin.

She stilled. Unaccustomed to touch, not just from a man's hand but anyone's, she froze. Even her breathing halted.

"Have you been crying?"

She pulled away from the warm, gentle touch. "I have gotten soap in my eye, is all."

"Lye? Let me see," he said as he stepped closer and lifted her chin. "It's a little red. We should take you to see Doctor Harden."

He released her, and Penelope pulled in a much-needed breath.

"It was only a drop from the back of my hand." She took a step back, not wanting him to inspect both eyes or he'd see that she, in truth, had been crying.

"Suit yourself. It's your eye." Beau glanced past her to the tub and the washboard. "You're washing clothes?"

The corner of her mouth twitched, and she pulled her shoulders back. "I am."

No need to tell him she'd failed and stained Esther's little gown with the blood from her raw fingers. Penelope buried her hands in the folds of her apron.

"There's a pile needs done if you're up to the task." His cheeks blushed. "Haven't had much time to wash them myself, between chasing criminals and children."

"I don't mind." Her hands fisted at the sting from her raw knuckles.

Beau pulled her hand from her skirt and held it up for inspection. "Looks like your dainty fingers mind. You know, there's a brush for scrubbing in the cupboard."

"Thank you." She slipped her hand from his and stepped toward it.

"Stop."

She turned, wide-eyed.

He pulled a spindled chair from the table as he dropped his hat on the crude top. "I'll hire someone to do the laundry."

"No." She shook her head. "I can do it."

His mouth formed a flat line and he motioned to her bloody knuckles. "When are you going to give up and realize Oak Grove is not for you?"

"I am not easily swayed to change my mind."

"I can see that." He laughed, and then tilted his head. "Miss Parker, this grand adventure that you've signed up for hasn't been so grand, has it? Let me guess, you're one of those ladies who spends afternoons reading romanticized Western fiction. I'm here to tell you it's not as glorious as written."

She sputtered on a gasp and then schooled her features and tried to hide her shock. Had Beau rifled through her luggage? Had he seen her precious books tucked beneath her neatly folded silk stockings?

"I will have you know, I typically spend my afternoons walking at the park." It was not an untruth. She spent her evenings reading, and not always romanticized Westerns. She had, on the occasion, chanced to read the local columns, until her name appeared one too many times on the pages. So she perused whatever else was available, including her father's business papers. Her mother's mind had failed too soon. Penelope had devoured every possible medical treatise on maintaining one's sanity. She'd attended lectures and consulted physicians on the matter. She would not suffer as her mother had done. She pursed her lips as she propped her hands on her hips. "Although I will admit to reading fiction, among other things. It does keep the mind sharp after all."

"I was only teasing." Beau laughed. "However, I must apologize for my behavior this morning. The children have been a challenge since they've arrived, and everyone seems to have an opinion on how they should be raised, even so far as suggesting I should take them to an orphanage."

"You wouldn't!" Penelope gasped. She'd been with

them only a short time, a few days really, and she knew they did not belong in a home for children. Images of small youngsters begging on the streets for bread played in her mind and churned her stomach. "How could anyone say such a thing, when the children have you? They should be with someone who loves them and cares for them."

He grinned. "Thank you for your confidence in me. Except it seems a few of the townsfolk believe I'm incapable, and truth be told, I can't help but wonder if they are right."

Penelope's eyes grew wide. How could a man as confident as Beau have doubts? Doubts just as she had. Somehow knowing he was just as vulnerable as she was made her feel less...vulnerable, less incapable. "Do not say such a thing. The older boys have lost their father and both the mothers they've known. What sort of grief would something like that do to an adult?"

Beau shifted his weight and nodded. "That is true. I lost my brother to an accident that never should have happened, and I blame myself. I was angry. Sometimes I still feel the anger."

She wanted to ask him about the guilt over his brother's death but sensed it would be better left for another time. If the opportunity arose. If he didn't send her back to St. Louis.

"They're so young, Beau. Who knows how the losses have affected them? And although I may not have experience, I hear that children can be difficult at best, and like I said earlier this morning, they're likely responding to their grief, maybe even a bit of fear that they'll lose someone else that matters to them."

"Or they could just be plain rotten."

Penelope giggled behind her hand. "Why, Mr. Garrett, whatever are you talking about? They are the most darling creatures I have ever had the pleasure of encountering."

Beau could not help himself. He stared at her when her entire face lit up with her laugh and her blue eyes illuminated. He didn't realize he was holding his breath until she quit laughing. He'd seen her smile, but it had been nothing more than a well-practiced movement of her lips and eyes. This genuine curve of the lips and crinkle of the eyes made her stunning. Her ability to tease him both surprised him and pleased him. He certainly wasn't expecting it from her. And strangely enough, the moment removed his irritation at her tossing his gift onto the table without opening it or offering so much as a thank-you.

How had this woman not procured a husband yet? What was wrong with her? Was she daft? Obviously, she didn't have all her wits about her if she was willing to respond to a mail-order-bride ad and travel to a rough-and-rowdy town, unescorted, and insist on hitching herself to a man she'd never met. Sure, he'd heard of strangers marrying through an ad, but never a lady of her breeding nor of her beauty, which served to raise his suspicions. Something must be wrong with her.

She quieted and covered her mouth with the tips of her fingers. "My apologies. That was very unladylike of me."

He peered at her through narrowed eyes. She didn't have any unsightly moles that he could see. No sign of illness. She didn't appear to have an awkward gait. "It was not unladylike, Penelope. Laughter is becoming on you."

He had not just said that.

Yes, he most certainly had. Seemed he was the one suffering from some sort of madness, and he blamed it all on Reverend Scott.

Her cheeks flushed a delightful shade of pink.

He reached out to touch a springy curl. She leaned back but not before he captured his prey. Soft and silky. He rubbed the strands between his fingers and poked his finger on a small clump of dried mud. The paper-wrapped scented soaps glared at him from the table where she'd discarded them. Why had she ignored his gift? "You need a bath."

She sucked in a sharp breath of air and slapped his hand away. She took two steps back, yet her soft perfume flowed toward him. Leaning forward, he chased the ebb and hoped to capture the scent. It reminded him of the Winterses' garden on a warm evening, which reminded him of Mama's garden. It was the one thing he missed from home. He pulled air into his lungs, and his eyelids began to drift closed. Like they did when a plate of Moore's fresh hot apple pie clunked on the table next to a steaming cup of coffee. He snapped his eyes open. He may need to call upon Doc Harden. Seems too many days in the saddle without adequate sleep were sneaking up on him. He was saying things and doing things that were not normal. He did not go about touching the hair of women. Nor did he inform them of their need to bathe.

Her question cut off his thoughts. "And how do you suggest I do such a thing?"

One corner of his mouth curved upward. He gazed into her eyes. Where Mary Ella's had been the color of his coffee before cream and sugar, Penelope's were the color of the morning sky, so light they were almost clear silver. "That there tub you've been washing clothes in is our bath."

She leaned around him and then glanced down the front of her apron. "That? It's not nearly big enough. It's hardly big enough for Luke."

He released the lock of hair and strode to the tub.

"You can be certain the urchin fits just fine." Barely. He'd seen the glimmer in her eyes when he mentioned the bath. A luxury she must miss, and one she had not afforded herself in recent days. He hadn't meant to sound rude or suggest that she smelled. But a lady like her was surely accustomed to bathing. The state of her hair proved she hadn't since her arrival in Oak Grove, another shortcoming on his part. He should have seen to her comforts immediately rather than selfishly seeking rest. "I'll boil the water if you're interested. We do have church in the morning. You want to be looking sharp, given the debacle at Moore's House."

He refused to remind her that the single Reverend Scott would be in attendance as well, and would probably give her another bouquet of flowers.

Her cheeks brightened with embarrassment, but she lifted her chin anyway. Beau warmed. He didn't know what it was about raising her hackles, but he sure enjoyed it when she took on a challenge.

"Mr. Garrett, I'll have you know, I always look sharp, even if my attire isn't up to standards."

"Now, Miss Parker, I do recall you waltzing into my jail, drenched as a soggy river bottom and muddy. Why, there isn't enough scrubbing a man can do in one day to remove the trail of chaos you left at the place."

Her nose rose a little. She narrowed her gaze. "A gentleman would never comment on a lady's state of dishevelment."

"You'll be hard-pressed to find any gentlemen here in Oak Grove, Penelope." He snagged his hat from the table. "Perhaps you should go home where there's certain to be a multitude of gentlemen to choose from."

He scowled.

"I cannot do that, Beau," she stated firmly. "Whether you like it or not I am staying in Oak Grove, and I will prove myself."

"To who?"

"Me. And perhaps you."

"And just what will you prove, my dear Penelope?"

"That I am a capable wife."

"I doubt that, Miss Parker. You can't even cook, which is a necessity for the job I'm offering."

"I can learn."

"From Matthew?" Beau hitched up his britches. "He'll have you frying worms in no time."

"Perhaps I'll fall on the mercy of a church lady."

His teeth ground together. The church ladies would be happy to teach Penelope how to be a proper minister's wife. They would reform her until she did as a proper helpmate should, and they'd make sure she never wore a man's britches again. He didn't know if he liked that idea. He covered his displeasure with laughter. "In case you've forgotten, you have made yourself a pariah when you chose to wear my britches to an establishment. Ladies do not wear britches."

Gravy, were those tears bubbling up on the rims of her eyelids? "I didn't mean it, Penelope. Well, they don't wear britches, but you did what anyone would do if they had no other options. Of course, most women would stay home, warm themselves by the fire and serve up a meal, but given you can't cook, I don't right blame you for making such a public display." He blamed himself for not being more considerate of her well-being. Even though the consequences could possibly devastate her later, he was beginning to think she did have the backbone to stay in Oak Grove.

He snatched the paper-wrapped box from the table and shoved it at her. "Here, scented soaps, if you'd like. And I am not giving them to you because you smell. Mr. Taylor at the general store suggested you might enjoy them."

"Oh!" Penelope lifted the box to her nose and sniffed. She turned it over and sniffed again. She swiped the tears and then clenched the box in her fist. "Was I supposed to wear my soiled and drenched gown or perhaps some of your long undergarments?"

"Ha, I would like to see that spectacle." Sass and fire. He liked it. He shouldn't, but he did. It made him want to hang around, to see what else would spew out of her little mouth or how she would dare do away with convention. The last time he'd gotten caught by the wiles of a lady, it nearly cost him everything, and he wouldn't make that same mistake again. No sirree. If he was to get a wife, he'd look for a practical woman, not one who wore silk gowns beneath soiled aprons to wash clothes. And definitely not one who captured his eye.

"If I must, I will."

"You wouldn't dare." He choked on air at the thought of her wearing his long underwear. The sleeves would hang to her knees. He gathered his senses.

"Circumstances have taught me to be practical."

"And did that practicality serve you well when you decided to chase down a husband you hadn't met?"

Her mouth worked around unspoken words, and her lips pressed into a thin line. Her eyes narrowed.

"Darling, *practical* among your social class and *practical* in Oak Grove are a long way apart. I stand by my judgment. You'll be running home before Sunday next."

As soon as the words were out of his mouth, he knew he'd regret them. Especially when she pulled back her shoulders and lifted that pert little nose of hers in the air. She was gearing up for battle, and for some reason, he felt more challenged by her than any enemy he'd ever faced. Including the burr in his saddle, Jessup Davis. And yet a spark of delight swirled in his chest. However, he best prepare himself for the backlash of her wearing his underthings. He hoped she didn't dare display them in public and that he would hear about such scandalous behavior only from the boys.

"Is that a challenge, Beau? And if I do not run home in a week's time?"

His jaw clenched tight. "You will."

"If I do not?" Her fists clenched at her sides, daring

him to accept the dare. "If I stay and prove I am capable of caring for the children?"

"Then you may remain." Hope lit her eyes, and a battle waged within himself. "As the nanny, with a monthly stipend, Penelope. Not as my wife."

Chapter Six

Penelope took one last look at the children, checked the clock on the mantel for the tenth time and then smoothed her pristine white gloves down her dark blue silk skirts. She tentatively touched each gold button on her jacket and released a nervous breath from her lungs at finding them all fastened. Her first impressions of Oak Grove were not the best, and she refused to embarrass Beau further. If she was to be his wife, she needed to be a proper wife. One who didn't disrupt court proceedings and wear britches in town.

Another furtive glance at the clock, and she bent her ear for a hint of Beau's horse. He'd joined them for breakfast yesterday and then returned in the afternoon—she assumed to make certain that she hadn't found herself locked in the chicken coop again. When he'd first entered the house, she had been uncertain and ashamed that she'd ruined Esther's gown. Despondent that she had met failure. Then they were laughing and joking, and it was nice. Almost as if they'd known each other much longer than a few days.

However, he'd ended up insulting her cleanliness. Bathing was most assuredly needed, albeit the need for it was not completely her doing. Although she could not argue his point. A proper wife needed to be tidy. She couldn't very well walk about town with clumps of mud falling out of her hair.

Still, the criticism of her person had had her lashing out in the most unbecoming manner. In fact, she had been downright shrewish, something she never would have dared in the presence of her father or Mr. Wallace, and he deserved her surly behavior if anyone did. Why, what lady in her right mind would threaten to wear a man's underwear? Obviously, her.

She was still shocked that Beau had so casually dismissed his insult as if he'd never said it and very kindly boiled water and filled the tub for her *after* he'd handed her rose-scented soap. A gift. Besides the flowers brought by the kind reverend and the ladies, she'd never been given a gift before. She wasn't certain how to feel. Offended because he'd said she needed a bath? She shook her head. He'd said the soaps had been a gift recommended by Mr. Taylor. Because ladies liked gifts such as those or because Beau had told the owner of the store she smelled?

What did it matter? The small present stirred a bubble of giddiness in her stomach. She sighed with her smile. Beau's thoughtfulness warmed her heart. And as if the soaps had not been enough, he'd offered her privacy and had taken the children out of the house so she could bathe. His consideration and kindness comforted her like tea. Was the marshal starting to thaw toward her, too?

She certainly hoped so.

The bath had been delightful, even more delightful than taking a soak in the large copper tub she'd had in St. Louis, even though she was only able to sit on the edge with her feet and legs in the water, as there was no possible way she would fit. But she did give herself a rosy scrubbing and thoroughly dunked her head into the water to wash her hair. The brushing of her locks while still wet served to gloss them into a right fine shine. There could be no question about it. She was the cleanest lady in all of Kansas.

"He's coming," Luke shouted, causing Penelope to jump. Harvey yipped at the excitement. The boy scrambled from his perch near the window and grinned up at her. "How'd I look?"

She smiled down at him and mussed his hair. "Handsome. All of you do. Now let's line up like we practiced."

She scooped Esther onto her hip and took John's small hand in hers. Beau's spurs hit the first step and struck a chord against her pulse, making it gallop. A firm, hard clop on the second step sent her knees to wobbling. Then the door swung open.

Penelope's breath caught. His wheat-colored locks were slicked back, revealing a high forehead. Dark brows arched over his blue eyes. He'd shaved, leaving only a dark mustache and goatee to outline full lips. A bit of lightheadedness stole her wits. She gaped at his considerable attractiveness. Beautiful words of prose came to her mind, words she'd memorized from *Jane Eyre*, a book neatly wrapped in a scarf at the bottom of her trunk. They'd stirred her upon the reading.

However, she had not fully understood them until this moment.

I sometimes have a queer feeling with regard to you—especially when you are near me, as now: it is as if I had a string somewhere under my left ribs.

That string pulled taut as if he pulled at it like a childhood game of tug-of-war. She snapped her mouth shut, severing the connection for the moment. It wouldn't do her any good for him to know that he affected her, not when he'd been staunchly adamant about sending her away. Nor would it do to give into this unknown pull on her strings. Sure, she'd read about it. She'd heard about it. Witnessed giddy-eyed foolish girls lose their heads over that feeling, but Penelope had had no understanding what it meant. Until now, and she wasn't certain how to think about it.

"Hey, Pa." Luke beamed. "We're in our getups and handsome."

"That you are." Beau looked from the smallest to the biggest. He offered them a gleaming smile. "Look at you, boys. Has there been a more handsome group of scamps this side of the Mississippi?"

He snatched Esther from Penelope's arms, leaving in his wake the scent of bay rum and mint. "And what of my beautiful lady?"

Penelope flushed from head to toe, even though she knew he hadn't been speaking to her. It was nice to hear, to pretend that he'd meant her. It also saddened her a great deal, as it would have been lovely to have the question directed at her. No one had ever called her *beautiful*. Not even Cook, who doted on her like a grandparent.

He pinched Esther's cheeks and then kissed the top of the infant's head. "Aren't you looking like a royal queen?"

Penelope swallowed. She'd washed all the clothes and pressed them so that the children looked their best. She'd even tackled Beau's clothes, which was strangely intimate, and she'd found herself blushing. "Your clothes are lying out on the bed, if you would like to change."

He didn't need to. He was as dashing as any man she'd ever seen spinning around a ballroom in formal wear. Of course, she'd been hiding in the corners and spying on them from between the leaves of potted plants. She couldn't help but imagine him taking her hand and leading her to the dance floor. Her pulse pounded in her veins. Then she envisioned stumbling over her own feet and crashing into the refreshment table. It'd happened once, and she'd vowed to never allow it to happen again.

As if he'd read her mind, his gaze touched hers and one brow rose in question. He held the look for a moment, and then his smile faltered. Penelope swallowed again as Beau turned to leave. She patted her hair. She glanced down at the front of her dress. She checked the gold buttons. Nothing seemed out of place, so what had she done wrong now? Dare she ask?

"Shall we go to church?" he asked.

She'd rather find a hole and hide. This, her most important Sunday in Oak Grove, was not meeting with her expectations. She'd hoped to erase her fall in the mud and her disgraceful evening at Moore's House. Considering the look Beau had just given her, she didn't think that was possible. There was obviously something about her that did not sit well with him. Was she about to embarrass him yet again?

The boys followed Beau outside. Once again, Penelope checked her hair and clothes. Had she chosen poorly? She sensed his disappointment, felt it to her bones. Knew it too well from the many times her father had chastised her for her lack of social graces or for dressing inappropriately for the occasion. One did not wear walking gowns to a ball. And one did not wear ball gowns to the opera. What did ladies wear to church in Oak Grove, if not their finest? How had her formidable walls crumbled around her? Back home, she'd given up caring what others thought about her when she'd realized it didn't matter how hard she tried to please them. Noses still had gone up and backs had turned whenever she'd drawn near. So why did it matter what Beau thought?

Matthew dipped his blond head through the doorway. "Pa said to get a leg on."

"A leg on?" She kicked her foot out from beneath her skirt and inspected her shoes.

Matthew rolled his eyes. "Come on. Pa is waiting. Says we're going to be late."

"We would not want that, now would we?" she teased, hoping to ease her own troubled mind. She held out her arm. "Will you escort me?"

Matthew's eyes grew wide. "I ain't ever done that a'fore."

Penelope patted the top of his head. "It is all right. Run along and I'll be right behind you."

She needed another small moment to gain her composure anyway. She'd entertained the masses before and poured tea for the mayor and a bevy of wealthy businessmen, all while their wives and daughters whispered about her behind their hands, and she'd never once experienced sweaty palms. However, Beau's dismissive glance had set her on edge. It had taken every bit of confidence from her shoulders and swept it under the threadbare rug. Why? Because today, just as the rest of the ones to follow, was a most important day in her life, and she couldn't fail. Not if she was going to succeed at becoming Beau's wife. Granted, she'd been in Oak Grove for only four days, but with each passing hour that she remained unmarried, she feared Mr. Wallace would find her and force her back to the altar.

She took one more glance at her gown, wondered if she should quickly change and thought better of it. Cook had always told her to never leave a man waiting too long. She pressed a shaky palm against her stomach and drew in a breath.

Penelope stepped onto the porch and out into the warm, spring-morning sun. Blue skies engulfed her, making the task at hand seem less onerous. She lifted her face and smiled. Today was going to be a grand day. A grand day, indeed.

If she could find one willing lady to teach her how to cook, and properly launder the clothes, and beat the dust from the rug, and fetch eggs while dodging sharp beaks, then all may not be lost with Beau. Her shoulders fell, and she sighed. Finding anybody willing to help her after her faux pas and the enormous task of learning all there was to learn in a single short week seemed impossible.

"Miss Parker. Penelope!"

She tore her gaze from the sky and met Beau's insistent stare from where he stood by the hitching post.

"Are you coming?"

He was a stunning man. His golden-honey locks sprung from beneath his hat, his stormy blue eyes sparked with irritation. She'd kept him waiting too long. She pulled her shoulders back and descended the stairs. She was Penelope Prudence Parker and she could accomplish anything she set her mind to. Even convincing her resistant groom to marry her before Sunday next.

With that settled in her mind, she walked across the yard and held out her hand for Beau to assist her into the wagon. His mouth twitched in irritation a moment before he gazed into her eyes and then lifted her around the waist and set her onto the wagon seat. He strode around the front. The springs gave way and the wagon lurched to the side as he climbed up and plopped next to her. His muscular thigh landed along hers. She grabbed hold of the side and tried to scoot over, but her skirt was trapped beneath his leg.

His close proximity shocked her sensibilities. Even his strong, capable fingers on her chin yesterday hadn't alarmed her as much as sitting this close to him. Her pulse raced. Her heart thumped against her chest, threatening to beat its way out of her skin. She snapped open the fan dangling from her wrist and waved it in front of her face.

"You all right?" Beau snapped the reins. The wagon

lurched and she fell backward. Beau swung his arm across her waist. "Whoa, there. You gotta take care if you don't want to find yourself ousted from the wagon. Guess I should have warned you. You're not accustomed to conveyances, are you, Miss Parker?"

She righted herself and smoothed her skirts. "Of course I am. Just none so...crude and rickety."

Beau eyed her. "I suppose not."

"That's not to say I rode in them often. We didn't have a personal one. Father never would spare the expense. He rather liked renting them to keep up with the latest fashions."

Beau turned down a lane and the horses increased their pace. "Is your father still alive?"

"Pardon?" She furrowed her brow.

"Your father?"

"Oh, yes." At least he had been when she'd left home. A moment of fear seized her. Had Mr. Wallace harmed her father when she'd jilted him at the altar? Certainly not. Still, Mr. Wallace was a dangerous man. "I think."

"You think?"

"He was when I departed home."

"And where exactly is home, Miss Parker?"

"East."

He laughed. "I gathered. You won't tell me where?"

"It does not matter, Beau. If I told you, you would send me home and I'm never going back."

"Why is that, I wonder? If we're to get along, we can't have secrets between us."

She blinked. Would he believe her if she told him of her suspicions? Would he send her back if he discovered she'd been promised to another man and had left him at the altar? "I don't think I can."

"Very well," Beau said as he slowed the wagon to a stop beneath an oak tree. He turned in his seat and held her gaze. "Tell me, is my family in danger from whatever it is you're running from?"

She diverted her eyes from his and noticed the ladies and gentlemen milling about the grounds surrounding the white church. She took in the simple skirts and bonnets. No wonder Beau had been displeased. She'd overdressed. She made a mental note to purchase a few wool skirts.

"Beau!" At the sound of the female voice, she turned to see a lady in a boisterous, floppy hat waving at Beau. She was young, petite and pretty. Short enough to barely reach Penelope's shoulders. Her flaxen hair captured the sun rays. One glance at Beau's beaming smile told her that he seemed to notice her beauty. A knot formed in Penelope's stomach, and she pulled the inside of her lip between her teeth and twisted with her gloved hands. It was always this way. A gentleman would engage her in conversation, and then a beautiful miss would approach and steal his attention. What's worse, Penelope couldn't help but wonder if she had interfered in a courtship. If Beau had set his cap on this young woman, Penelope would have no choice but to release him from their agreement. Then what would she do? Find a man in Oak Grove willing to marry her?

"Bobby Jean, how are you this fine day?" Beau jumped from the wagon and walked around to Penelope's side and offered her his hand. "Bobby Jean, may I introduce you to Miss Parker. She is here for a short while to care for the children. As I'm sure you already know, given you had a hand in altering my ad."

"Oh, Beau, what makes you so certain it was me?"

Beau angled his head and quirked his lips. "You didn't expect the boys to not out you, did you?"

"I imagine not." The lady laughed, and then held her hand out to Penelope. She smiled. "My pleasure, Miss Parker. I do hope you've given Beau a hard time since your arrival."

Beau grunted.

Penelope offered her best smile as she stepped down. She schooled her features and tried not to show hurt over Beau's introduction. It was obvious he was upset over the ad and blamed this lady for her arrival in Oak Grove. She accepted the lady's hand. "How do you do? So you're the one who posted the ad."

"I only helped a little!" Bobby Jean smacked Beau's arm with her fan. "A lady with manners. How charming." Miss Bobby Jean looped her arm with Penelope's, and as she guided her toward the church, she leaned in next to Penelope's ear. "Now, you never mind that incident at Moore's. You've been the talk of the town, and I have to say it's refreshing. You certainly put Beau on his ear, and it's about time, too. Why, just look at you. You are darling. Lovely, lovely, lovely, darling."

Beau lifted Esther into his arms and caught a whiff of Penelope's rose-scented perfume. He buried his nose against the baby's crown and took another sniff. "You smell like sunshine, baby girl."

He glanced past the running boys toward Penelope as she was swept away by Bobby Jean. They were as different as night and day in looks. He'd always appreciated Bobby Jean's straightforward demeanor, and it seemed Penelope was cut from similar cloth when it came to dueling wits with him. Those two ladies were the most direct women he'd ever met.

The hair on his arms just about stood up when he caught sight of their heads bent together. How had he not considered this scenario? All morning long he'd envisioned rectifying Penelope's situation. She wanted a husband and he intended on finding her one. After their meeting with Reverend Scott, he had realized the preacher was entirely unsuitable for a strong-willed lady like Penelope. She'd run him over, and the poor man would never have a say in their marriage. He was doing Scott a favor by scratching him off the list of potential husbands.

There was the new banker and Brian Gannon as prospects. However, he wasn't certain either one would protect Penelope from the viperous tongues, since spotless reputations meant everything to them. Which meant it was up to Beau to shield Penelope from the gossiping masses as they talked behind their cupped hands about her stunt at Moore's. At least he'd thought it would be up to him. He hadn't foreseen Bobby Jean sweeping in and taking over his plan, but he should have known better. After all, it was Bobby Jean's interference that had him in his current predicament.

He should be grateful Penelope was off his hands, but he was fit to be tied after he'd given himself mental preparation for the battle, not to mention a fresh shave and a clean set of clothes.

"Well, I'll be," he said as he swept his hat from his

head and smacked it against his thigh. Dust rose up and Mark coughed. "Sorry, scamp. I didn't realize you were so close. I thought you'd gone off with your brothers."

Mark wiped his eyes. "Why'd Bobby Jean take Penelope from us?"

"I don't rightly know, Mark," he said, surprised that the boy had uttered much of anything. He rarely spoke and usually only when spoken to.

"I wanted to hold her hand."

Beau gaped, even more surprised by the child's desire. The boy always turned away from affection. "I imagine Bobby Jean wanted to welcome her to Oak Grove and introduce her to the ladies, just like she did with you and your brothers your first Sunday here."

His words didn't seem to lift Mark's spirits any more than they had his. Beau knelt in front of him. "I tell you what, how would you like to sit next to Penelope?"

A rare smile curved Mark's lips, and he nodded before skipping toward the church.

Beau understood the child's disappointment, and his elation. How many times had he imagined walking Penelope into the church with her on his arm? When he'd plopped down money for the scented soaps. When Reverend Scott and the church ladies had shown up. When he'd seen her clear blue eyes looking up at him with gratitude as he'd rescued her from the chicken coop. And why did any of that matter? It wasn't like he was going to marry her.

He readjusted John's hand in his and felt a sense of loneliness he'd never experienced before. He was certain it had something to do with Penelope's absence from his side. Not only had he wanted to walk her into church, he'd pictured sitting by her in the pew as a family, her skirts trapped beneath his leg, her scent caressing him like the morning breeze. He stopped the mental picture from forming. What was wrong with him?

Ever since Penelope had staunchly defended the children when they'd locked her in the henhouse, the thought of courting her had entered his mind. And after seeing her efforts at laundering, a fleeting thought that marriage to Penelope wouldn't be so bad had taken hold, which he'd quickly stomped under his boot, because he was not in need of a wife.

But that did not mean he wanted to see Bobby Jean coming to Penelope's rescue. That was his responsibility. And he definitely did not want Bobby Jean giving Penelope wind in her sails and helping her succeed in becoming Mrs. Beau Garrett. Because that would never happen. Thinking about courting Penelope and marrying her was entirely different than actually doing the deed. He'd decided when Mary Ella had deceived him that he would never risk his heart again, not even for a lady like Penelope. Marrying for convenience, perhaps. But there couldn't be a spark of desire, which took Penelope out of the picture. Then, he knew there was a secret she refused to tell him. However, he sensed she was good and pure of heart. And even if he was willing to take a chance, Penelope needed china and silver. She needed gowns. She needed a home suitable for a lady, not a hastily put-together cabin.

Beau ducked through the church door and allowed his eyes to adjust. He found Penelope cornered near the pew, Bobby Jean by her side like a sentry, as several gentlemen pressed in, including Brian Gannon, Miller's

brother, and one of the bachelors he'd thought to introduce to Penelope. Now he wasn't so certain. Seeing
them side by side, they didn't suit each other.

Bobby Jean's elderly mother pinched Penelope's
cheek with gnarled fingers. To her credit, Penelope
didn't flinch. Instead, she smiled at Mrs. Danner and
then took the lady's hand in hers.

She nodded toward Brian, and Beau's insides turned
all upside down. Never mind the fact he'd suggested
Gannon introduce Penelope to Brian only a few days
ago. He ought to throttle Bobby Jean for getting him all
tied up in this mess. He'd pick a bone or two with her
for interfering with his newspaper ad and now because
she was bending Penelope's ear.

As if Penelope needed help.

She absolutely did not. She was the nanny for his
children, not up for grabs by every eligible Tom in the
county. Besides, if he hoped to send her home by next
Sunday, which he wasn't certain he wanted to do, he
needed to steal her away from them.

Sheesh, he was starting to sound like an indecisive
ninny. His desire to ship her back warred with his desire
to keep her in Oak Grove. His thoughts on the matter
flipped around faster than Dusty when given free rein,
and he didn't seem able to bring them under control. It
was like watching a runaway stagecoach veering off the
cliff. One thing for certain, though, she'd be staying in
Oak Grove as another man's wife over his rotten bones.

The elderly Mrs. Danner caned her way through the
throng and stopped in front of him. She thumped her
stick on the floor. "You've a fine lady there, Garrett."

Beau warmed at Mrs. Danner's approval and then

groaned. He'd given Penelope a week to prove her abilities as a nanny, not as his lady, and he needed to make sure he remembered that.

"Porcelain skin," Mrs. Danner continued. "Never touched by the sun. And charming to boot. Best take care, boy. She seems to be popular with the men of this town. Is it true she wore britches to Moore's?"

Beau glared. He could see with his own eyes just how the fellows gathered around her, like Brian Gannon, who was a right fine person and hardworking. Then there were those he'd never had the chance to meet in Oak Grove, so didn't know if they were the appropriate sort for Penelope.

Were they new arrivals planning on making a life here or those who oversaw the railroad? Brian didn't have much more to offer Penelope than Beau did. The railroad men, though, in their fine, tailored coats were right up there with Reverend Scott—debonair. The sort of gentleman she, no doubt, aspired to have for a husband. Not some dried-up marshal living on the outskirts of town. He swallowed the lump in his throat and tried not to worry over them. Would it be such a bad thing if one of them took an interest in Penelope? Well, any of them besides Brian. His friend had roots here, and if Penelope hitched up with him, she'd stay. A railroad man, on the other hand, would keep heading west, taking Miss Parker with him. And by the look of their suits, any one had the coin to keep her in top fashion, or at least in better fashion than he was capable of doing.

His stomach soured at the thought. He'd given Penelope one week. A trial period he'd been reluctant to offer. Not because he thought she'd acquire the skills to become a worthwhile nanny but because he feared after another week in her presence he wouldn't let her go.

He dragged his eyes from Penelope and focused on Mrs. Danner and answered her question. "Yes, ma'am, Miss Parker did wear britches to Moore's House," he said. Mrs. Danner might be an old, prudish crone, but she held sway in Oak Grove and when she gave her opinion, most of the ladies agreed with her.

Over by the pew with Penelope, a gentleman in a dark-colored suit guffawed. Loudly, obnoxiously. The noise grated Beau's nerves. None of the men around her seemed to be bothered by the gossip surrounding Penelope, which shouldn't bother Beau, but it did. Deep in his gut. Maybe they had not heard about her antics. His mouth twitched. Or maybe they found her practicality admirable, as Beau had. Still, the gossip he'd heard while making his rounds yesterday had been disparaging and vicious.

"Caused a stir, I hear," Mrs. Danner grumbled.

It certainly did. It's why he'd returned home yesterday afternoon when he had. He'd barely turned a corner, after visiting the general store and purchasing the scented soaps he intended to give to Penelope as a gift, when a lady whispered to her companion about Penelope's incident at Moore's, and she hadn't pointed out the britches but rather the condition of her hair and the splatters of mud on her cheeks. The soaps felt like an insult in his hand, but he'd already spent what little coin he'd had on the present. He'd stopped in his tracks and dug in his heels to defend his lady's honor. They questioned him about what sort of woman he'd invited to Oak Grove. One who certainly did not understand etiquette and bathing. Before he released a tirade and added more fuel to their tongues, he'd tipped his hat and bid them a good day. Their impertinence had set a fire under his boots, and he'd quickly gone home to take another gander at Penelope. To make sure she hadn't received any curious, good-intentioned visitors.

He couldn't fault the ladies in their observations. Penelope had been a mess, but it was no fault of her own. It wasn't like she'd had a looking glass available to her. Beau had never found the need for one. And since he'd left her in charge of five children with nothing but their names and the expectation that she feed them, it wasn't like he'd given her the opportunity to tidy herself up before she entered Moore's House.

The scandal she'd made could be set solely on his shoulders. When he'd arrived home to remedy the situation and found her on the floor in front of the wash bucket, her knuckles tinged red, he'd become frustrated and angry with himself for neglecting her needs. His lack of care for her person had forced her to take desperate measures. He hoped to right the ill he'd done since her arrival by acting as her defender today.

Mrs. Danner tapped her cane against the floorboards as if she had more to say. He waited patiently for her to burn his ears and to make her opinion known on the matter. Most likely to bid him to send such a scandalous woman back to where she'd come from. Beau was ready to argue that it was her daughter, Bobby Jean, who had invited Penelope to Oak Grove in the first place.

"Good for her." Mrs. Danner laughed, which surprised Beau. "About time someone came along and put a wrinkle in the old biddies' starched noses."

It hadn't just been the old biddies' noses Penelope had wrinkled. It'd been the young biddies-in-training, too. Beau smiled at the image. "I suppose you are right, Mrs. Danner."

"Them gals need fodder to keep their lively twitters going, and your gal is just the one to do it. Now, I know what you're thinking there, Marshal. Idle hands are the devil's work, but I guarantee gossip keeps a community alive and interesting. You mark my words, if ladies quit nattering, the town is dead. I've seen it happen before."

"Seems to me, gossip does nothing but cause problems." Especially when there was little to no truth in the words. Like when Mr. Moore heard his roses had been dug up by Mrs. McCoy's hound. It hadn't happened, but that hadn't stopped Mr. Moore from marching over to the McCoys' and demanding restitution. Upon investigation, it had been discovered Mrs. Moore was seen to be petting the hound while she was trimming the bushes.

"Mama, are you bothering the marshal?" Bobby Jean swept up beside her mother. "Beau, I daresay Penelope is as charming as they come. She didn't bat an eye or even remotely blush at the interrogation. And how delightful that she quietly dismissed her audience when the children stole her attention. She'll make a wonderful mama for them. You've made an excellent choice."

Beau cleared his throat and wondered if he could be as charming and efficient at handling the ladies of Oak Grove as Penelope was proving to be. "About that choice, Bobby Jean, you know very well I had very little to do with it."

Bobby Jean beamed at him. "Why, Beau Garrett, whatever are you talking about?"

Beau shook his head. "If you weren't the judge's wife and my cousin, I think I'd throttle you."

She laughed as she waved her fan in front of her. "In a week's time, you'll be thanking me, and then later, naming your firstborn after me."

Beau narrowed his eyes. "Bobby, whatever you're planning, you have to stop. You of all people know why I don't want a wife. Why I can't have one."

"As I of all people know why you need a helpmate, Beau." Bobby Jean slapped his wrist with her fan. "She's not Mary Ella. Give her a chance."

"She has one week to prove she can properly care for the children. As their nanny. Nothing more." Before he continued the conversation, Beau turned on his heel and made his way toward the family pew, where he found Penelope surrounded by the boys. On her left side, Mark sat with his fingers entwined with hers. She seemed oblivious to the stares she received from the men watching her. Something inside him warmed. She had no idea the beauty she held, and the children were taking to her. He'd seen them act more like children in the last two days than he had in the last two months. It was as if their burdens had disappeared, and he sensed given time, his might, too. Problem was he didn't know if he wanted them to. He'd carried them for so long he feared what life would be like if they disappeared.

He slid sideways onto the pew, next to Luke.

Penelope motioned for him to lean close. "Is this appropriate? I understand that the family sits in assigned pews. Should I move to the back?"

"No." He'd thought about this moment all night, only then, they didn't have a child between them. Besides, he wasn't sending her to the back where the gentlemen who'd been vying for attention milled about. "Here is where you should be. You're with the family." For a week, at least.

Beau glanced over his shoulder. There wasn't one bare spot in a pew. The church was packed on this warm spring day. He'd never seen so many of the townsfolk gather on a Sunday, except when the ladies made pies. Even then, it wasn't this full, which proved the curiosity over Penelope had spread like a wild grass fire on a windy day.

He noticed a few newer folks toward the back, with the handsome gents in right fine suits, and he made a mental note to steer clear of them after service. He grimaced. It wasn't that long ago he'd determined to find her a groom if she remained insistent on staying in Oak Grove. Now he couldn't stomach the thought of her vowing to honor and cherish another man.

Miller Gannon tapped him on the shoulder and leaned in. "Word has it Jessup has a place up on the north side of the river a mile or so. Might be where he's hidden the stolen money."

Beau handed Esther to Penelope and rose. He eyed the men in suits and sighed. "You're certain?"

"No, just hearsay."

"Whose word?"

Gannon's mouth curved upward. His cheeks blushed. Given his deputy marshal had been spending time at Moore's House, Beau wondered if he was sweet on the proprietor's daughter, just like Jessup was.

"You don't need to say anything." Beau shoved his hands in his pockets. "Given your source, we can wait until after service to check it out."

Gannon nodded. "Sure thing, boss. Wouldn't want you leaving your family behind." He nodded toward Penelope. "She sure is a beauty, cleaned up."

"I thought you weren't looking for a wife." Beau grimaced at how short his words sounded. He didn't like his friend noticing Penelope. When he'd first seen her this morning, she'd stolen his breath and every bit of his resolve to keep his distance. He hadn't expected her to shine as she had in her jacket with the gold buttons. To look so beautiful with her hair artfully piled upon her head and tendrils curling down her nape. Fool that he'd been, he'd touched her locks yesterday. Now he couldn't get the sensation from his fingertips.

"I'm not."

"Good, because I suspect she can't cook, and you need a woman who can fill that belly of yours."

Miller patted his stomach. "I do right fine at Moore's. No need for a wife."

"Not even to wash your clothes?"

Gannon chuckled. "They do just fine at the bath house."

"By the way, why is it so packed this morning? Is there a picnic I wasn't told about?"

Gannon eyed him and then scratched the back of his head. "You don't know?"

"Know what?" The hair on his nape stood on end. He had a bad feeling.

"They all come to see your gal."

Beau swallowed past the knot in his throat. It was as he'd suspected. "My gal?"

"Yep, all sorts of jawing going on about her. How she done wore britches and raised a ruckus in Judge Greg's court. And then I see Mrs. Bobby Jean cozied up to her. That can't be nothing but trouble."

Beau rolled his eyes. "You're telling me."

The pianist struck a chord, and all chatter clattered to a halt. Gannon nodded and then slipped into his assigned pew next to the judge. Before the children arrived, Beau had sat in the same pew with Miller, Judge Greg and Bobby Jean. Now he had his own pew, with very little room to spare. He'd gone from a single man with no responsibilities to a single man with five mouths to feed, now six. Perhaps he should heed Bobby Jean's advice and start looking for a new wife. A practical wife who didn't set his teeth on edge or make him want to linger in the scent of her perfume longer than he should or to act like an inappropriate fool wanting to touch her porcelain skin or her silky black hair.

If he was to agree to a wife, she'd have to know how to gather eggs and make a hearty breakfast, pull weeds and grow a garden. She had to know how to wash clothes without scrubbing her delicate knuckles raw.

Reverend Scott walked down the middle aisle, shaking hands as he went along. His black Bible hit the pulpit with a distinct thud over the high-pitched, musical notes. A scowl formed on his lips and dark brow, and Beau knew for certain in that moment that Penelope would never make a proper wife for the preacher. In the year since the pastor had arrived, Beau had never seen him anything but happy and kind. A complete bore, and

Beau had a feeling they were about to see a very serious, and perhaps angry, side to the minister's character. He was right to scratch the man off his mental list
of potential husbands.

The banker, who happened to be sitting in front of
them with his mousy sister and her children, buried his
nose into a handkerchief and blew. The sound rever-
berated in the church, even amid the piano music. Penelope's eyes grew wide, and Beau crossed the man's
name off the list, too.

Reverend Scott glanced at the pianist and sliced his
hand across his throat to halt the music. "I am appalled!"

Beau leaned back at the man's red-faced rage.

"You, who call yourself a part of this congregation
and good Christian folk, who gather together and support your neighbors in times of need, who applaud yourself at your good deeds and your charity…" Reverend
Scott stepped to the side of the pulpit and leaned his
elbow against the corner. "How dare you call yourselves
brothers and sisters of Christ when you toss stones? Our
Lord, Who was pure and just and had every reason to
throw stones, did not. He did not condemn the sinner."

Gasps cluttered the air. Fans fluttered faster. Beau
wrinkled his nose and wondered if the minister was
pointing a verbal finger at him for arresting Jessup
Davis for thievery. But Beau had no choice, not while
wearing the badge. He'd gathered a posse to go after
the man who'd robbed the bank and then Taylor's Store,
leaving clerks tied and patrons shaking in their shoes.
He had found it odd, though, that the young man's deeds
had escalated over the last two weeks, going from a
minor scoundrel to a full-fledged crook.

"I have it on good authority that many of you have dared to refuse a gracious welcome to our newest resident, Miss Parker." The minister pointed to Penelope, who blushed. "Instead you have slain her reputation based on the attire she chose to wear out to dinner on her first evening here."

Beau silently applauded the minister's staunch defense of her, but then jealousy quickly took hold. He should be the one defending her, not this foppish man of God.

"Have you considered walking in her shoes? Did a single one of you offer her a kind hello or a meal after an onerous day's travel?"

Beau swallowed. He was guilty as charged. Not only did he not welcome her, he'd left her with children she'd just met and selfishly went on his way. He should have done more.

"I hear tell she was left in the rain and soaked to the bone. She had no means of retrieving her luggage for a change of clothes and made do with what she had. Mrs. Daniels, did you not wear your husband's britches to fetch your hound stuck on the muddy bank of the Neosho? Yet nobody saw it as a sin worthy of malicious gossip. They applauded you for your ingenuity and your practicality. Why is it any different for Miss Parker, who obviously had no other choice but to don Marshal Garrett's britches?"

"They were not her husband's," Mr. Daniels grumbled.

The congregation laughed. Penelope's shoulders fell, and Beau witnessed a small tear on the edge of her lashes before she buried her head against Esther's neck.

The tear tore at him, ripped off his reservations about her. He'd stood by the wayside as Bobby Jean championed her and strange, handsome men fawned over her. He'd listened to Scott's defense of her actions, each moment heating his jealousy to a boiling point. Now was his chance, his chance to protect her, as he should have protected Mary Ella from the enemy's schemes. This was his opportunity to settle things between him and Penelope and let her know exactly where he stood where she was concerned.

Beau jumped to his feet. "No, they were not, Mr. Daniels. However, they were her fiancé's."

Murmurs flew through the church building and echoed off the walls. Beau took John and Esther from her lap and grabbed her hand. He lifted her to her feet. "Let me introduce you to my bride-to-be, Penelope Parker. She answered my mail-order-bride ad, and after a few correspondences, we agreed to marry." He held the reverend's steady and pleased gaze, and Beau wondered if he'd been bamboozled by the minister. Was the man of cloth in cahoots with Bobby Jean? "My apologies for causing a stir, Reverend. We'd hoped to speak to you after service about our nuptials. For the time being, Miss Parker is staying at our home with the children while I take up residence at the jail. All is proper, you see."

The reverend smiled. "As it should be, and we can certainly perform a wedding after service this morning, if there are no objections."

Beau glanced around. The congregation was filled with shock. Only the back row of bachelors leaning against the wall seemed to carry a different set of emotions. Disgust and disappointment. Good. He grinned like the boys had with their first taste of candy. "No objections here, Reverend. The sooner the better."

"Now, shall we get on with today's message?"

Beau and Penelope took their seats. The war that had been waging inside him since her arrival subsided. Lightness overtook him, and he had half a mind to grab his intended bride and waltz her down the aisle, right now for all to see. He stole a glance at her. She kept her head down, and he couldn't help wondering if he'd done something wrong. Of course he had. He'd agreed to a marriage to save her reputation. Something he hadn't been able to do with Mary Ella, and he'd loved her. No doubt his confession had caught Penelope by surprise, as he'd caught himself by surprise. Of course, his jealousy had a good deal to do with the spur to his actions. But he wasn't about to tell her that.

What was wrong with him? He needed air. Perhaps now would be as good a time as any to make his excuses and see if the rumors about Jessup's hideout along the river were true. Now that he had the man locked up, he should recover the money, if at all possible. He glanced at Penelope and knew he couldn't leave her, not like this, not now.

Reverend Scott moved on with the message, but Beau barely paid attention. His focus had been solely on Penelope. Her every move. Her every breath. The slight sniffles and dab of her kerchief to the corner of her eyes. He thought she'd be elated over his unexpected announcement. He expected a victory smile. Something. Anything but the tears sliding down her cheeks.

He was the one who should be shedding tears. Why,

he'd barely acknowledged his need for a wife, and it hadn't been the likes of Miss Penelope Parker. He spent too much time thinking about the black-haired beauty and not enough time considering how to keep Oak Grove safe from mischief.

He leaned across Luke and touched the back of her gloved hand. A jolt sliced up his arm and straight to his chest. "Are you all right?"

She didn't even look at him, just nodded.

"Well, I'll be," he muttered under his breath and then scratched his head. They were to be married in a short time, and his future bride acted like she was being led to the altar by the end of a shotgun.

Chapter Seven

"**A**men," Reverend Scott ended his prayer, and Penelope's palm moistened inside her glove. She dared a quick glance at Beau and prayed beneath her breath he'd forgotten what he'd said. She prayed he'd sweep little John into his arms and walk right out the back door.

"Marshal Garrett, Miss Parker, are you ready for your nuptials?"

"Penelope?" Beau's gaze burned the side of her face as she twisted her hands.

She turned to him and swallowed. "You've been adamant about not taking a wife since the moment I've arrived."

"I've changed my mind."

How? Why? She hadn't even had the chance to prove herself to him. What if she failed? He couldn't take the vows back once they were said before God and witnesses. "I don't understand."

He took her hand in his and helped her to her feet. He leaned close, next to her ear. "There is nothing to understand. You are in want of a husband. I am in need of a nanny, and I will not have the lady caring for my children behaving in a scandalous manner. Certainly, you of all people understand the consequences of such uncomely behavior."

Her cheeks flamed hot, and she nodded. She did. She'd been the focus of gossip since she'd come of age, although not because she'd done anything untoward.

"This is the only way I see to rectify the situation. Don't you agree, Miss Parker?" His gaze bore into hers. "Think of the children."

"Yeah," Luke said as he tugged on her skirts. "I need a ma."

She looked from Matthew to Mark. One looked hopeful, the other frightened.

She drew in a nervous breath, her nose tickled by a flowery scent. The lady in front of her stared. Penelope glanced around. They all stared. Even the stragglers leaning against the back wall. She hadn't the proper attire for a wedding. Still, it was why she'd traveled to Kansas. It was what she wanted. Being married was necessary to save her from Mr. Wallace. However, couldn't she have a day or two, perhaps another week, to prepare? "Do we not need a marriage license? Aren't there laws about this sort of thing?"

"No need to worry, Miss Parker. The documents can be signed afterward. If the reverend doesn't have one available, I do." A tall graying man that she recognized as the judge from the courtroom her first day in town crowded in behind them. He nodded to Beau. "Is this what you want, Beau?"

Beau's jaw ticked. His lips formed a flat line. He nodded.

The judge turned to her. "Miss Parker? You already agreed to marry the marshal?"

The letters remained tucked in her reticule, every line, every precious word branded in her thoughts, and they weren't even his doing, but composed by another hand, by Bobby Jean.

"Well?"

If she said no, she'd cause a scandal and risk being sent home. If she said yes, Beau just might discover her the biggest disappointment in his life. She swallowed her reservations and nodded. "I did agree to marry Beau Garrett before my arrival in Oak Grove."

"Very well," the judge grumbled. "Reverend Scott is waiting for you, and I'm hungry, so let's get this marriage done."

Beau looked relieved.

Hoots and hollers from the congregation echoed off the four walls and Penelope didn't think her cheeks could get any hotter. Heat crept down her neck and up her ears.

"Judge, would you mind?" Beau handed John to the judge, and then he stole Esther from her and handed the baby to the judge, as well. He gently tugged her hand and pulled her in front of the pulpit, and then he glanced over his shoulder and waved. "Matthew, Mark, Luke, come along. Let's get you boys a new ma."

"Whoopee!" Luke jumped off the pew.

Penelope wished she felt the same excitement. She needed to feel the same excitement. In all her daydreams about her wedding, she never imagined it quite like this. In fact, once she'd turned twenty, she'd lost all hope of ever finding a suitable match. By the time she'd turned twenty-two, she'd lost hope of marrying at all. When her father announced her impending marriage to Mr. Wallace, Penelope had had no desire to plan for her special day, outside of wearing mourning clothes. After all, she was quite certain the probability of her demise would most likely have followed the "death do us part," as it had with all of Mr. Wallace's previous wives.

She stood in front of Reverend Scott. Beau's palm warmed the curve of her back and calmed her somewhat. She took one breath. Two. Spoke several words and absently nodded and vaguely recalled saying "I do."

Beau turned her around to face the congregation. Townsfolk of her new home. The reverend spoke loudly. "May I introduce you to Mr. and Mrs. Beau Garrett? Marshal, you may kiss your bride."

Penelope panicked. She'd never known the touch of a man's lips on hers. Beau reached for her hands and wrapped them around his neck. He circled his arms around her waist and drew her in. He held her gaze for a moment.

"Are you ready?"

His words were quiet, a bare whisper. Before she could draw in a breath Beau's mouth was on hers and he tugged her closer. Her knees wobbled, and just when she thought she'd faint, he pulled her tight against his muscled chest, supporting her with his strong arms. Then, before she knew it, the moment was over.

Beau pulled back, lifted her chin to meet her eyes and smiled. "That wasn't so bad, was it?"

She managed a shake of her head.

"Marshal!" A shout from the back pulled her from her haze.

"Fred! What has happened to you?" Beau asked.

She glanced toward the door and noticed a man with blood running down his face, his hand pressed to his forehead. "It's Jessup. He's escaped."

Beau swept another kiss across her lips and left her standing in front of the pulpit, surrounded by the children and the judge. The sight of blood and the realization that she'd married a lawman hit her all at once. What if something happened to him? And without her proving to him that eventually she could make a suitable wife? Her seven days had disappeared and turned into one. She didn't have to prove anything now, not to Beau. She had his name and his protection. However, she wanted to please him, to demonstrate to him and to herself that she could be a good wife. But what if he didn't return safely? What if she became a widow only moments after she'd become Mrs. Beau Garrett?

A dark silhouette formed in the church door, hidden by the glare of the sun, but she'd know the size and girth of the man who'd just entered anywhere.

Mr. Wallace had found her.

Was he too late? Or… They hadn't signed anything yet. Could he claim her marriage to Beau illegal?

"Beau?" His name came out much weaker than she'd intended. She couldn't breathe in enough air to speak more. Her hands shook. The room spun, and she reached out to grab the pulpit. She swayed forward and then backward. Then her knees crumpled beneath her and she hit the floor.

Beau heard the bare whisper of his name a moment before he raced out of the church, and then he heard men mumble and a few women scream. Had Jessup entered the church through the back? Did the outlaw seek to torment the townsfolk in a house of God? He turned on his heel and rushed up the stairs. A circle of people gathered near the pulpit. He pushed his way through until he saw his wife in a heap of skirts on the floor. Mark knelt beside her with silent tears streaming down his cheeks.

"Ma, Ma." Matthew shook her shoulders violently.

Luke peeled back her eyelids. "Wake up, Ma." The boy tipped his chin up, his long blond curls a mess over his brow. Blue eyes pleaded with him.

"Penelope?" Beau crouched on his haunches. Worry replaced the exhilaration he'd felt moments ago at saying "I do," giving him a sense that marrying her had been the scariest decision he'd ever made but also a good one. For the children's sake. And for his. Now that she was Mrs. Garrett, he no longer needed to worry about another man paying her attention. He removed her glove and held her hand. It was warm. He tapped her cheek. "She'll be fine, boys. Smelling salts?"

"Too much excitement for the day, I say." Mrs. Danner shoved through and fanned Penelope's face.

"I agree. I should get her home."

"What about Jessup, Marshal?" Judge Winter grumbled. "He's too dangerous to remain on the loose."

Beau cleared his throat. This was one consequence of having a wife he hadn't foreseen, especially a wife of Penelope's delicate nature. He warred within himself. How could he leave his new wife of less than fifteen minutes to chase a villain? Because it was his duty. And what of his duty to her and the children, he argued to himself. "Judge? Bobby Jean, will you see to my family?"

Doctor Harden pushed in and knelt on the other side of Penelope. "Go, Marshal, before he gets away. I'll tend her and see her settled with Judge."

Beau drew in a deep breath. Penelope's soft rose-scented perfume swirled into his lungs. He bent over, kissed her brow and then jumped to his feet. He shook Judge's hand. "Please, take care of her."

"Of course," Bobby Jean said.

"As if she were my own lovely new bride." The judge clamped his hand over Beau's shoulder. "Now, go get Jessup."

He took one last look at his family and rushed out the door.

"I took the liberty of fetching Dusty." Miller Gannon tossed the reins to him as he stepped into the street.

"Thank you, friend. Let's go get Jessup." Beau swung onto the saddle and nudged his horse. "Any word on where he was last seen?"

"Headed north, across the river."

Beau ground his back teeth. "I can't even get married without the rotter ruining my day."

Gannon chuckled. "He's usually interrupting your morning coffee or night's sleep. Never thought you'd get married, Beau."

Beau shook his head. Had he really gone and got married? Yep, he sure had. Strange as a newborn kitten in a hen's nest, he didn't have any regrets. He rolled his shoulders and then his neck.

"What happened? How'd he get out?"

"Seems he has some help, Marshal."

Beau nudged Dusty faster. Strange he hadn't felt the sickening thud in his stomach he'd expected upon saying the words *I do*. Of course, he wasn't being coerced into the nuptials. Not that he sensed anyway. In fact, he'd had to do the convincing and even had used a tactic he hadn't been proud of. He'd pulled the scandal card, but only because he thought it mattered to her, especially given her upbringing, and when that hadn't worked, he'd used the children. He never thought he'd have to convince any lady to marry him, most certainly not one arriving in town with demands that he do right by her and abide by their agreement per correspondences he'd never seen.

A swirling knot formed in his stomach, but it wasn't the expected sickening of being saddled for the rest of his life to a woman like Penelope. Beautiful, charming, tempting. All of his regret came from her uncertainty and the tears. Had she changed her mind? Once she'd seen other options of eligible bachelors in Oak Grove had she decided against him?

"Beau!"

Beau shook her from his thoughts and ducked in time to miss a low-hanging branch. He pulled up on the reins. "That was close."

Miller halted beside him and adjusted his hat. "Remind me to never get me a wife."

"What for?"

"I like my head where it is."

Beau narrowed his gaze. "And what is that supposed to mean?"

"You've been riding willy-nilly, not paying attention where we're going. And you about took yer head right off with that there branch. I'm thinking your thoughts are turned back to the church and your pretty bride that you said you didn't want." Gannon twisted his lips. "What got into you anyway? One minute you're saying nope, uh-uh, and then you're telling the preacher she's your fiancée. I don't get it."

Beau scowled. However, he couldn't deny the truth of Miller's words. And he'd been exactly afraid that Penelope would distract him from his duty to Oak Grove. At least this time it had nearly got him killed and not someone else. "Anyone ever tell you that you talk too much?"

"That's what my mama said." Miller grinned. "Shall we keep on or turn back to check on your wife?"

Beau nudged Dusty. "Where's this hideout?"

"Up yonder a ways. Hear it's hidden in the side of a hill."

"Are you talking about the old trapper's hut?" Twenty years or so before Oak Grove became a town, a trapper built a cabin to trade with the local Indians. It'd been abandoned for quite some time, and last Beau had seen it, there wasn't much left. But for an outlaw it might make the perfect hideout.

Chapter Eight

Penelope kept her spine straight as a broom, even though what she really wanted to do was sink into the upholstered wing chair. Had she really seen Mr. Wallace at church? Had her new husband left to ride straight into danger?

She forced herself to speak when her hostess, Mrs. Bobby Jean Winter, entered the salon. "Thank you for the hospitality."

Instead it was Mrs. Danner who spoke up. She peered at Penelope through her wire-rimmed glasses as she poked a needle into her fabric. "I might have to readjust my opinion of you, gal."

"Oh, Mama, be nice. She is our guest." Bobby Jean set a silver tray on an end table and poured a cup of tea. "The children are outside with Judge. I dare say he acts like one of them at times. Tea isn't much, but it should calm your nerves a bit."

Penelope took the cup from her hostess. "Thank you. You have a lovely home. Your kindness at church is appreciated."

"Certainly. It was my pleasure and now that you've married Beau, we'll become fast friends." Bobby Jean beamed. "Judge let me do the decorating. I must admit I like simplicity, but I do love my comforts. You must miss your home."

"No," she responded a little more hastily than she should, and then she released an unladylike sigh.

Mrs. Danner chuckled. "Now, that is more like it. Lean back, relax."

"My apologies. There are things I miss, but having been away, I cannot recall what those things are."

Her fear over seeing Mr. Wallace overshadowed any other thoughts.

"It can't be easy for a lady such as yourself to chase after five little ones, not to mention marry a man such as our marshal." Mrs. Danner grinned.

"I'm married." Even as she said the words, she had difficulty believing them. However, she'd been there. She'd said "I do," as had Beau. She'd been kissed. Her first kiss. She lifted her fingers to her lips as she recalled the sweet gentleness of Beau's lips upon hers. She was really married. Finally, after all these years of waiting. She gave in to the supple upholstery. Her head sank against the pillowy softness, and she closed her eyes.

"You certainly are correct about that," Mrs. Danner twittered. "The entire town bore witness to that kiss."

Penelope's cheeks caught fire. Her eyes flew open and she sat up straight. Had Mr. Wallace seen the kiss? It didn't matter. She was truly married, and there was nothing Mr. Wallace could do about it. Was there?

That kiss had taken hold of her senses and her muscles. It had turned her knees to liquid and curled her toes inside her boots. Were all kisses as such, or only Beau Garrett's? She feared the blame lay solely on Beau's mouth, which caused her a great deal of anxiety. What if he hadn't felt the same knee-wobbling sensation about kissing her? What if he'd kissed another before her and longed for a very different wife? A wife he actually wanted instead of one who nearly ruined him and his children with scandal? She worried her bottom lip and demanded her fears be quiet. However, with Mr. Wallace in town, it was difficult not to imagine all the bad things that could happen. Beau could easily toss her aside for another. Divorces were not unheard of. Although that would only cause another scandal, and she didn't think Beau would risk one on a grander scale than her wearing britches to a café.

"Oh, Mama, honestly, must you pester Mrs. Garrett?"

Penelope wrinkled her brow. "Mrs. Garrett?"

She'd spent time practicing penning her name but had never once said it aloud. Mrs. Garrett. She had to admit it had a nice sound.

Bobby Jean sat on the sofa beside the chair and patted her hand. "Does that bother you overmuch, my dear? That is why you came to Oak Grove. To marry Beau."

She nodded, and then she shook her head. The tears she'd fought so hard to keep hidden welled. "I don't know. That was before, when I believed he wanted a wife. He doesn't."

How many times had he told her he didn't want to be married? More than she cared to count. He believed he was getting a nanny, but because she wore britches to Moore's House and caused a scandal, he had a wife.

"Seems he has one now, and without too much pro-
testation from the man." Mrs. Danner poked the needle
through the fabric.

"Mama, do be quiet. I would hate for Judge to send
you to my brother's home."

Mrs. Danner scowled. "Can't help my mouth. It likes
to get away with my thoughts sometimes."

Bobby Jean leaned forward. Her face was kind and
gentle. "I know Beau very well. After all, he is my
cousin. He wouldn't have married you unless he wanted
to."

With a shake of her head, Penelope said, "He didn't
want to. He was afraid my scandal would cause the
children harm."

Her new friend sat back a little. "I'm certain that is
not the case. However, that is a matter for Beau to correct, of which I shall not interfere."

"I beg your pardon, Mrs. Winter, I mean no offense,
but is that not how we're in this mess, because you chose
to interfere with his correspondence?"

Penelope opened her reticule and pulled out the letters addressed to her. "These are not real, not as I had
thought. The man I believed I was to marry did not
write these letters. They are not him. I sensed a great
deal about him through his words, and now I discover
that they are not his own."

Bobby Jean bowed her head. "They may not be
Beau's words, but every word would have come from
his heart if he'd only known what he needed. I remind
you that I know Beau very well. With the children underfoot, he needed to find a wife, not a nanny. It is not
my place to tell his story, dear, and I'm not sorry one

bit for what I did. It all may seem like trouble now, but you'll see, everything will work out as it should. Beau will make a right fine husband."

Penelope could not deny the fact that he was proving to be a right fine individual and would no doubt make a wonderful husband. It wasn't him she was concerned over. It was her. What sort of wife would she make him? One that met failure at every turn?

"Now, for the trouble I caused," Bobby Jean said, clapping her hands and smiling, "I owe you a great debt. What can I do to repay you?"

Penelope reached for a tea cake and sniffed. Lemon, her favorite. She took a nibble just as she began to shake her head, and then she froze. She chewed. The confection was moist and sweet. She did not feel the need to choke down the cake with a quick swallow of tea as it did not stick to her tongue or her throat. "May I borrow your cook?"

Mrs. Danner guffawed. Bobby Jean giggled and laid her hand on the arm of the chair. "Oh, dear, I have no cook. That is my own doing."

One of Penelope's eyebrows arched. "Yours? Do you make biscuits and chicken and potatoes, too?"

Her new friend nodded. "Among other things."

"Can you teach me?"

Bobby Jean jumped to her feet and clapped her hands. "That is a most excellent idea! Now, when shall we get started?"

"How about today?" The judge said from the doorway, Esther fast asleep on his shoulder. "I'm starved."

Bobby Jean danced across the room and kissed her husband's round cheek. "You're always hungry, my love.

How about some cakes to hold you and the children over until dinnertime?"

"As long as you fry me up some of your chicken, I can bide my time with cakes," he said as he ushered the boys into the salon. "Find a spot and kick up your feet."

"Oh, no, they are covered in dirt." Penelope reached for Luke's britches and began dusting him off.

The judge laughed. "As am I, Mrs. Garrett, but that won't stop me from sitting on my own furniture."

"Oh, dear."

"Don't fret yourself, gal." Mrs. Danner eyed her from over her glasses. "It's only furniture."

Penelope glanced from one child to the next, each hesitant and waiting for her response. She calmed her nerves. Cook would have had a switch to her backside if she would have entered the house as filthy as the boys were, but if the Winters were fine with it, who was she to say any differently? Besides, she didn't want to cause the boys any unneeded anxiety. They were children after all. "Very well, but mind your manners while I help Mrs. Winter with dinner, all right?"

Luke hopped onto the sofa next to the judge, a cloud of dirt flying into the air. Penelope thought she might faint again, but the judge laughed and then speared his fingers through Luke's blond mop of hair. "Thatta boy. That's the way it's done."

Mark found a vacant chair near a window. Matthew collapsed onto the floor and kicked his feet into the air. Penelope smiled. She worried over Mark, staring out the window, but she'd seen glimpses of him opening up. Like this morning at church when he'd sat beside her and curled his hand into hers. She'd sensed he needed connection, so she'd gently removed her glove and let their palms touch. He hadn't smiled, but he had scooted closer and almost leaned his head on her arm.

She walked over to him and pressed her lips to his brow. "Would you like to join us?"

· He shook his head.

"All right, then. If you need me, you know where to find me."

He barely moved, but it was something.

"I'm up for chess," the judge said. "Anyone wish to join me? Not you, Mother Danner. You do not play fair."

"You can't prove a thing, son." Mrs. Danner laid her needlework aside. "Would you boys like to outwit a judge?"

Matthew jumped up and sat on the sofa. "I can outwit a fox. That's what Pa tells me. I ain't ever outwitted a judge though."

Penelope sighed. She'd correct Matthew's grammar another day. He was enjoying himself too much.

Bobby Jean looped her arm through Penelope's and took her into the hallway. "Shall we, then? They will be fine."

"I know," Penelope said as she followed Bobby Jean from the family-like gathering. It gave her pause, knowing the judge wasn't the children's father, yet he treated them as if they were, just as Beau did. Her feet were hard-pressed to move. She wanted to linger a little longer, to watch and learn how family should interact. As far as she knew, her own father had never held her like the judge did Esther, and he'd certainly never invited her to play games. Only to serve as his hostess or entertain his guests with music and mindless chatter.

She bit the inside of her lip. "Do you have other children besides your daughter?" she asked Bobby Jean.

"Of course. Our daughter is married to a miscreant meant to be a lawyer and our son is off exploring the West."

Penelope's eyes grew wide. "Adult children. You look too young."

Bobby Jean's soft smile warmed her. "Would it help if I told you Judge and I married when I was sixteen? Both my parents had passed due to illness."

"I'm sorry."

"Don't be. Even if they hadn't, Judge had already come courting. He's older, but sake's alive he put a curl in my toes with his lazy drawl and his witty humor. I knew the moment I met him that I was going to be Mrs. Winter. Of course, don't tell him that. I made him give a good chase and let him think he won, which is exactly what you should do with Beau."

Penelope shook her head. "We're already married."

"Yes, my dear, but love is a-coming."

"Love? What does love have to do with marriage?"

"Oh, dear. You've heard of love, right?"

"In books, yes, but never in reality. My own parents married for gain. My father needed money, and my mother needed his reputable name." There weren't many men willing to marry a woman with melancholy. At least Papa hadn't sent her directly to the asylum, not until she was beyond the help of doctors.

"Dear, I forget you come from a very different world." Bobby Jean added flour to a bowl and then used a fork to pull a piece of chicken from a bowl of water. "Have you ever had a pet? Of course, you do!

What was I thinking? Mrs. Moore came for tea yesterday, and all she spoke about was your darling Harvey. Should I have Judge fetch him? I fear you'll be here for some time. Beau isn't likely to return until after nightfall. Unless they capture Jessup sooner."

"I don't wish to be a bother."

"No bother. Judge," Bobby Jean shouted and waited for him to appear in the kitchen. "Will you have someone fetch Harvey? I've been curious about the little guy and the knot he's put in Mr. Moore's pants."

"Of course, my love. I'd offer but I'm enjoying the children too much." He swaggered across the floor and kissed Bobby Jean's cheek.

Penelope watched Bobby Jean dunk the meat into the dough and flop it around while she thought about the interaction between Judge and Bobby Jean. Was it normal for a husband and wife to adore each other?

"I adore Harvey, but I cannot understand how love has anything to do with a pet."

"What about a favored servant?"

Penelope smiled as her heart warmed. "Cook and Wren."

"See? The look on your face says you have great affection for them both."

"I do, Cook fed me and scolded me whenever I stuck my finger in the batter." Penelope laughed. "And Wren sat with me while I read my books."

"Imagine that affection on a grander scale. You've only known the children a few days, but I see the love you feel for them in your eyes."

"Empathy. Pity, maybe. I can relate. My mother

died when I was young, and my father was never much around."

"Siblings?"

"An only child."

"I should have remembered from our correspondence." Bobby Jean's cheeks turned a pretty pink. "Yes, I wrote on behalf of Beau, and I am not sorry. Although I'm sure I'll have my comeuppance." Bobby Jean dusted her hands off on her apron and wrapped her arms around Penelope.

Penelope froze. She blinked. She tried not to pull away, and just when she believed she couldn't handle the touch another moment longer, Bobby Jean released her.

"I'm certainly thankful you are here, and I have to admit, it didn't take Beau as long as I thought it would to come around to making you his wife. I wonder why."

"Reverend Scott's scolding and lecturing on a scandal, no doubt."

Bobby Jean considered Penelope for a moment and then dropped a piece of chicken into egg batter. She shook her head. "No, definitely not. It must have had something to do with the gentlemen I introduced you to before service. Nothing sets a fire under a man's foot and has him racing for the altar like another man talking to his lady."

"But I wasn't his lady. He made that clear on multiple occasions." Even now that she carried his name and in the aftermath of that kiss, she didn't feel married. She still had to prove herself to him. Prove that she could care for the children. *Their* children now. Her hand flew to her mouth. "Oh, my"

"What is it, dear?"

"I'm a mother. A mother of five."

"You're not going to faint again, are you?" Beau's deep voice echoed in the kitchen.

She spun around so fast the room swam with her. She focused on Beau. His hair curling beneath his hat. His vest and denim shirt, the silver badge and trousers. His dusty boots. Not a single spot of blood. She rushed to him and squeezed her arms around his neck. His arms hung at his sides. "You're safe."

"Of course I'm safe."

"I feared you'd get shot."

He laughed. "And why would you think a thing like that, darling?"

"The man at church, he was covered in blood." And that hadn't been all that had unsettled her. With Mr. Wallace in town, she'd have to warn Beau so there weren't any surprises.

Beau glanced between Bobby Jean, and then he arched a brow. "What man are you talking about?"

Penelope stepped away from him, away from his solid strength and warmth and walked across the room. She fisted her hands at her sides, frustrated that he would act as if she'd seen things. "The man at church. The one who stormed in after our wedding and boomed at the top of his voice, 'It's Jessup. He's escaped,'" she said, deepening her voice for effect.

Both of Beau's brows inched upward, and then he massaged his brow with his fingers. "Oh, that was Fred. Sometimes he sits at the jail while Miller and I attend services. He hadn't been shot, and it was only a small scratch."

"A small scratch?"

Beau laughed, but she sensed it was forced and nervous. "Only bashed on the head by a woman. Like I said, a small scratch. Seems Jessup might have a small gang of thieves with him."

She stomped her foot. "Beau Garrett, this is not a laughing matter. You could have been killed or worse."

"I'm sorry, Penelope. I didn't see the danger. It's part of the job." Beau sauntered toward her and took her shoulders in his hands. Penelope tilted her head back to look at his face. He was so very handsome. And he smelled ever so good. Like fresh air and horses and spicy cologne.

"What could be worse than getting killed, Penelope?"

Her lips parted. She clamped them closed and blinked. Running into Mr. Wallace.

He inched closer. The toes of his boots touched the toes of her shoes. "Penelope, what could be worse than being killed?" he asked again when she did not reply.

She blinked, uncertain how to respond. She wanted to tell him the truth about Mr. Wallace. She had to tell him, but all she thought was how awful it'd be if he became angry and turned from her because she hadn't told him about St. Louis. And how awful it'd be if she never felt his lips on hers again. Her heart screamed that the worst was never knowing what it was like to be part of a family. However, she could not say any of those things. He'd just laugh at her, especially since they'd just met only a short while ago. Had it been only a short while? It seemed like weeks, months, even.

"Penelope." He brushed a strand of hair behind her ear. "You didn't answer my question."

"Leaving the children fatherless, again," she blurted out.

He stepped back and swept his hat from his head. His chest rose high, then fell. "I suppose you are correct. Where are they?"

"In the parlor with Judge Winter," Penelope said.

Bobby Jean spoke up as she wiped her hands on her floured apron. "Penelope has offered to help me make dinner, Beau. How about you join Judge and the children and stay a while? It'd be nice to visit, and the house feels less empty with the laughter of children."

Beau squinted. "Your manipulation isn't needed, Bobby Jean. Of course we'll stay." He looked at Penelope. "That is, if it is fine by you."

She was taken aback. Rarely had anyone considered her wants, and she never recalled being asked. She wasn't certain how to respond. "Certainly, it is."

Without another word, Beau took a step to leave the kitchen.

"Beau, wait," she said and he turned toward her with a brow raised. "Did you catch Mr. Davis?"

His lips twitched. "I'm afraid not."

He slipped into the shadowed hallway. The air seemed to cool. Her emotions turned less confused but also bereft. She missed him. Such a silly notion since he'd just been here.

"Well, that was a mite interesting," Bobby Jean said.

Penelope propped a hand on her hip. "Pray, tell me what was interesting?"

Bobby Jean waved a chicken leg in the air. "That. The conversation. He's taken with you."

"I don't see how you can gather that from one small

conversation." Penelope dipped her hands into a watering bowl. "What may I do to help?"

"First, you can try to deny the sparks between the two of you."

Sparks? Penelope glanced down the front of her dress and inspected it for scorch marks. "I don't understand. There was nothing on fire between us."

Bobby Jean giggled. "Not literally. Well, not exactly literally. Here," she said as she tapped her chest, leaving more flour on her apron. "Didn't you feel it?"

Penelope tilted her head. Her knees had gone wobbly again, and her breath had tangled up in her lungs, and of course the skin around her ear where he'd tucked her hair still felt warm from his touch. "I'm not certain what it is I felt or what I'm supposed to be feeling."

Other than a great deal of fear that Mr. Wallace would arrive any moment and demand she return to St. Louis with him.

"It looks like I have my work cut out for me."

Penelope's eyes grew wide, and she shook her head. "Please do not cause any more chaos between Beau and me. It is obvious he is irritated with the interference." They didn't need any more help. She was a wife to a man with a dangerous job, and her husband was stuck with a wife he didn't want, all to save himself and the children from scandal, and now Mr. Wallace was in town. Beau would have been saved from so much trouble if Bobby Jean hadn't changed the ad.

"I'll take care with my actions. All I ask is that you be you. Don't try overly hard to be someone you're not, and Beau will fall in line just fine."

Penelope didn't see how not trying to be a good wife

would work to her advantage. If she couldn't cook, the children would starve. If she couldn't wash clothes, they'd be filthy, and if Beau's toes didn't curl like hers did when they kissed, she feared he'd look elsewhere, and then what would happen to her?

Beau hung his hat on the coat tree outside the parlor and shoved his hands into his pockets. When he'd agreed to be marshal, he'd had no responsibilities. Now he had six. Five children, five orphaned children, left to him by his brother, and Penelope, an innocent who had no idea what she'd agreed to when she'd said "I do" before Reverend Scott and Oak Grove's townsfolk. He'd laughed off getting shot to ease her worries and concerns. Since the children had arrived, he'd been aware of the danger he faced every time he encountered a rotter, but he didn't want his wife fretting over the danger, too. Truth was, every time he settled his gun belt on his hips, his day of reckoning for all his sins was closer. And he had a lot to answer for, especially since the death of Mary Ella and then his brother. Making sure the children were raised right, with family and a caring mother, was a start. It's the reason he'd decided to marry Penelope. He'd seen her care and attentiveness to the children. She may not understand domestic duties, but from all he'd witnessed, she understood the children. More than he did. All he'd needed was Reverend Scott's prodding to do the right thing.

He ducked through the parlor door. "How are my boys doing?"

Harvey lunged off Judge's lap and darted for Beau's

legs. He scooped the mutt into his arms and scratched the silky fur between his ears.

"Pa!" Luke raced to Beau. The child hit with a force that nearly knocked him off his feet. The welcoming was a good sensation. It warmed his heart. It also solidified in his mind what Penelope had said about leaving the boys without yet another parent.

"Whoa there, partner." Beau swung him into his arms. "What have you been up to?"

"We saw a pony and fed the goats. Can we get a goat? I want a goat. Mr. Judge sent a groom after Harvey, and he brought us treats. See?" Luke stuck out his tongue for Beau's inspection.

Beau crooked his knuckle under Luke's chin and closed the boy's mouth. "We have chickens," Beau said, placing the boy back on his feet.

"Chickens stink."

"That they do."

"How'd it go, Marshal?" Judge looked over the rim of the spectacles perched on the end of his nose.

"Not so good. No sign of him this time." Beau sat on the edge of an upholstered wing chair and took note of the vast differences of Judge's home compared to his. Differences he'd noticed but barely paid heed to until Penelope entered his life. The small cabin had been suitable two months ago. Before he had a family and a wife. A wife who was used to comforts. He shook his head. What had he been thinking when he'd taken her on? "I suppose it's too late," Beau muttered.

Judge concentrated on the chessboard as Mrs. Danner moved and efficiently took the judge's queen. "See there, boys? That's how it's done. Now, how 'bout we check what the gals are up to in the kitchen."

Mrs. Danner ushered the boys out of the parlor, and before she closed the door, she gave Beau a narrowed glare. "It's never too late, but before you go and decide anything stupid, know you've got yourself a right fine gal. She ain't no ninny, that's for sure. You tell him, Judge. A right fine gal, she is."

The door closed. Judge leaned back against the sofa and fished a cigar out of his pocket. "Would you like to step outside with me a moment? Bobby Jean will have my hide if I light up in the house."

Beau unfolded his length from the chair and followed Judge through a set of double doors leading out to a small garden area.

"Sure are some good boys, but that Luke is full of energy."

Beau laughed and leaned his hip against the white-painted column holding up the roof. "Did they give you any trouble?"

"Not one bit. Although I half expected it. Mark sure is a quiet boy."

Beau nodded. "Hasn't said much since he arrived in Oak Grove."

"He sure lights up when Penelope is around."

Beau's heart warmed.

"So do you."

He massaged the back of his neck and thought about denying Judge's observation, but he couldn't, unless he wanted his friend and mentor to call him an outright liar.

"You're not having regrets, are you?" Judge lit his cigar. Smoke rings lifted into the air as he puffed.

Beau drew in the scent and thought of his father, thought of his home and his mother. Then he thought about his brother and the life he'd given up to save their family from scandal all because Beau wouldn't marry Mary Ella after he'd discovered her treachery. Zach had traded a life of comforts for a life of toiling in the dirt, all so he could die at a young age. "I can't give her this," he said as he motioned with his hands toward Judge's house.

"Has she complained?"

"No. Not even when her knuckles bled from washing clothes, or when the boys locked her in the henhouse." The corner of his mouth lifted when he recalled how she'd taken him to task. "She even chastised me for my anger when I threatened to punish the boys. She didn't even do it in front of them and supported my decision to dole out a reckoning for their misdeeds, but her wisdom made me second-guess the right and wrong of it."

"She's a good woman, Beau. Reminds me of my Bobby Jean. And hardy."

Beau pushed from the column and cupped a white flower from a bush in his hand. "Not so hardy, Judge. She's petite and delicate. You should have seen her the day she came to town."

Judge chuckled. "I did. Barged right in on my court-room, fiery mad because she'd been left to wait in a storm."

He dropped the flower and ran his palm over his freshly shaved jaw. The scent reminded him of Penelope.

"Allow me to ask you a question, Beau," Judge said

as he blew out a smoke ring. "What'd you marry her for?"

Beau's lids closed. "Can I lie, Judge?"

"I think you know better."

"I saw the railroad men gathered in church fawning over her, and I knew they could give her a better life, give her the things she's used to. The thought of not having her around soured my stomach. I didn't think the boys could stand another loss, and they've taken to her so well." Judge pierced him with a hard look. "And if I'm to be fully honest, I was jealous."

He didn't know if he could stand losing her either, but those words were best left burning on the tip of his tongue.

"What about you, Beau?"

"I didn't want to give them a chance to woo her with their money and social status."

"Did you ever question why she answered the ad? Certainly, she had ample opportunity to marry. My guess is she's running from something."

Beau raked his fingers through his hair. "What, I wonder?"

"Why don't you ask her?"

"I did. She ignored my question, which gives me pause."

"And yet you made her your wife. Can't be too bad, Beau. You're a good judge of character. It's why I suggested you for the job. With Abilene caught up in a rise of lawlessness and railroad men looking to build through here, I wanted efficiency and I wanted someone who could keep the law before things got out of hand."

"Right, and I'm doing a great job of it. I can't keep Jessup Davis locked up."

Mark shuffled through the double doors. "Mrs. Winter said it's time to wash up for dinner."

Beau reached out to touch his shoulder. Before he second-guessed himself, he gave the boy a gentle squeeze. Mark didn't flinch and he didn't jerk away as he'd done previously, which surprised Beau. "Thank you, Mark. Will you tell Mrs. Winter and Penelope we'll be along shortly?"

Mark dipped his head and traipsed back through the door.

"You're doing right by those young'uns," Judge said as he smashed his cigar against the underside of the handrail and then rose from his chair.

"Thank you," Beau replied, not quite feeling his friend's compliment. He was doing the best he could, but it seemed it wasn't enough. "Shall we?"

"Beau," Judge called.

Beau stopped and glanced over his shoulder. "Bobby Jean is bound to be up to something."

"When isn't she, Judge?" Beau pulled the door open.

"Can you find it in you to forgive her if she oversteps? She means well."

"She's already overstepped a great deal, and now I have a wife I don't need and didn't want." Beau massaged his neck and stared at the tip of his boot. "I know she means well, Judge. I just don't take too kindly to being manipulated."

"What man does? However, you just might find she did you a favor."

Before he knew it, he was entering the Winterses'

dining room. It was a place he'd been in many times before with Miller Gannon. Except this time he saw it through eyes of guilt and shame. The sparkling chandelier. The curtains that held a lady's touch. The china laid out in perfect order. The pictures on the wall. The rich mahogany tabletop with matching upholstered chairs. They were all things he'd taken for granted growing up in Indiana. All things he'd thrown away when his father had threatened to disown him at his refusal to save the family from scandal and wed Mary Ella. They were all things his brother had been accustomed to, not the hard labor of plowing a field. And they were all things Penelope had left behind. Had she expected fine possessions upon her arrival? Had she hoped for a home like the Winterses'?

His bride glided around the room and dished out food onto plates for the children. She smiled at him. "I hope you don't mind. I requested Mrs. Winter place you between Luke and John. I'll sit between John and Esther's highchair."

He saw the practicality in her arrangement. He applauded her for the foresight. However, he'd hoped to sit beside her since it was their wedding day. To smell her perfume. To brush his hand against hers as they reached for the gravy bowl at the same time. The pale creaminess of her neck called to him. He leaned forward and touched his mouth to her nape. "I don't mind, Penelope."

She shivered. The fork in her hand clattered to the table.

"Are you all right?" Beau pulled away from her and looked to her pale face.

Her mouth curved as she pasted on a smile. "Yes,

of course. Why wouldn't I be? We're about to share a lovely meal with the children and your friends. Your kiss caught me off guard, is all."

"Our friends. What's mine is now yours, Penelope." He wasn't certain he liked the way she'd distanced herself from the children and the couple he'd hoped would be her friends, too. Was it her way of distancing from him? He circled her wrist.

She spun around. "Beau! What are you doing?"

"Touching my wife's hand."

Her eyes grew wide.

He leaned in and inhaled the scent lingering on her neck. "Are you disappointed to not be sitting beside me on our wedding day?"

"Pa!" Luke burst through the door. "Look what Mrs. Winter let me carry."

Beau turned in time to catch the flying gravy bowl as Luke tripped over his own feet.

Chapter Nine

Penelope's spoon hovered above her soup bowl. Beau stared at her from across the table. She sipped her soup and then slipped her napkin from her lap to wipe her mouth. Esther reached for a roll, and without taking her eyes from Beau, Penelope broke off a piece and handed it to the infant.

"We don't sit here often. I forget how nice it is." Bobby Jean lifted her glass to her mouth and took a drink.

Judge shoved a bite of chicken into his mouth. "I agree. It's not often we have guests. Beau and Miller used to visit every Sunday. Since he's taken up with you scoundrels," Judge said, eyeing each of the boys, "we don't see either of them much."

Beau laid his spoon aside. "I hadn't realized Gannon had been skipping out, too."

"Is Miller the other marshal?" Penelope asked.

Beau chuckled. "I suppose you can call him that."

"He's what we call the deputy marshal. We have

several part-timers, but Miller is always on duty. Just like Beau, here."

"Well, when Judge puts it that way, I guess Miller is pretty much the other marshal. He has the same authority I do."

"Now, don't go selling yourself short, Beau." Judge sipped on his tea. "That boy can learn a lot from you and has. He also seeks your advice before making too many decisions. He respects you, and that's what makes you the marshal."

Penelope tried to focus on the conversation, but she couldn't stop thinking about the man covered in blood this morning or the fact that Beau had run out of the church headlong into danger. She'd fretted and worried. Twisting her hands together, smothering the boys when they were near, until Beau had arrived and she'd seen for herself that he was well. However, what about next time? The worry. The fear. What if he didn't return?

"Mrs. Garrett, tell me, where do you come from?"

It took Penelope a moment to realize that Bobby Jean was speaking to her. She finished chewing and then wiped her mouth with her napkin. "St. Louis."

Beau's fork hovered. "Missouri? A slave sympathizer?"

"Yes, Missouri." She softened her gaze. "We did not own slaves. Nor did I agree with the matter. Not that a woman has much say in politics."

"It must have been very difficult for you," Beau said.

Her brow furrowed. "I'm not certain I follow. What must have been difficult?"

"Living among friends and neighbors who opposed your own beliefs."

She darted her eyes from his and focused on spooning a bite of vegetables into Esther's mouth. "I had no friends, my neighbors were societal pawns whose opinions ebbed and flowed with the opinions of whomever they entertained that evening, and my father, the only living family I have, cared for nothing but his next dollar."

Silence held the room captive. Penelope lifted her head. "My apologies. It has been some time since I've dined with polite company, or any company other than my own. I daresay I've forgotten the etiquette of conversations. Will you forgive me?"

Judge burst into laughter. Beau's chair scraped against the hardwood floor as he scooted back. He stretched out his legs and crossed his arms over his chest. Penelope blinked.

"I daresay, dear wife, you are refreshing. Like a dousing rain after a hard drought. Although, with your expensive clothes, I am hard-pressed to believe you actually don't care for the upper echelons."

"Why should I? My clothes have nothing to do with whether or not I like someone. As I mentioned, other than my former maid, I had no friends. Only acquaintances."

"Well, Penelope," Bobby Jean cut in, "that is about to change. I believe we'll make fast friends, and you're already proving to be a wonderful cook, wouldn't you say, Beau? After all, she did make those biscuits you've had five of."

Beau grinned. "Five? Is that all? I believe I'll have another one."

An ache filled her chest at his lack of acknowledgment. She'd been anxious over the biscuits and the dessert. It would have been nice to know whether or not Beau actually liked them. She supposed it was a good sign that he was eating more than one. Could she re-create the recipe at home and without a stove? She'd certainly give it a try.

"I have a grand idea." Bobby Jean beamed and folded her hands together. "It's been entirely too long since we've had children in the house. How about Judge and I keep them for the evening? After all, it is your wedding night."

Heat crept up Penelope's neck and burned the tips of her ears. Cook had talked to her about the ways of a man and woman on their wedding night, right before she was to be married to Mr. Wallace. It wasn't something she quite understood, but the intimacy embarrassed her. "That is not necessary."

"We wouldn't want to bother you," Beau added.

"It's no bother," Judge said. "I think it's a wonderful idea."

Beau tossed his napkin onto his plate. "Very well, after we help clean up, we'll take you up on your offer."

Penelope thought she'd faint again.

It didn't take them long to clear the dishes and put the kitchen back in order.

Judge stopped them in the hall with a large document in his hand. "Before you leave, we should finalize this marriage."

She shivered in nervous excitement. She was about to officially become Mrs. Beau Garrett. The moment she had waited for since she'd left home was finally here, and it was nothing more than a mechanical scrawl of her name. All her penmanship practice came down to nothing more than a breath of air. Although the weight bearing down on her shoulders since she'd ran away from home seemed lighter, there was no elation and no celebration. Before she knew it, she was kissing the children's cheeks and walking next to Beau while his horse clopped behind them. A sense of foreboding pricked her nape. She needed to find a way to tell him about Mr. Wallace. She shivered against the cool air.

"Are you cold?"

"I don't think so. The wind caught me unaware."

He grunted, and then they walked in silence. He didn't say a word. Neither did she, as she didn't know how to approach the subject of her former intended. How was she to tell Beau she'd left a man at the altar and that he was here in Oak Grove? Would Beau annul their marriage as fast as he'd raced out of the church this morning, hot on the heels of Jessup Davis? Given he'd married her only to save his family from scandal, it was possible. If he found out what she'd done, he might send her back to St. Louis and not care about the scandal. With her out of the way, the gossip would soon die anyway.

She feigned interest in the evening sky and the few stars that were beginning to make their presence known. She bent her ear to the musical hum of a frog. Soon they were standing in front of their home. A shack compared to the Winterses' home. A shack compared to what she'd been accustomed to. However, it was home, and she found it quite comfortable.

Beau looped Dusty's reins around a hitching post

and placed his palm at the small of her back. He led her up the pathway, up the stairs and to their front door.

"Beau, I have something to tell you," she whispered when he gazed into her eyes. She began to tremble. How would he respond once she told him about Mr. Wallace?

He must not have heard her, for he opened the door and then swept her off the ground. She yelped. He settled her against his chest, her legs dangling over his forearm. Their eyes met and for a moment Penelope believed their marriage was real and not a facade to save his children from scandal. She could not blame him for his efforts. She'd seen disgrace destroy families, and she didn't wish for the children to suffer any more than they already had. But she couldn't help but wish for more in a marriage, something akin to what she'd read about in books. She had no grand illusions of love. Outside of what she'd witnessed between Bobby Jean and Judge, she'd not seen nor heard of love within the bounds of matrimony nor had she known the emotion from her own father, but she'd hoped for something more.

"Shall we, Mrs. Garrett?"

She nodded, and yet she had no idea what it was she agreed to.

Beau ducked through the door and deposited his bride onto her feet. A little hastier than he should have or had intended. Her blue eyes had held his, and emotion stirred within his chest, beating against his breastbone with the fierceness of a thunderstorm. His palms moistened and he found it difficult to breathe, or to even reason. All he could think of was to rid himself of her presence, the sooner the better before he tugged her against him and repeated the kiss they'd shared at church earlier that day.

He released her and offered her a teasing bow. "Your humble abode, madam."

She remained steady, but the look on her face left him lingering. Did she want him to kiss her? He cupped her chin and pulled her close. His mouth hovered above her lips. Her eyelids fluttered shut. Her breath caressed his. He leaned closer until the moist warmth of their mouths touched. Fire shot through him like a bolt of lightning. He released her with such haste she almost fell backward. He snatched her hand and held on until she quit swaying. "Happy wedding day, Wife. I'll be in the barn if you have need of me."

He turned and left, shutting the door behind him. What had he been about, kissing her like that? They'd agreed to marry, and as such, he had every right to stay with her this night. However, he wasn't certain she fully understood the fullness of their vows. She needed time. He needed time.

He took Dusty into the barn and gave him a bucket of oats. He found a blanket and laid it on a pile of hay. Although he'd left her with the children while he'd found his bed at the jail, he didn't dare leave her alone now with Jessup on the loose.

He propped his head in his hands and stared up at the rafters as he thought over the events of the day. He had a wife. A beautiful wife used to comforts, the same comforts he had walked away from after his father demanded he wed Mary Ella. He'd refused. He hadn't done anything to warrant such accusations from her, and when he'd discovered she'd caused the death of

his fellow soldiers, and nearly his own due to her trai-
torous actions, he couldn't justify marrying her. He'd
known Mary Ella most of his life and had no idea of
the things she'd been capable of, such as acting a spy
for the South, reporting their positions. He knew even
less about Penelope. Only that he sensed she was running from something and that he had an overwhelming desire to see her protected. He also found himself
desiring to give her some of the luxuries she deserved.
Maybe even a new home containing a parlor and a dining room with curtains and chandeliers.

He left his bedroll and leaned against the door frame.
He'd been content sleeping beneath the night sky on
nights like this. He took in his cabin. The rough logs
he'd cut himself, the crude chinking. He'd been proud
of the accomplishment when he'd completed his abode.
Now he wanted more, even a white picket fence with
a garden full of roses and lilies. Drawn to the house,
he buckled his gun belt around his waist and walked
around to see where additions could be made, and he
formulated a plan. Tomorrow he would consult a few
of the men in town that had already made changes to
their homes to see what could be done to his. He neared
a window and caught sight of Penelope's shadow. It
looked as though she pulled a brush through her long,
luxurious curls.

His mouth turned down. She'd made no protests
when he'd left her alone. Had she expected them to
share their wedding night together? His thoughts were
cut off when he heard a thud. Her shadow bent over just
as a bloodcurdling scream rent through the open window and tore through his chest.

He raced around the house and burst through the door, his pistol in hand. He turned the corner to the bedroom. Penelope stood trembling on the mattress.

She shifted toward him. Her eyes wide with fright. "S-s-snake!"

He bent his ear but did not hear the telltale sound of a rattle. He leaned forward and peered over the iron bed frame. A large black snake slithered up the side of the wall. The front half of the smooth ebony body curved along the windowsill.

"Wait there."

"No! Beau, you can't leave me here with that."

"I'll be right back," he said as he sauntered out of the room and grabbed the iron poker from the fireplace. He hefted the snake's body and pushed it outside and then slammed the window closed.

"You didn't shoot it."

"No, think of the mess." He reached for her and swung her off the bed. He began to place her on her feet, but she clung tight to his arms, and for the life of him, he wanted to pull her closer.

"What if it comes back?"

"It just might, but that kind is the friendly sort and will help keep rodents away."

"Oh." She squeezed her arms around his neck. "I was scared."

"I know, but I'm here now." He pulled her from his neck, and setting her on her feet, he glanced into her frightened eyes. "I was only outside, sleeping in the barn."

He wasn't about to tell her that he'd been looking for ways to expand their humble home when he'd caught sight of her brushing her hair through the window. He'd watched her for far too long and should have left the moment he'd seen her. After all, they'd been married only a few hours, not days or weeks.

"Will you be all right?"

"I—I think so." Her voice shook.

Beau applauded her attempt at bravery. "The children usually sleep in the loft. Would you prefer I make a bunk there?"

She looked toward the spot the snake had been. "May I? Sleep in the loft and you take the bed? After all, it is your bed."

Before he knew what he was about, he nodded. "If that will set your mind at ease."

She nodded. "As long there are no critters up there."

He shoved his hands in his pockets. "Would you wish I inspect the loft before you take up residence?"

"That would be satisfactory."

He slipped off his boots and placed them by the door. He climbed up the ladder and inspected every cranny. Much to his surprise the area was tidy, for a place usually filled with wild boys. He pressed his palm onto the mattress to look under the bed and realized the donated bed had much to be desired in the way of softness. He sat on the edge and then kicked his legs onto the frame as he laid back. Definitely not suitable for Penelope. He was certain she was used to a soft mattress, not a lumpy and poky one.

"Beau? Are you all right?" Her soft voice, so innocent and sweet, rang into the rafters.

He jumped to his feet. He wondered if the one in his room was much better. Since he often slept on his roll under the stars or on a thin hard cot at the jail, he hadn't paid heed to how his mattress might feel to a lady like Penelope. He climbed back down the ladder and hit the floor with his stockinged feet. "No critters."

Her hand fluttered to her chest. "That is a relief."

Her silky black curls glimmered in the firelight as she spun around, seemingly looking for something.

"There are blankets. The mattress is on the lean side, so if you'd prefer I kick my feet up there, I am more than willing."

She shook her head, and her soft perfume danced between them. "I'd sleep better knowing I was far from the ground." She glanced at her folded hands. "Although I would worry about you."

Artifice knew no residence with Penelope. She wore her heart on her sleeve. Her displeasure. Her anger. Her joy. Her sadness. Her concern for him. It had been more than evident when he'd returned from hunting down Jessup. There was no facade. Her concern was genuine. His chest swelled. "Would you like to sit awhile? I can make us some hot cocoa, if you'd like."

Her eyes sparkled as the corners of her mouth turned upward. "Cocoa? I've heard stories of its deliciousness but have yet to try it."

"You're in for a treat." He chuckled and knelt before the fireplace. He stacked logs and busied himself with starting the fire. Moments later, a pot of water boiled above the open flames.

"It sounds nice."

He pulled out one of the spindle-backed chairs tucked under the crude table and motioned for her to take a seat. "With the children underfoot, we haven't had much time to discuss things, let alone the nature of our marriage."

Her dark, thick lashes brushed against her flushed cheeks.

"Although we have married for differing reasons and in haste, our vows should not be taken lightly. I will honor them, Penelope, and I ask you do the same."

Her heart-shaped chin bobbed. "Of course. You will have no cause to worry where I am concerned."

One of his eyebrows arched upward. "Must I remind you that it is the consequence of your scandalous behavior that has placed us in this position?"

"I'm sorry." He noticed the pools forming on her lashes before she bowed her head.

He leaned forward and lifted her gaze to meet his. "Don't. I do not fault you. It is what it is. Never apologize for actions you deemed practical and most likely will repeat. Understand?"

"I do not wish to disappoint you, Beau." A tear slid down her cheek.

It was in that moment he realized just how sensitive and soft her heart was. However, he'd seen her strength and boldness just yesterday. She was a woman who deserved to be cherished. He only wished he had it in him to be the man to do so. "I do not disappoint easily, Penelope. I can become frustrated and irritated, but only because I lack some foresight where you are concerned. You are not like the ladies I've become acquainted with over the years."

Her mouth gaped.

"I've spent my fair share of time dodging matchmaking mamas in ballrooms. I've also spent my time courting a woman I believed to be my future." His jaw hardened at the memory. "So trust me when I say that you are not like them, and yet your outer layers look the same. It will take me some time to ascertain what is written on your pages, Penelope, as well as what your book cover looks like." He scrubbed his palm over his chin. He had a feeling she didn't know how her cover should look either. Had she been forced into a mold that was not meant for her?

"Thank you, Beau."

He took her hand in his. "For?"

"For giving me a chance."

"I cannot say it'll be easy, Penelope. I will need much grace from you as we move forward. Can you do that?"

"I can."

Beau rose to his feet and leaned over her. He kissed her crown. "Now, are you certain you wish to sleep in the loft?"

She stood and nodded. A hint of mischievousness sparkled in her eyes. "It will be fun. I've never slept in one before."

He sighed and watched her climb the ladder in her ankle-length dress. A chill washed over him when she disappeared, and the cabin seemed to grow dim in her absence. He turned toward the bedroom and realized he'd forgotten to make her cocoa. He'd just have to remedy that tomorrow.

He turned down the lanterns and hunched down in front of the fire. He spread the logs farther apart. The glowing embers reminded him of Penelope's eyes when the light hit them. He shook his head. Next thing he knew he'd be seeing her face in split wood and a muddy bank. That produced a smile. He wouldn't ever look at the Neosho River quite the same. He'd always see her standing in his jail with all that finery dripping wet and muddy. She'd been stunning that day, and this morning standing in church in the midst of eager bachelors, she'd looked even more beautiful.

He unfolded his length and traipsed to the bed. The edge sank with his weight and he allowed his body to collapse the rest of the way. The softness hugged him. He released a yawn and covered his eyes with his forearm. He drew in Penelope's soft scent caressing his pillow, and like a content kitten with a full belly of milk, he drifted off into the deepest sleep he'd had in months.

Chapter Ten

Early morning light streamed through the window down below, and Penelope stretched her aching muscles. Beau hadn't lied about the mattress, and she wondered how the boys had fared so long with such a poky bed. But then, they were much lighter. Their little bodies probably didn't sink into the harsh straw as much as hers did.

She eased onto the edge of the bed and listened for any signs of Beau stirring. She descended the ladder, and when she saw that he wasn't about, she thought he'd left sometime during the night. However, the loud snores coming from the bedroom told her otherwise. She smiled. A sleepless night had given her plenty of opportunity to think on a plan of action. She might be Beau's wife in name only, but she was determined to be worthy of being his wife and maybe even gain some of his affection. First, she'd start off by making his coffee and then conquer the henhouse. With great care, of course. She did not wish to have another encounter with a slithery beast.

She stared at the cold logs and berated herself for not paying closer attention when Beau started the fire last evening. Certainly, the water in the kettle would not heat itself. She wrinkled her nose in what was certain to be a most unladylike manner and smiled. The freedom to release herself from social strictures lightened her shoulders, and she felt the need to dance across the floor without any inhibitions.

The rooster crowed. It wouldn't be long before Beau tumbled out of bed and took over the chores. Grabbing the basket for eggs, she slipped out the back door and made her way to the beady-eyed hen. Whistling a little tune, she swung the door open and stepped inside. "Hello, my lovelies. Have you been waiting long?"

She slid her hand beneath one hen and then another. Her confidence grew with each egg she laid in the basket, until she stood in front of the mean one. The hen stared. She squawked. Penelope startled. She glanced at her pickings. The children were with the Winters. There were plenty of eggs already for Beau to have a hearty breakfast. "Very well, then. I'll leave you to your nest."

She latched the door and breathed a sigh of relief. She'd done it. She'd gathered eggs, and now she could wake Beau with a delicious breakfast. As long as her attempts at cooking them as Bobby Jean had shown her were successful.

"Ma'am."

Penelope yelped. The basket flew in the air and she watched in horror as her precious eggs painted the dirt bright yellow.

"My apologies, ma'am," a gentleman about her age said as he dismounted. "I didn't mean to startle you."

Hand to her chest to still the fierce beating of her heart, she glanced down at the stranger as he gathered her basket and handed it to her. She was thankful the stranger was not Mr. Wallace come to take her home.

"There's still one survivor," he said.

Her thankfulness quickly abated as a dark look passed in the man's green eyes. Had Mr. Wallace hired someone to kidnap her? A shiver raced down her back. She looked toward the house and prayed Beau would come outside. "May I help you?"

"No, ma'am. I was just passin' through. Saw the place here and it reminded me of home. Are you alone?"

"No, my husband is around here somewhere." It wasn't an outright lie. Beau was here; he was just sleeping like a log.

"Is that so?" the man drawled.

"Yes. I'm certain he'll be along shortly."

"Well, then, I guess I'll be going." He swung into his saddle and tipped his hat at her. He turned his gray-spotted horse around and then said, "I didn't realize the marshal had married. When he comes round, do me a favor, sweet gal, and tell him Jessup Davis stopped by, will you, darlin'?"

At the moniker, she felt a shiver race up her spine. She sucked in a sharp breath and watched the man ride away. It had been much different when Beau had said it to her yesterday, pleasant. Hearing Jessup call her that made her feel assaulted. She clenched her fists to halt the shaking, but the more her nails bit into her palms, the angrier she became, the more scared, too. He'd been within reach. He could have hurt her, and what of the children? Thankfully, the children were with Judge and Bobby Jean. Her gaze flitted to the house, and she breathed a sigh of relief Beau had been inside, as she was certain Mr. Davis had come to cause her husband harm.

"Penelope," Beau said as he opened the door. He stood on the front porch in his stocking feet. His eyebrows dipped when he saw the yolks on the ground. "Are you all right?"

She dropped the basket. She gathered her skirts in her hands and raced across the yard and threw herself into Beau's strong arms. "I am fine."

He leaned back. "Why did you pounce on me like a cat on a mouse? The broken eggs? Did you trip coming out of the coop?" He looked over her shoulder. "I need to fix that step. You're shaking."

"No, no. I startled, is all." The overnight growth of beard caught the sunlight. She couldn't resist the urge to feel the prickles beneath her fingertips. His blue eyes flitted to hers and held her gaze a moment, and she nearly lost her breath.

"What startled you so bad that you're shaking like a timber rattler about to strike?"

She tugged her bottom lip between her teeth. Telling the truth may mean she'd have to watch Beau chase after that dangerous man. Lying would be easy. It would also mean their marriage would start off with deception between them. The secrets she kept hidden already weighed heavy on her shoulders. She stepped out of his arms and folded her hands together. "Mr. Davis was here."

Beau shoved her behind him and scanned the house and yard. "Where? How long? What did he want?" He swung toward her and grasped her upper arms. "Are you all right? Did he hurt you?"

"No, Beau. I'm fine, really. He was here when I stepped out of the henhouse. I dropped the basket when he said hello, and then he asked me to tell you he stopped by."

She didn't wish to tell him how close Mr. Davis had gotten to her or how scared she'd been when she'd realized who he was.

Beau stepped back and speared his fingers through his hair. "It's taking everything in me not to give chase." He tossed a look over his shoulder at her. "I can't leave you here alone. What if he is watching?"

"Certainly he would not harm me."

Beau kicked his stockinged feet into the dirt. "I wouldn't put it past him if he could get to me. He's been taunting me since I started wearing the badge and I can't quite figure out why. At first it was a brawl at the saloon, then he stole a pig and some other animals. Two weeks ago, he robbed the bank. Each time he commits a crime, he leaves a message for me. I had him in jail and he broke out, and the first thing he does is come to my home and speak with my wife. It's downright frustrating."

"Beau," she said, reaching for his hand, "I was frightened when I realized who he was. However, my fear came from the idea that he was here to harm you or the children. Not for myself."

"I'm afraid you should fear Jessup. I'll do my best to keep you safe." He clenched his fists. "You never should have come here. I should be sending you back, but I have a sneaking suspicion you wouldn't go."

"No, I wouldn't, Beau. This is my home now. I am your wife." The children were her family as was Beau. "I'm not going anywhere. I can learn to shoot. I'll protect the children if he shows up again."

"A gun in your hands causes me a great deal of worry, Penelope. I fear I would rather take my chances that Jessup wouldn't cause you harm if I'm not around." He shook his head. "Get presentable. We're going to Judge's and we're fetching Miller and Brian for reinforcements. It's time for a meeting. I hope you don't tire of me being underfoot, my dear, because with the Millers and Judge's help that is exactly where I'm going to be until Jessup is locked up for good."

Penelope was excited to see the children and her new friend, but she wasn't too sure about the idea of Beau being underfoot, as he called it, since it wouldn't afford her the opportunity to learn the domesticated duties expected of a lawman's wife. However, she couldn't be too disappointed having him around. At least she'd know he was safe. She just wished she knew how to help protect him.

Beau hadn't realized how anxious he'd been until he gave Esther and the boys each a big squeeze, including Mark, who hadn't pulled away. Their smiling faces solidified his resolve. He had to capture Jessup and lock him up for good. For the safety of his family.

Judge puffed on his cigar. Miller leaned on the edge of the rail, whittling on a piece of wood. Beau gazed through the open doors at Penelope sitting on the floor playing with John and Esther. He rubbed his sternum with his knuckles.

"You all right, there, Marshal?" Miller asked.

"Yeah," Beau said as he pulled his attention from his wife. "Why?"

"The way you're massaging your chest, it looks like you might fall over dead on us," Brian Gannon said from his perch on the porch steps.

Beau's mouth twitched. "Indigestion."

"The wife trying to do you in with her cooking already?" Judge chuckled. "Took my Bobby Jean some time to make a decent meal, but you best believe I ate every spoonful with a smile and made sure to compliment her. Even when my toast was black as night."

"I remember Sarah's first meal. Too much salt." Brian laughed and then sobered. Beau knew he was thinking about his late wife, taken by the illness that had ravaged Oak Grove the year before last.

Beau decided not to tell them that Penelope had yet to attempt a meal on her own. "I'll keep your advice in mind, Judge."

"I don't think I could do that." Miller blew a shaving from his carving. "I can't lie to save my life. Any woman I marry better know how to cook. It'll be my number-two requirement."

"What's your number-one?" Beau asked, uncertain if he really wanted to know.

"She better know how to shoot. I can't have a woman what doesn't know how to shoot."

"Agreed," Brian said.

Beau grumbled as he scrubbed his palm over his face.

"What's this little meeting about, Beau?" Judge

pierced him with a hard gaze. "It's no coincidence Miller and Brian are here, too, is it?"

"No, sir." Beau sat on a white-painted chair and rested his elbows on his knees. He told them about Jessup's visit. "I can't risk the children."

"That's why you should have married a shooting gal, Beau. Any man in his right mind wouldn't mess with a lady who can hold a gun with a steady hand."

"It's a little late for your opinions on what type of woman I should marry. What's done is done with that matter."

"You could always teach her to shoot," Brian added.

"I'm afraid that'll take time." Beau leaned against the back of the chair. "Besides, a gun in Penelope's hands is enough to frighten me to my grave. I can't leave her at home with the children while I do my duties as marshal. Before you get any wild ideas, Gannon, I'm not ready to give up my badge. I have a responsibility to this town."

"You have six responsibilities in there, too," Judge reminded him.

"That I do, Judge." Beau stretched out his legs and crossed his feet. "And I don't know what to do about them."

"Simple," Miller said. "Judge has twenty bedrooms."

"Not so many as that, young man."

Miller ignored Judge. "They can stay here with Mrs. Bobby Jean and whichever one of us is available. If we need to posse out, Judge can keep watch."

Beau twisted his lips. The thought of seeing his family only in the company of others soured his stomach, especially after last night. He and Penelope had spent only a few hours alone together before they'd found their separate beds, but he'd enjoyed the conversation, and when he'd woken this morning, his first thought hadn't been pouring a cup of hot black coffee but seeking out Penelope to wish her a good morning. "I don't know. I certainly do not wish to impose."

Judge waved his hand. "No imposition. Bobby Jean will be glad of the company, and she knows her way around guns."

"What about you, Beau?"

Penelope's disappointed, quiet voice cut through him like a fork slicing melted butter, and he wasn't certain why. He looked up at her as she stepped out onto the porch. Her long black locks curled around her shoulders and to her waist. She'd chosen a simple gown of pink that turned her cheeks a rosy hue. Her dark lashes rose and fell, as if waiting for his response. He didn't know what to say. Fortunately for him, Judge was rarely at a loss for words.

"Of course Beau will stay here when he can." Judge relit his cigar. "But you must know there will be nights he's needed to keep the law."

And nights spent sleeping on the hard ground while on Jessup's trail.

She nodded. "Of course. I understand."

Beau didn't think she looked like she wanted to understand. He reached for her hand and gave it a squeeze. "I'll be fine, as you and the children will be fine, too. And it won't be a long time. Miller is the best deputy marshal a man could ask for."

"And Beau's the best marshal this side of the Mississippi. We'll catch Jessup, and no harm will be done." Miller tucked his piece of wood into his front pocket.

"I cannot help but worry."

Beau rose to his feet and drew Penelope into his arms. "Allow me to do the worrying for you, darling. See this as a temporary reprieve. You'll find the comforts and luxuries you are accustomed to, but once Jessup is captured, you'll be expected back at our humble home."

"And to that awful mattress." She teased. She leaned back. Her blue eyes sparkled. "I love our humble home, Beau."

"It's too small for all of your luggage."

"It's cozy." She smiled. "I could do without the critters and the pecking hen, but I'll take them if I must."

He kissed the tip of her nose. "We are agreed then. You'll stay here with the children?"

"We are agreed."

"Good. Just promise me you won't get too comfortable here and refuse to come home when it's time."

"As long as you promise to stay here whenever it is possible. I fear the children have had too many changes as it is. Being in a new place without their pa, they'd miss you dearly."

"And what of you, Penelope, will you miss me dearly?"

Of course she would miss him. However, it was not something she wished to share. Especially when she feared he toyed with her affections. They'd known each other only a short while, and yet she could not remember a day without his presence in her life, except for the looming reminder that Mr. Wallace was in Oak Grove.

She no longer feared Jessup Davis. The bigger threat

seemed to be the new stranger in town. Although she didn't completely fear Mr. Wallace as she once had. His condescending nature had been replaced with Beau's kindness and care. But still, she did fear what the future held and prayed Mr. Wallace would not bring harm to Beau or the children. She wished she could be confident of Beau's intentions for their marriage. Rejection had been so deep-rooted in her soul that she feared the slightest mistake on her part would have Beau sending her packing.

Would she miss her husband dearly? How to respond to his question? She settled on a diplomatic reply. "Your absence will be noticed."

Beau risking his life to bring Mr. Davis to justice set her nerves fraying. What would she do if anything happened to him? Her heart beat heavy against her chest. Fear for Beau's life, fear of the unknown rattled her. Was this what she'd read about in books? This emotion, was it love?

She drew her cheek in between her teeth. Mr. Wallace waiting in the shadows scared her, but he was the least of her worries. Losing Beau was taking over, and she needed to find a way to tell her husband about her past before he was given cause to distrust her. And before Mr. Wallace did something rash and unpredictable.

"So, you'll miss me, huh?" A glimmer of a challenge sparked in his eyes. "Is that right?"

"Of course. Who will corral the children when they act out?" She leaned in next to his ear. "I dare say, Mrs. Winter's eggs are far superior to yours. Come to think of it, I am not sure I will notice your absence at all. Judge keeps the boys busy and Esther adores Mrs. Danner. I will have plenty of help with the children, and my belly will be fully satisfied with Bobby Jean's cooking. Hmm, I don't think I'll miss you at all, Marshal."

"You best watch your step, darling, lest you tempt me to throw you over my shoulder and give you a good switching for your impertinence. There is nothing wrong with my eggs or my biscuits."

A soft chill raced over her limbs, not the sort that caused her fear but the sort that made her want to laugh. "Is that so? As I recall, your last efforts at making biscuits were on the brown side."

He burst into laughter. "However, they did not require a pail of water to douse the fire."

Her cheeks heated as the memory of the awful smell tinged her nostrils. The house had filled with smoke, and she'd been certain she'd burned their home down. "That was not my intention."

"I do not think anyone intends to burn their breakfast, Penelope."

"I have much to learn." She pulled back and glanced at her folded hands. She was far from the wife he'd longed for, far from adequate, and it made her weary and sad.

He lifted his gaze to hers. His beautiful gray eyes sought to make her understand something. "Penelope, I didn't expect you to cook straight off. Although you did claim to have knowledge. I'm surprised by your ability to boil water and to gather eggs without being henpecked to death."

"Beau Garrett! You are funning me."

"I am, darling. It gives me great pleasure to tease

smiles out of you." He winked. "In case you're curious, I will miss you greatly while I'm gone."

Her eyes grew wide as she sucked in a breath.

"I need you to promise that you will not leave the Winters' house without my escort." He squeezed her hand. "Promise me. For no reason."

She couldn't utter the words, but she nodded.

"Thank you." He touched the tip of her nose with his finger. "I pray it won't be long till Jessup is captured."

"And what of you, Beau?" She bit her bottom lip. "I don't mean to worry, but I do. He seems like a dangerous man."

"Which is why I must go after him. Do not fret overmuch. I have captured men with more salt than Jessup and have come away unscathed."

His words did little to ease her concern. "I will do my best not to. And I promise to protect the children, too."

"That is all I ask. Now, would you like to stay while we discuss our plans or would you rather help Bobby Jean with luncheon?"

She was surprised by his offer. Whenever her father spoke business, she was forced to leave the room, and when she entered to serve his guests tea and cakes, they pretended to speak of nonessential things, such as the weather or the most recent horseflesh available on the market. Since she could not fault Beau for deciding that she and the children stay at the Winterses' and since she had nothing more she could offer, she chose to decline his invitation. "Thank you, Beau, for considering me. However, Mrs. Winter is making refreshments, and I'd much rather learn of her business than yours. Do take care with your plans. I would hate it if anything happened to you."

He kissed the back of her hand. "Likewise, which is why after Jessup's visit this morning, I intend to make the safety of my family priority."

She warmed and felt giddy. "And I will make it my priority to be the best mother and wife, my husband."

After another kiss to her hand and a slight squeeze, she left him to formulate his plans with Judge and the Gannons. She picked Esther up from the floor and made her way to the kitchen, where she found the boys sitting on the floor in a circle eating jellied biscuits.

Bobby Jean greeted her with a smile. "How are you doing?"

"I am well, although I remain slightly shaken from my encounter." She realized the children were bending their ears to her conversation, and she approached her friend. "I fear for Beau's safety."

"I can understand. When Judge decided to join the War Between the States, I was terrified. He's not a backline kind of man. When he left, I was so afraid that the next time I'd see him would be in a pine box."

"Oh, Bobby Jean, I cannot fathom it. Although he is my husband, I've only known Beau a brief time, and the fear quaking my knees is almost unbearable."

Bobby Jean wiped her hands on her apron and took Esther from her arms. "I prayed, a lot. And I tried to trust, but most importantly, I believed in my husband's love for me and our children and that he would do everything in his ability to come home alive."

That was where Beau and Judge differed. Beau couldn't possibly love her the way the judge loved his wife. Whenever Bobby Jean walked in the room, his eyes glossed over with pure adoration, and he rarely took his gaze from her. That was the sort of love Penelope had longed for but reality told her was not possible. Ladies of her social class rarely married for love. She certainly had not. She'd married out of necessity, for survival. If she hadn't feared for her life, she wouldn't have left Mr. Wallace at the altar. She would have married him because her father demanded it. Not for love.

"Would you mind stirring the dough for a time? I want to hold this sweet child a moment." Bobby Jean nuzzled Esther's neck and received adorable giggles.

Penelope gripped the silver spoon and stirred. Flour exploded into the air and coated her face and hands. She coughed and sputtered.

"I should have warned you. I forget you haven't much experience. Sink the spoon to the bottom and move it slowly until the dough begins to moisten."

Penelope made another attempt. She giggled at her success. She turned and jabbed the spoon until the dough formed together. "What shall I do next?"

"Sprinkle some flour onto the butcher block, turn the dough on it and begin massaging with your hands. Perfect! Keep that up for a time. I'll take the children to the men, and then we'll make a pie crust and biscuits."

Penelope worked the dough and thought about how much she wanted to be a good wife to Beau. She'd been raised for socializing, balls and extravagant dinners, at which she'd failed miserably. She had been shown how to sit and walk properly. Head high, back straight. She knew how to pick out linens and dishes, and how to barter with seamstresses for the best clothes at the cheapest prices. She knew how to play the piano, and her needlework was above par, but she'd never known the satisfaction of making a pie, or even biscuits.

She recalled Cook's beaming cheeks whenever she placed a meal on the table. She took pride in her concoctions, and Penelope had savored every morsel. The spices and the texture had always been to perfection, and from all she'd tasted of Mrs. Winter's cooking, her friend was cut from the same cloth. Penelope prayed she could learn and see Beau's pleasure when he took a bite of something she'd made.

"Well, look at you."

Penelope startled. Bits of dough flew up at her face. She turned and all the tension she hadn't realized was plaguing her shoulders rolled off like water when she saw Beau. "Beau, you frightened me."

Before she knew it, he meandered toward her until the tips of his boots disappeared beneath the hem of her gown. He reached up and plucked dough from her hair. "I'm sorry. I couldn't help myself. You look awfully adorable dusted in flour."

She scooted back and glanced down at her dress. She frantically swiped the flour from the fabric. "I'm a fright."

Beau touched her nose with the tip of his finger. "Beautiful."

His strong arms wrapped around her waist and pulled her close, and her hands pressed against his chest. Her cheeks warmed. "Beau, what are you doing?"

"Greeting my wife."

Chapter Eleven

Penelope entered the dining room with a crockery full of steaming scrambled eggs. She settled the pot on a trivet in the middle of the table and pasted on a smile. She'd hoped Beau would find the time to visit and share Sunday breakfast with them before heading to church. It had been near a week since she'd seen him last, since she'd become his wife, and she hadn't even had the chance to prove she was capable of being his wife. What bothered her more was it'd been seven days since the children had seen him. She'd found it quite disconcerting that the boys had quit asking after him by day three. Did they wonder, like she did, if Beau would return?

"Smells delicious." Judge folded his paper and tucked it beneath his coffee cup. "Dare I hope my wife is coming with a chunk of ham? A man cannot live on eggs alone. He must have sustenance."

A genuine smile curved her lips. "I can attest ham is on its way. However, I fear it may not be up to Bobby Jean's perfection."

A bushy brow arched upward. His mustache twitched

as he fought laughter "I suppose I can sacrifice a meal or two for the sake of Beau's future."

"Speaking of Beau, have you heard news from him? I try not to worry. But after a week with no word, it does cause me a bit of anxiousness."

"I do imagine, especially being a new bride and all." Judge sipped his coffee. "It's not unheard of for the posse to be out for weeks. I'm certain we'll learn something soon."

"Learn something soon about what?"

At the sound of the deep voice, Penelope swiveled, her skirts swirling around her legs. "Beau!"

"Darling," he said, leaning in to kiss her temple. "Dare I say you've missed me?"

She swatted his arm and rolled her eyes with a great deal of exaggeration. He'd called her *darling* a time or two, but this time it seemed almost intimate. At least her thundering pulse and shaking knees believed so. She took a couple steps back and breathed. "Miss you? Why, *darling*," she teased, elongating the syllables, much like he had, "I have nary the time to breathe, let alone miss a man I've been married to no more than a week and haven't seen in nearly just as long." She took a breath. "Why, there's been the cooking lessons and the children. The gathering of wood and learning to start fires, washing clothes. Gardening and the children. And shooting lessons." She rushed her words when a dark shadow passed through Beau's eyes. "Did I mention the children? I've hardly found the time to sleep. And you dare ask whether or not I've missed you?"

She swept past him and made for the door. His fingers drew down her arm and captured her wrist. His gaze held hers. "Excuse me, Judge."

Beau leaned close; his breath tickled her ear. "Dare I say, I've missed you?"

Her eyes grew wide and then fluttered closed. His arm circled her back and he pulled her in. Her heart pounded against her chest. She thought he'd kiss her, like he'd done on their wedding day, and she melted against him. But then Judge cleared his throat and she heard the slap of bare feet in the hallway, and Beau released her from his arms.

"Pa!" the children sang in unison. Beau lurched forward and nearly tumbled over Penelope.

"You're home." Matthew pushed between them and hugged Beau tight.

A spark of happiness warmed Penelope's heart when Beau knelt in front of the boy and gathered him into his arms.

"I am. Just for the afternoon. What shall we do?"

Luke jumped on Beau's back and snaked his arms around his neck. "Fishing. Ain't been since we moved."

"Haven't been," Penelope corrected.

"Haven't been," Luke said as he rolled his eyes.

"We've been fishing, Luke."

"Not since we moved to Judge and Bobby Jean's." The boy's mouth twitched. "I like it here, but I miss our old home."

"Oh, Luke," Penelope said, taking his hand. "We're only staying for a short time. We'll go back soon enough."

"That's right." Matthew beamed. "Soon as Pa catches the bad guy. Right, Pa?"

"That's right." Beau unfolded to his full height with Luke clinging to his back. "Soon, too, I hope. After church we will go fishing. Have you ever been fishing, Penelope?"

She shook her head. "No, but I'd love to come along. How about I pack us a lunch, then?"

"Well, isn't this a nice surprise?" Bobby Jean bustled in with two serving dishes. "You're just in time for breakfast. I hope you're hungry."

"Matthew, will you fetch Mother Danner, John and Esther?" Penelope took one of the dishes from her friend and laid it on the table. Judge stood and held a chair out for his wife. Mark and Luke filed into their chairs.

"Yes, ma'am."

"Wow," Beau said with a low whistle. "Ma'am? No matter how many times I tried, I couldn't get the boys to address Mrs. Wheelwright appropriately. You're doing well with them."

"I'm afraid it is little of my doing and more of Bobby Jean and Judge's."

"You'd get round to it, child." Judge patted Bobby Jean's hand. "Is that not correct, dear? You can't expect to fully mother after being a mother a short time. We have a few years on us."

"And a lot of respect and sway." Penelope poured Beau a cup of coffee and then sat in the chair he held out for her. "The children adore both of you, as do I."

"And I," Beau said as he stole the seat next to her. "I do not know how to thank the both of you for what you're doing."

Bobby Jean waved off his words. "Nonsense. It's a

joy to have a houseful, and Penelope is eager to learn and does more than her share."

Beau turned to his wife. "What is this about shooting lessons?"

At his question, Judge sputtered and Bobby Jean quickly shoved a bit of biscuit in her mouth. Unable to reply, Penelope stared at her plate. Was he displeased that she was learning to protect the children?

"She did right good, Pa," Mark said around a piece of ham.

Penelope blushed and glanced between the normally quiet child and Beau. By the look on her husband's face, he was just as shocked as she was by the conversation. She nearly held her breath but feared the silence would move the boy back into his shell. "Thank you, Mark."

"That is good to hear," Beau said before looking to Judge.

"Mark has the right of it, Beau. She's a real natural."

Bobby Jean passed the tray laden with bacon to Beau. "She can shoot a tick off a hound's tail if she were inclined to do so."

"Y'all talking 'bout Ma's shooting?" Matthew raced into the dining room ahead of Mrs. Danner and Little John. He handed the baby to Penelope and began to dig into his breakfast as soon as he'd jumped onto his chair. "Never seen anything of the sort. My old pa couldn't shoot so well. And my other mamas wouldn't get near a rifle, not even when the barrel was cold."

"I suppose that is good news." Beau cut off a piece of ham. "I thought we'd discussed Penelope shooting. As I recall, I didn't think she was ready for the task. It just isn't safe."

Penelope clenched her fists beneath the table. Her cheeks flamed, this time not from Matthew's compliments or from Beau's attentions. She was irritated. "How do you expect me to defend *our* home and *our* children if you do not allow me to learn the skills needed?"

"Well," Beau said, and then took a sip of his coffee.

Stalling would get him nowhere. "*Well* might get you a ways with other people, Marshal, but not with me. I would like a good, honest answer. It's not like I can beat a scoundrel off with a broom, especially not the one hanging by our hearth. It would splinter to pieces before I made contact."

Judge chuckled.

"My apologies for my outburst. However, it is high time everyone quit expecting me to break like a piece of china. I'm not fragile, and if I'm to be your wife," she said as she pointed a finger at Beau, "and their mother in this barely civilized town, then I must be capable of defending my home." She pushed her chair back and rose. "Now, if you'll excuse me, I've lost my appetite."

She swept out of the dining room and rushed up the stairs before anyone witnessed the frustrated and angry tears streaking down her cheeks. No sooner had she closed her bedroom door than the torrent of tears poured from her eyes. She'd hoped Beau would be pleased, proud even, and that she could take the children back where they belonged. It was evident from Luke's conversation the children needed stability. They needed their home back, and as much as she enjoyed staying with the Winters and was very grateful for the couple allowing them to, she needed her home back, too.

* * *

Beau jumped from his chair and stared at the blur of blue skirts swishing down the hall and up the stairs. He leaned back and glanced at the occupants in the dining room.

"What'd you do that for, Pa?" Matthew asked.

"Do what?" As if he hadn't already gotten himself hip deep in the muck and mire, but he was mighty thankful Penelope was out of hearing. However, in his defense, he truly did not understand what on earth he was guilty of doing. By the looks of Bobby Jean and Judge, he should. "What did I do?"

Bobby Jean opened her mouth to speak, but Judge shook his head.

"Allow me, my dear." Judge rose from his seat and adjusted his britches. "That gal of yours has worked tirelessly to gain your approval. She was right proud, too."

"Real good," Luke said as he stole another biscuit from the bowl.

"I'm sure she was, Luke." Beau crossed his arms. "I mean no disrespect, Judge, but she is a lady, and in my opinion, ladies don't shoot."

Bobby Jean tossed her linen napkin onto her plate and jumped from her chair. Her hands propped onto her hips. "Now *I* take offense. What am I?"

Judge chuckled.

"You've done it now, Pa," Matthew said.

"That he did, young man." Mrs. Danner spooned a bite into Esther's little mouth. "I wouldn't want to be in your shoes, Marshal."

Beau rolled his eyes. "You're a lady, Bobby Jean, but she's—"

"What?" Her eyebrows lifted.

"Best tread lightly, Marshal. My wife knows how to shoot."

"As do I," Mrs. Danner piped up. "Take care your thoughts don't run away with your mouth."

He raked his palm over his face. "She's my wife, and they're my children. It is my job to protect them, not hers."

Gravy, he would not fail in safeguarding them like he'd failed safeguarding Mary Ella from herself.

"And whenever you're not around, then what?"

At the sound of Penelope's barest whisper, he turned around. His heart lurched at her red-rimmed eyes and tear-stained cheeks.

"I'm to sit inside a house not my own and do needlework?"

"Penelope," he said as he took a step forward.

"Don't." She held up her hand. "I am not weak and easily breakable. I've been hiding in corners behind potted plants for way too long, Beau. I won't do it anymore."

"I'm not asking you to." He took her soft, warm hand in his.

"Then, what is this?" She pulled from him and motioned around them. "We have not seen you in a week's time. I am grateful for the company, but how am I to learn to be your wife and their mother without the doing of it in our home?"

He realized in that moment that she wasn't at all like most upper-class ladies.

"I'm not asking to return home at this moment. I understand the need for our safety. However, Beau, there will come a time when we'll need to go back. What if I encounter a rattlesnake, or another scoundrel comes knocking on our door? Should I not know how to shoot? You can't keep us locked up forever."

The corners of his mouth turned upward. He held his hands up in surrender. "All right, I give up."

"Are you certain, Beau?" Penelope looked at him with a great deal of doubt. Did she worry he'd go back on his word? He couldn't blame her, since he'd vowed to be around as much as possible. A week-long absence wasn't keeping his promise well.

"Yes. How about after service you show me just how capably you can shoot."

Her beautiful face lit up. Her eyes shone with delight. Good, he'd finally done something right.

"All right!" Luke hopped from his seat. "And fishing?"

"Yes, Luke, and fishing." He ruffled the boy's mop of curls.

"Now that's settled, may we finish our breakfast before Reverend Scott sends out a posse looking for his wayward congregants?" Judge dug his fork into his eggs.

Chapter Twelve

Penelope tied the apron around her waist and slipped a pair of scissors into her pocket and then made her way to Bobby Jean's garden. It had been two days since Beau had left again, and she couldn't help wondering how long he'd be gone this time. She prayed fervently each night with the boys for Beau and Mr. Gannon's safety and that Mr. Davis would be captured quickly. However, the last couple days had seemed to go on for weeks, and it almost felt like her prayers were going unheard. Even Reverend Scott's Sunday message on patience did little to comfort her, which is why she'd decided to break from her morning routine of helping Bobby Jean in the kitchen and make her way to the garden.

Of course, discovering a single flower on the wing chair in her bedchamber had had a lot to do with her decision. Hope had filled her and propelled her to the garden with haste. Would Beau be there waiting? Would she catch his lingering scent? Perhaps even feel the warmth left by the tips of his fingers when he touched a bloom, as she'd seen him do when she interrupted his conversation with Judge. That day seemed to be months ago.

Bobby Jean had taken her and the boys to the garden several days ago and showed them which flowers to cut for the table and which ones to cut for Judge's library. With a great deal of patience, she showed them the correct place and angle to snip. Surprisingly, the boys were attentive to the instructions and very careful with the delicate blooms, just as their father had been. They also seemed to enjoy the task, which pleased her greatly.

While walking about, Penelope took note of the various blooms. The white blooms with yellow-and-red centers were her favorite. Not only did they fill the air with a lovely, sweet aroma, they reminded her of her walks in St. Louis, one of the few small pleasures she'd been allowed. With her host's permission, she thought to add some cheerfulness to her borrowed bedroom, to complement the flower left by Beau.

She walked along the shaded cobblestone path and took delight in the various bursts of colors. Perhaps one day, Beau would allow them a garden of her own. If he ever returned. She feared his prolonged absence the first week meant he regretted their marriage. However, when he'd returned Sunday morning and told her he'd missed her, most of her doubts had dissipated. Most of them. Did all brides have such insecurities, or had hers been magnified because she'd married a stranger? She tried to take heart from bits of conversation between Judge and Bobby Jean when they spoke of Beau and her marriage. Still, she couldn't quite connect the words they used with the stated emotion. It was frustrating, to say the least. How could she understand what they spoke of with little to no experience of her own? Moreover, how could she describe what was going on in her heart when she did not understand?

She tried not to fret that she was the cause of Beau's absence. Maybe he was hot on Mr. Davis's trail, like Judge said. Still, Beau had promised to return the next day, or to at least send word that he remained alive. Was the flower his message? Had it even been Beau who'd left it on her chair? Her jaw trembled. What if Beau hadn't been there? Was he out in the hills somewhere, wounded or, worse, dead?

She turned on her heel and rushed to Judge's library. She lifted her hand and knocked on the door. Unnerving silence met her ears. She rushed into the kitchen and stopped in her tracks. Beau sat at the kitchen table next to Judge. "Beau!"

He scooted back his chair and approached her. "Good morning, Penelope."

She drew in his scent with a breath of air, and her shoulders lost their tenseness. "You're home. Dare I hope you've captured Mr. Davis?"

His smile fell. A grim shadow crossed his brow. "No, not yet. But one of the locals saw him near the Belfry Monument, which could mean he is closer than we first believed."

"Does that mean you'll be around more?" Hope fluttered within her chest.

"That is my hope."

She wrapped her arms around his neck. "Thank you for the flower."

Beau pulled back from her. He squinted. "What flower?"

"The one you left on my chair in my chamber." Gooseflesh attacked her nape. A sickening feeling churned in her stomach. "The white bloom with the yellow-and-red center. They're my favorite. Although I'm not certain how you would have known that, unless we have the same taste in flowers." Her shoulders sagged. "Oh, Beau, please tell me you put it there."

His shook his head and then glanced at Judge, who shrugged. Penelope's knees shook. "Bobby Jean?"

"Yes," her friend said as she entered the room with a kettle of hot water. "I heard my name."

"Did you leave a flower on my chair this morning?" Her friend's brow furrowed. "No, why?"

Beau stormed out of the room and stomped up the stairs. Penelope lifted the hem of her skirt and chased after him. "Beau, the children. You'll wake them."

He kept moving with long strides. The bedchamber door banged against the wall. Beau appeared in the hall with the flower. Three sleepy children filed out of their own room, rubbing their eyes. Answering the question that had been burning her tongue. The boys had not left the flower either.

She clasped her hand to her throat.

Beau's cheeks reddened. His jaw twitched. The stem bent in his clenched hand. "When did you find this?"

"Moments before I came down. I went to the garden thinking to find you, and then I—"

He searched her gaze. "You what, Penelope?"

"For a small moment, I thought maybe you didn't leave the flower." She pulled her bottom lip between her teeth. She didn't wish to tell him why she thought such a thing. How did she explain that she didn't believe his affections ran deep enough to grant her a gift, even as small as a flower? "I became worried, scared even, so I ran to find Judge to see if he had had any word of your well-being."

The flower petals sprinkled to the floor. "I'm going to end this now."

His shoulder brushed against hers as he swept past her. He took the stairs two at a time, until he met the foyer. Sunlight burst through the front door and disappeared with a slam.

He hadn't even said goodbye.

Beau clenched his fists until his fingernails bit into his palms. "I'm so firing mad I could spit bullets."

"Marshal, that sort of anger won't get you anywhere." Brian Gannon leaned against his porch cleaning his nails with a penknife.

"I don't know, Brian," Miller said. "I'd be right angry if someone broke into my house and taunted me the way Jessup did. 'Specially when he was so close to my wife. Why, he could have—"

"Enough!" Beau snapped. "I've considered every possibility that could have happened. I don't need to hear them voiced aloud."

One woman he'd cared for already lay six feet beneath the ground in a cold pine box. He wouldn't allow it to happen again.

"What's the plan, Marshal?" Brian asked.

Beau tore his hat from his head and slapped it against his thigh. He glanced at Miller. "I thought we had one."

"Seems we didn't think everything through." Miller downed the contents of his metal cup. "Can't rightly blame Judge though. Good thing he taught Penelope to shoot. Now she just needs a pistol by her side at all times."

"Over my rotten bones, Miller." Beau puffed out his chest and jammed his fists on his hips, his hat crumpling in the process.

"Now, Marshal, my brother has the right of it. If your gal can shoot as well as you boasted, she should be armed."

"It's not a good idea."

"Neither is leaving her unarmed and unprotected." Miller grinned. "You need to choose one. Either you stay with her or you give her a pistol."

His stomach turned. He couldn't stay, not when he needed to see Jessup locked up for himself. And, well, giving her a gun didn't sit right either. "Brian, how 'bout you stand guard at Judge's?"

"What about my son?"

"Take him with you."

"Marshal, you're not thinking with your head," Miller spouted.

Beau's jaw locked and he ground his teeth. His friend was right. "I'm sorry."

"Don't be, Beau. You know I'd do anything for you, but I can't rightly place my boy in danger. Besides, I intend on riding out with you as soon as the plans are all settled. Benjamin will stay with Mrs. Wheelwright." He pocketed his penknife and shoved from the wall. "What about Reverend Scott? He's a former Pinkerton, if you didn't know. He'll get right down to business."

Beau didn't like the thought of Reverend Scott being the man to protect Penelope, but he seemed to have little choice in the matter. "What about one of the Wilsons or Granby? McCullough?"

The Gannon brothers laughed.

"What?"

"Beg pardon, Marshal, but they're either married, toothless or downright cranky." Miller's grin was a little ornery.

"Your point being?"

"Seems to us," Brian said as he motioned between him and his younger brother, "you don't want the handsome reverend anywhere near your wife. Which makes me wonder what you think about me?"

"First," Beau said, glaring at Brian, "you don't want a wife any more than I did, and you'd stay clear of Penelope." He wouldn't bring her flowers or charm her with poetic sentences. How the reverend had survived Pinkerton was beyond him.

"And two?" Miller prodded.

"It's Scott's fault I'm in this mess. If it wasn't for his preaching, I wouldn't have been married in the first place and Jessup wouldn't be using my wife against me."

As he spoke the words, he knew them for the falsehood that they were. He would have married Penelope eventually. How could he not? She was pure and good. Her heart precious and delicate. If anything happened to her, it would devastate the children. And maybe even destroy him.

Chapter Thirteen

A lone lantern flickered in a single upstairs window, welcoming, beckoning him home. If only it was his home and his wife waiting up for him after a long, hard day. After another solid week on Jessup's trail, sleeping on the hard-packed ground, he was ready for a soft mattress and a pillow beneath his head. Even more so, he longed to see his wife.

He stretched his saddlesore muscles and then dragged himself up the stairs. The first night he'd spent under the stars, it had taken everything in him to not race back to Oak Grove. He'd practiced patience and hoped the need to hold her in his arms would dissipate. It had not. The need to taste her lips and feel her slender arms had grown only stronger with each passing moment.

Thunder rumbled across the sky and lightning flashed in the distance. Another day, a time before he'd held Penelope in his embrace, he would have been content with making his bed on the earth's floor. He would have kept on his prey like a hound on a squirrel and welcomed the wakening downpour. However, tonight, at the first sign of an incoming storm, he gave up his search for Jessup and made for the Winterses' home. The coming tempest was but an excuse to see his bride.

To see to his wife and assure himself she was well.

Beau fished the key from his pocket but found the door remained unlocked, which unsettled him a great deal. He'd have to remind Judge to be more vigilant. He wondered if the door had remained unbolted the night the flower had been deposited in Penelope's room.

He hung his hat on the coat tree and made his way to the room he'd taken whenever he stayed with the Winters. He swung the door open and found three children's blond heads glistening in the dim lamplight. He strode across the floor and gazed upon the sleeping boys. Harvey's furry head popped up from Mark's chest, and Beau smiled to see the pooch giving some extra attention to the boy. Beau wasn't certain why Mark hid within himself, but he was glad to see him peeking out of his shell a bit, and he had a sneaking gut suspicion it had a lot to do with Penelope and even the four-legged critter curled up with Mark.

Beau's heart ached to gather them in his arms and hold them tight against any more cruelty the world thought to offer them. He remembered back to his conversation with Penelope. She had been right; he needed to do all he could to protect them as well as himself. They couldn't lose another parent, not well before time called an end to his place on earth, or Penelope's.

He turned the wick down until the room was completely dark. He slipped out of the room and eased the door closed. He made his way to the next guest room and opened the door. His beautiful wife slouched in a wing chair next to the window where the lantern remained lit. She'd waited up for him after all. Or at least tried. Her hands were relaxed in her lap, her eyelids firmly closed. Soft snores filtered into the air. He unbuckled his gun belt and laid it in the top drawer of the dresser and then hung up his vest before gathering his wife into his arms. She was taller than most women of his acquaintance, but she weighed no more than a feather. She snuggled against his chest. Her soft silky curls teased his neck. He drew in her scent and had a sense of home. A sense of home like he hadn't had since before he'd left his parents' house, and that had been before the War Between the States.

He gently laid her on the bed and drew the covers to her chin. She mumbled and curled onto her side as she sank into the mattress. He longed to lie beside her and hold her in his arms, tight against his heart. He no longer wanted to keep distance between them. He wanted to kiss her mouth, and not to just seal a vow made between them in front of God and church. However, he was exhausted to the bone. He sank into the chair, kicked off his boots and stretched out his legs. His gaze stole to his sleeping wife. Her hand curved beneath her chin. Her shoulders rose and fell with her even breaths. Peaceful, serene. Graceful. She was a lady through and through, deserving of things he could not give her, but in that moment, he knew he'd done the right thing, marrying her.

He kept his gaze upon his slumbering wife until he drifted off to sleep.

* * *

Penelope stretched her arms above her head and then curled into a ball and snuggled deeper into the covers. A strange yet familiar scent tickled her nose. She drew in a breath. Dusty. The horse had a distinct smell, like hay and fresh air. What was he doing in her room? Beau? Her sleepy haze cleared from her mind. Her eyelids flew open.

The soft glow of the lamp illuminated her husband, making him seem like a figment of her imagination. She stared, afraid if she moved, he would disappear. Her gaze roamed over him. He reclined in the wing chair by the window, his stockinged feet kicked out in front of him, his ankles crossed. She watched his chest rise and fall for several moments. Her eyes shifted to his jaw and to his high cheekbones. She stole a breath and blinked. Her husband was a beautiful man—not just ruggedly handsome, but beautiful.

A flash of lightning, accompanied by a snap of thunder, startled her. She hated storms. Always had, even as a child. She'd spent many nights huddled beneath the covers, quaking in fear as the tree branches scratched at her widows while rain and hail tormented her with their presence.

Beau jumped from the chair and bent over her. "Shh, darling." His hand settled on her head and smoothed down her hair. "You're shivering. It's just a storm."

"I know." She hated the way her voice shook. She disliked the display of weakness. "The children?"

"Are fine. They have Harvey to comfort them."

Oh, just as she had had many tempestuous nights.

The little beast had no fear and had often brought her comfort whenever it had chanced to storm.

"Scoot over," he said as he pulled back the covers and sat on the edge of the bed. She did as he bid, and before she knew what he was about, he had her in his arms. His chest a firm yet comfortable pillow. "Are you all right?"

"Yes," she said without a moment's hesitation. It wasn't even a bit strange being held so closely to this man. In a matter of days, she'd learned to crave his presence, like she did her morning tea and evening reads by lamplight.

His hand stroked her hair, welcoming her to snuggle deeper into his solid warmth. His lips caressed her forehead and she sensed his caring nature. She sighed.

"Are you all right?" he asked again.

She didn't trust her words. How could she tell him that she'd never been better, and yet at the same time, she'd never been so scared? Unfortunately, the storm had nothing to do with her fear but with the feelings stirring in her being for him. Feelings she'd never experienced before and didn't know how to lay claim to. Worse, what if this man who'd shown her more care and consideration than anyone ever had was acting only out of his good nature and not because he actually cared for her? She feared the emotions overwhelming her and the questions begging to be answered. Would it destroy her when she discovered the truth? After all, her own father had found her of so little value that he'd tried to marry her off to Mr. Wallace, an act that would certainly have led to her demise.

"I'm right here, darling. I'm not going anywhere."

She took some comfort in his words. Their vows bound them together, until death parted them. At least she prayed so. But would that change when she told him about Mr. Wallace?

Chapter Fourteen

Penelope glanced at herself in the mirror and then gripped the doorknob. She stopped in her tracks and took another look in the mirror. She shifted her gaze over her eyes, her nose, her mouth, her long, slender fingers. Her waist. Something was different. However, she could not put a finger on it. She seemed lighter.

Unfettered.

She leaned in closer and drew a finger over her eyebrow and down her cheek until her hand met the collar of her dress. The harsh lines etching her face for so long had eased. Her mouth was no longer tense and her brow no longer stressed from the constant stoical demeanor she'd been taught from nursery. All seriousness had evaporated like the morning dew beneath the sizzling sun.

She pulled in a breath as she held her palm to her stomach. She was almost—dare she say?—fetching. Perhaps not like the beauties strolling the ballrooms she'd been forced to endure to further her father's business ventures, but she wasn't displeasing, as she'd once believed. She had a feeling that it had something to do with Beau.

Oak Grove seemed to be agreeing with her appearance, which was fine by her. She didn't miss St. Louis. Not even a little. Now, where had her husband gone off to? When she'd first woke, she had believed she'd dreamed his comforting presence, but his scent lingered on the pillow beneath her head.

She left the room and made her way down the stairs and into the kitchen. Beau sat with Judge at the small table, and Bobby Jean stood over the cookstove.

"Good morning, darling."

"Hello. My apologies for oversleeping."

Beau's chair scraped against the floor as he rose. He meandered toward her. "No need to apologize. The storm disrupted your sleep."

The corner of her lips eased upward. "Not while you held me. Thank you, Beau."

He kissed the tip of her nose. "My pleasure. Now, Bobby Jean has been anxiously waiting to share her latest recipe and I need to be off. The rain halted our search last night, but we have an idea where Jessup might be holed up."

Dismay weighed her shoulders down, but she nodded.

"Are you overly disappointed?" he asked her.

"Of course I am. However, I understand. I cannot pretend you didn't have a life before I arrived in Oak Grove, and I should not expect it to halt due to my arrival."

"Penelope, as soon as Jessup is back behind bars, I promise to take some time for you and the children."

She shook her head. "There is no need."

He cupped her jaw and held her gaze. "There is. I should have known my wife fears storms and needs the comfort of my arms." He teased her again.

"You had no way of knowing."

"I intend to learn all there is to know about my wife, Penelope."

Her ears burned as images of Mr. Wallace pressed into her mind. Jessup was not the only threat to her new family. "There are things I need to share."

He touched her nose with the tip of his finger. "Can it wait until I return?"

"Of course."

He leaned in, kissed her and bid the Winters farewell. She turned and watched her husband exit the kitchen and then stared out the window as he rode off into the early morning light.

"Beau tells me he promised you a cup of hot cocoa and failed to carry it out," Bobby Jean said. "Would you like to take some with me in the garden before I begin my daily chores?"

"Oh, the chickens. I'd forgotten about them." For nearly two weeks she hadn't paid them one thought. "Who has been gathering the eggs?"

"Several of us have been taking turns checking them."

That bit of information concerned Penelope. "What if Mr. Davis goes to the house?"

Judge scooted his chair from the table. "That is our hope, dear."

"I hope no one gets hurt." Most certainly not Beau. What concerned her even more was Mr. Wallace.

"The boys know what they're doing, and they know Jessup. It won't be long before his arrogance gets him caught. Mark my words."

Bobby Jean swept from the cookstove and toward her husband. She kissed his rosy cheek. "Enough business, Judge. I'm stealing Penelope away for a time. We have a party to discuss."

Penelope tilted her chin and considered her new friend. "A party?"

"Yes, once all of the nastiness with Davis is complete, we must celebrate your marriage to Beau."

She chewed on her bottom lip. "I don't think that is a good idea."

Bobby Jean scooped up a tray of hot cocoa and beckoned Penelope to follow as she walked past her. "Whyever not? I think it is a splendid idea."

Her friend might like parties, but Penelope despised them, especially when she promised to be the focus of attention. The dinner parties she'd been forced to attend were spent sandwiched between chatty gentlemen who lacked social graces as much as she had or were spent in awkward silence. On occasion, a host would place her between gentlemen who were far more superior to her, just to make fun and have lively gossip over Penelope's many faux pas. Eventually she learned to ignore the senseless chatter and pretend she was not bothered by it. "I should speak with Beau first."

"Nonsense. He is occupied." Bobby Jean laid the tray on a small table between two outdoor chairs before she sat. "Now, isn't this lovely?"

Penelope perched on the edge of a seat and took the cup of dark cocoa offered to her. "It is. My father's gardens were sparse. He cared little for the expenditure, although I dare say his gardener's house rivaled our neighbors' and is larger than Beau's cabin."

"Is your father a kind man?"

The rich, sweet chocolate slid down her throat. It was delicious. She stared at soft white blooms basking in the morning sun and took another sip. "I fear I do not know my father enough to say. He was not unkind. However, our relationship was never anything more than business."

"Dear, I am sorry."

"No need to be, my friend." Penelope blew the steam from her chocolate. "I did not know any different and, therefore, do not miss what I did not have."

"And your reason for responding to an ad when you so obviously could choose a gentleman from your ilk?"

Her smile slipped. "It was not so easy as that. Father wished to use me for gain, which is common and would have been acceptable had there been a willing man. Except I fear I lack beauty. So much so my father's fortune was not enough to entice a marriage proposal."

Bobby Jean gasped. "Certainly that is not true."

She considered her new friend and wondered how much she should tell her. "Not entirely. There was one man. A widower."

"That is not so horrible."

"No, that in and of itself is not. But to the best of my knowing, he had five wives and more children than anyone knew for certain."

"The best of your knowing?"

She tugged her lip between her teeth and drew in

a slow breath of air. "Some say he may have had as many as ten."

"My, and your father approved?"

"It was business."

"Am I to assume you left before the wedding?" Bobby Jean's warm hand touched her arm. "I don't mean to pry, but Beau means a great deal to us."

"I understand." She did not wish to confide in her friend any more than what she had, not before she'd spoken to Beau. "Yes, I left before the vows were spoken."

"Are you certain you don't want a party?"

She did not wish to disappoint her friend. Once Beau found out about Mr. Wallace, would there even be a marriage to celebrate? "Not until things are settled."

Bobby Jean beamed. "Most certainly."

Mrs. Danner poked her head through the open door. "Judge says we've company and asked for some tea in his library."

Bobby Jean rose from her chair and glanced down the front of her gown. "I am a mess."

"Allow me." Penelope jumped to her feet. "Serving tea is one thing I am accustomed to doing."

"Are you certain?"

Penelope was pleased to help her friend. "Yes, it will take no time, and then I'll meet you in the kitchen for my next lesson in cooking."

Bobby Jean embraced her and pecked her cheek. "Thank you."

Penelope gathered the tray and made for the kitchen. She added two new cups to the tray and refilled the white porcelain kettle with hot water. She followed the sound of men's voices and pushed the door open with her hip.

Judge rose from his seat. "Hello, dear. I have to say I'm disappointed my lovely wife did not attend us. She is a sight for these old eyes and warms my heart like the morning rays. Mrs. Garrett, may I introduce you to my guest, Mr. Wallace?"

Penelope swallowed. Her ears roared. Certainly, she had not heard correctly. The man rose from the intricately carved chair and turned toward her with his hand stretched out. The tray in her hands wobbled. The cups clanked against each other. Air rushed into her lungs, stinging the back of her throat. She coughed and sputtered. Hot water splattered down the front of her gown, right before the tray fell from her hands and clattered to the carpet.

Gunshots jerked Beau from his sleep. He spun away from his bedroll and ducked behind a tree. He scanned his surroundings, basked in early morning light, and found Miller crouched behind a rock while Brian took shelter behind a tree. Another gunshot echoed through the valley and the bark of a nearby pine exploded, a fragment piercing his cheek. He lowered his hat to shield his eyes and then peered from his hiding place. Light flashed with another blast, this one hitting Miller's rock. Seeing Brian creep along the left flank, Beau darted from the tree in an attempt to distract Jessup. It worked. Two shots hit the ground, one in front of him, one behind him. He rolled back to the tree.

For a moment, there was silence. He noted two things in those seconds. First, Jessup was a better marksman than he'd first believed, and second, the scoundrel obviously wasn't looking to harm anyone.

"Jessup! Give yourself up and let's talk about this."

"Marshal!" Brian hollered from where the shots had been fired. "There's nobody here."

"How can that be? He was just shooting at us." Beau rose to his full height and cautiously peeked from behind the tree. Early morning light eased across the hills like warm honey on a biscuit. He shifted his gaze for any moving being. "He has to be here somewhere."

"All that remains is a campfire and four bedrolls," Brian called.

Beau slapped his hat against his thigh. Jessup wasn't alone? No wonder he'd been able to frustrate their efforts at finding him. He had help. Beau and the Gannons had been so close. If he would have kept on instead of getting distracted by thoughts of Penelope, maybe they would have captured the rotter. Beau shook his head and ground his teeth together. He shouldn't be upset with himself. It was natural for a husband to let his mind wander to his wife on occasion. However, it hadn't been the most opportune moment. In fact, it had been the worst moment possible.

"Miller, scout the area for tracks," he snapped. "If they stumbled on our camp and were caught off guard, they may have made haste and been careless."

"Yes, Marshal."

He ate up the distance between him and Brian and glared at the camp. The fire was cold. The beds freshly rumpled. Beau shook his head. "What are your thoughts, Brian?"

"Seems to me we've been bamboozled."

"Seems that way." Beau lifted his head to the sky. "In all the accounts of Jessup's antics, not one indicates anyone besides Jessup. A lone man."

"Maybe that's because the others didn't make themselves known. Or maybe there is only Jessup and this camp is a deception."

"What do you make of that?" he asked, pointing at an abandoned blue ribbon.

Brian shook his head. "Think he has a gal with him?"

"Possible. I suppose it could be a joke."

"I don't think so, Marshal." Brian knelt near the end of the bedroll where they'd seen the ribbon. "From these prints, I'd say there is a person of a delicate sort, perhaps a lady. By the looks of things, she's wearing serviceable shoes, yet they have a small heel on them."

Beau pursed his lips as Penelope's footwear came to mind. He had yet to get her appropriate shoes, which meant she was still doing household chores with dangerous heels. What sort of woman would make camp with criminals?

He inspected the area. Four cups, four plates piled, four sets of utensils. The bedrolls were crude and threadbare, except one. Beau knelt beside the bedding. It was new. Recently bought. Or stolen. Although Beau didn't figure Taylor's General Store carried as fine a fabric as what covered this bedroll. Come to think of it, Jessup had held up the general store. Still, it was a question to ask Taylor. For some reason, he didn't see Jessup caring whether or not he had a soft cushion to rest his bones.

A thick cigar caught his eye. The end had been neatly cut, not sawed off with a blade. Beau picked up the rolled tobacco and sniffed. Not the kind that could be found in Oak Grove. This cigar was the sort purchased in a big city and cost a good deal of coin. Whoever had been here with Jessup wasn't accustomed to sleeping outdoors. And what of the owner of the blue ribbon? Had she been accustomed to the outdoors? Was she a servant at this man's beck and call? Perhaps even another pawn?

Something burned at the edge of Beau's thoughts. Was Jessup a pawn in someone else's devious scheme? When had Jessup's law-breaking activities escalated? Only recently had he robbed the general store and then the bank. Crimes that had accelerated since the railroad men came to town. The expense of the cigar fit with their tailored coats and slicked-back hair. He poked through some of the belongings near the head of the fancy bedding. A leather satchel had fallen over, spilling some of the contents on the ground. Beau's heart plummeted to his stomach when he spied several dried petals sprinkled atop a pamphlet. The petals were browning along the edges, but they came from the same flower Penelope had found in her room. He swept his hat from his head and slapped his thigh. Hot air blew from his nose. He had a feeling this was no longer about Jessup tormenting him but rather something more sinister.

He picked up the pamphlet with an engraving of a cathedral. The words St. Louis Cathedral were scrawled below. Wasn't that where Penelope was from? He scratched his head beneath his hat and then unfolded the paper.

Mr. Karl Wallace
&
Miss Penelope Prudence Parker

He didn't need to read the rest. He knew what it was. The date printed there was only a month before Penelope's arrival in Oak Grove. He crumpled the paper in his fist. What was going on? Had he been duped? Or was his bride on the run?

He pocketed the cigar and the wedding announcement. He choked down the knot forming in his throat and then raked his hand over his face. How could he have been so gullible? Again. He should have learned his lesson long ago, that pretty ladies were dangerous.

However, he hadn't lied when he'd told her he was a fair judge of character. There wasn't a deceiving bone in Penelope's body. Not intentionally. He knew that for certain. She was as pure and sweet as his own mother. Sweeter than Bobby Jean. Which meant she'd come to Oak Grove on the run, and by the looks of it, she was running from a man who was dangerous.

He stood up and barked an order to Brian. "Wait for Miller to return. See what you two can gather from the camp. I've got to go."

"Where arc you going?"

"Home." He needed to see his wife. If she was even legally his wife. And if she wasn't, well, then he'd arrest her for polygamy until he could figure out the facts of the matter and see if her marriage to Mr. Wallace could be dissolved, because he had a feeling the man stalking his bride wasn't a nice man.

He strode through the high grass and saddled Dusty. He nudged his boot against the horse's side and rode hard toward Oak Grove.

Chapter Fifteen

Penelope peered through the sheer curtains at the men below. Judge shook hands with Mr. Wallace, and she couldn't help wondering what business they had concluded. She wrung her hands together and chewed her bottom lip. Had Mr. Wallace told him about her? About their relationship? Had he made demands that she return to St. Louis with him?

Mr. Wallace turned to leave and just as she heard the door close below stairs, he swiveled and glanced up at the window. He stared for a hard moment and then tipped his hat. Fear churned in her stomach. Bile stung the back of her throat. She had not experienced such a reaction to him, not even the day she was supposed to have become his wife. Perhaps it was due to the fact that she had not known Beau nor had she known such kindness could come from a man. Now that she did, the revulsion to Mr. Wallace was more than she could bear.

She collapsed onto the thick cushion of the wing chair. How had Mr. Wallace found her? She'd been careful. Hadn't she? Signing her grandmother's name on the ledger when she purchased passages and keeping her face hidden when she'd ventured onto the train. Unless Wren... She shoved her knuckles against her mouth. Had he gotten hold of Wren?

Penelope jumped to her feet and smoothed her sweaty palms down the front of her skirt. There was no other way Mr. Wallace would have found her.

"Oh, Lord, what am I to do?"

Her stomach swam with nausea and she fought to keep her wits about her. If Mr. Wallace had Wren, it would not go well for her friend. If he hadn't harmed her already, he would soon. Penelope had to discover Mr. Wallace's direction. She sank onto the chair again. The only way to find out that information was to ask Judge, which would lead to questions. Questions she wasn't certain she could answer. And if Judge knew about her past, would he chastise her and send her away before she had a chance to explain anything to Beau?

"Beau, I wish you were here. You'd know what to do."

She should have told him from the beginning about Mr. Wallace. However, fear had held her prisoner. She was afraid if Beau knew the truth that he'd send her back to St. Louis and the fate waiting for her at Mr. Wallace's hands. A fate that seemed to have caught up with her.

What was she going to do?

Certainly, he wouldn't harm Wren, would he? Not if she complied with his wishes, which she imagined meant returning to St. Louis with him. Tears welled in her eyes. She did not want to leave Oak Grove and the family she'd come to care for. The children she'd promised not to abandon. Beau.

If only there was another way. She thought again of Beau. Could she wait for his return? He'd been gone for days, and the time before that, weeks. No one knew how long he'd be away this trip, especially since he was bent on capturing Mr. Davis after he'd left the flower in her room.

Her heart jolted to a halt. Had that even been Mr. Davis? Could it have possibly been Mr. Wallace? She stood and paced the room. Had he been in her room, mere inches from her? A hallway across from the children? She shivered, and then anger rushed through her limbs. Mr. Wallace was more dangerous than she'd first believed. Entering a home not his own and leaving her a message. Had she ventured farther into the garden, would he have kidnapped her?

Most assuredly. Her nails bit into the flesh of her palms. She would not stand by and allow him to threaten her family or her friends. And this morning's visit was, no doubt, exactly that.

She could not leave Wren to Mr. Wallace, and she would not allow him to pay another visit here and risk the children. "Oh, Beau! Where are you when I need you?"

Perhaps she could request Judge's assistance in getting word to Beau, but even he didn't know where her husband had taken off to. And she could not trust that Judge and Bobby Jean would not get hurt if they interfered with Mr. Wallace's plans. As long as she heeded his warning, he would leave well enough alone, and maybe even spare Wren, too. All she had to do was to leave the Winterses' house undetected.

She glanced out the window and gauged just how far the house was from the copse of trees. Too far in her current state of dress and heeled shoes. She should have ordered a more practical pair, but time had gotten away. Besides, she hadn't been allowed to leave the Winterses' premises for the very reason she was about to depart. Beau wanted her and the children safe, but now she was about to amble right into the lion's den and there would be no rescue for her.

She sat at the desk and pulled open the drawer. She found a sheet of fine paper and dabbed it with a hint of her rose water. She dipped the quill into the inkwell. Her heart ached as the words bled onto the paper. She left notes for each of the children, and she hoped they would one day understand just how much she truly loved each of them.

She pulled out another sheet and scrawled Beau's name at the top. She sniffed. A tear plopped onto the sheet and collided with the black ink. All those hours of practicing writing her name seemed wasted now. Pain formed in her chest until she thought it would tear her apart. She hiccupped, choked and then a stream of gut-wrenching sobs poured out of her. If only there was another way, but she knew if she did not do as Mr. Wallace wished, her life wouldn't be the only one at stake, and she couldn't risk Beau's or the children's.

The words flowed onto the page as fast as the tears streamed down her cheeks. How could she tell Beau what she didn't even know? Apologies and farewells, and words of love. She stared at the page a long while and then crumpled it up. She yanked another sheet from the drawer and simply wrote:

Dearest Beau,

Please accept my humblest apologies. As it turns out, Oak Grove is not for me. My only wish is that I would have discovered this truth prior to our nuptials. I will pen Judge Winter to see about an annulment. To soften the children's transition, I ask that you care for Harvey.

Yours,
Penelope Prudence Garrett

She wiped the wetness from her cheeks and stared at her penmanship through the tears blurring her vision. She blew across the ink and waved the sheet back and forth. She gathered the notes written to the children and tucked them into the drawer beneath the newer sheets. One day, when she was long gone and back in St. Louis, and perhaps even gone from this earth if Mr. Wallace held true to form, the letters would be found and the children would know that they had been loved by her.

She rose from the chair, slipped out into the hallway and sneaked down the stairs.

Beau jumped from Dusty and took the stairs two at a time. He threw the door open. Judge stood in the foyer, his brow wrinkled.

"What is it? Where is Penelope?"

Judge scratched his beard. "I don't quite know."

Beau stalked toward his friend and mentor. "What do you mean, you don't know?"

Bobby Jean appeared at the bottom of the stairs. "Oh, Beau! I'm glad you're here. She's not in her room."

"She's not in the garden either," Judge added.

"She left this for you." Bobby Jean fished a folded note from her pocket. Her hand shook as she handed it to him.

Beau unfolded the sheet and skimmed the lines. "What happened?"

"Nothing," Bobby Jean said.

Judge cleared his throat. "I'm not certain. I had a visitor this morning. One of the men with the railroad."

Beau clenched his jaw. "Someone please tell me what happened to my wife?"

"Nothing out of the ordinary. We spoke for a bit. Penelope brought us tea, and when I introduced Mr. Wallace to her, she dropped the tray, apologized and ran out of the room."

At the mention of the name, Beau felt his breath seize. "Mr. Wallace? I have reason to believe the man is here to cause my wife harm."

"What makes you say that, Beau? He was quite the gentleman."

"I'm certain he was." Beau jammed his hand into his pocket and handed the crumpled pamphlet to Judge. "He sent a message to my wife. Seems the flower in her room wasn't enough."

"Where did you find this?" Judge asked after reading the pamphlet.

"Jessup's camp. Inside an expensive leather satchel. A satchel surely belonging to a well-to-do gentleman."

Judge squinted. "She deceived you. And us. She's married."

"Yes, to me." Beau growled. "After the time you've spent with Penelope, do you think she is capable of trickery?"

Bobby Jean sobered. "No, of course not. She confided in me about this man. Widowed many times. She feared him."

"You've kept this to yourself?" Judge questioned.

"She confided in me, and I had no reason to believe he would come here. I do not believe there is deception in Penelope. Only uncertainty and fear."

"Are you certain she wasn't already married, Bobby Jean?" Judge asked his wife.

She nodded.

"I agree," Beau said. "I've reviewed every interaction I've had with Penelope over in my head as I rode here. She was hiding something, but I cannot believe she's hiding a marriage. I don't believe she'd insist on wedding me if she was already married. I concluded that she needed our union for protection." He clenched his fists. "A fine right job I've done of it, too."

Just as he'd left Mary Ella defenseless, so he'd left Penelope. He saw his past unfolding before his eyes all over again. This time there had been no words of love for his wife, but he loved Penelope more than he thought possible. He realized now that his love for Mary Ella had been nothing more than a young man's foolish obsession. What he felt for his wife was much more, much deeper.

"I can't believe she would just leave," Judge said.

Neither could he. He glanced at the words Penelope

had written on the sheet of vellum. There was not one single word of affection, but the small blot bleeding through the ink spoke more than any word could. A tearstain. "She didn't. She wouldn't have left unless she had no choice. Not after the trouble she went through of running and hiding from Mr. Wallace."

"What are we going to do?"

"We find my wife."

"Pa!" Matthew and Luke barreled in from the hall with Harvey at their heels.

The pooch reminded him of the letter left by his wife. Was the gift of leaving Harvey behind a selfish act or one of selfless love? The panting, happy beast had eased the children's burdens. No doubt he would relieve the pain Penelope's departure would cause them. If only the dog could ease his heartache, too.

The boys' shouts echoed against the walls. "Pa, we can't find Mark."

Beau's stomach sank to his feet. "Did you check the garden?"

The boys nodded.

"We were playing outside, and then he was gone. I lost him," Matthew cried. He threw his arms around Beau's waist and hugged him. "We looked everywhere, Pa. You've got to find him."

Beau knelt and held Matthew to him. He understood what it was to be the oldest and have the responsibility of the younger brothers. Beau knew the guilt and the turmoil of failing. He would do everything he could to keep Matthew from experiencing those emotions. "It'll be all right. It's not your doing, son. I'll find him."

The front door opened, and for a moment, relief

washed over Beau with the hope it was his wife. But Judge and Bobby Jean's daughter stood in the doorway with her husband. Both pale as moonlight.

"What's happened, Susan?" Beau asked.

"A man—" she started, and then began crying.

"Found one of the railroad men dead on our property." Calvin buried his wife's head against his shoulder.

"Dead?" Judge shouted.

"Shot in the head."

"My son and wife are missing, and now this." Worry and fear ate at his core. "Think they're related?"

"Hard to say, Marshal, but Jessup's horse was near."

"Bobby Jean, get my guns." Judge hitched up his britches. "I've had enough of this business."

Keeping his arm around Matthew's shoulder, Beau rose. "I appreciate the help, Judge, but you're crossing the line and I can't allow that. Allow me to find Penelope and Mark, and then I'll investigate the murder."

"Marshal, I understand you're the law and I'm the judge, but there is a child involved, and family. You won't stop me from assisting you in finding them. I've sat around long enough as it is. The people of Oak Grove and those who visit our fine town will know their judge means business. Calvin, leave Susan here with her mother and take the buckboard and bring the man to town. We'll see to things once we've finished this other business."

Bobby Jean handed a set of revolvers to Judge and then spoke to her daughter. "Come along, Susan. Help me with the children." She grasped Luke's and Matthew's hands. "I'd volunteer to go with you, but I suppose you'd argue someone should stay here and help Matthew guard the house."

"You're supposing right, dear," Judge replied.

Beau dipped his head in appreciation, grateful she had given Matthew an objective. "My appreciation, Bobby Jean."

"I hope you appreciate this old woman's efforts, as well, Marshal." Mrs. Danner swept in with Esther on her hip and head high. Little John followed behind. Some of the tension left Beau's shoulders at seeing John and Esther. Mark was the only one missing.

Beau reached over and kissed his infant daughter's head and hugged Mrs. Danner. "Of course, and there is nobody in all of Kansas more capable of protecting my children."

Mrs. Danner grinned. "I like you, boy, but I'd like you a mite better if you'd fetch your bride and child back to this house faster than a hound on a squirrel."

"Yes, ma'am." He settled his hat on his head and walked outside. Judge's boots sounded behind him.

Beau climbed in the saddle. Dusty danced beneath his anxiousness as they waited for Judge to saddle his mount. If he didn't respect the man and appreciate his help, he would have galloped away. However, he also knew rushing into anything in haste could end badly.

As his patience was about to near an end, Judge rode out of the barn. "You ready?"

Beau nodded and they set off.

"Where should we go first?"

"Church?"

Judge glanced at him. "I'm a praying man, Beau, but I don't think now is the time to seek the altar."

"No, sir," Beau said through his clenched teeth. "Reverend Scott will be of some help, and if I know the First Congregational ladies, they'll be gathered for their weekly meeting, and they'll get word out quickly."

"Smart man. That's one reason I suggested the city hire you."

"I'm certain it didn't hurt that I'm kin."

"Not at all. But don't think for a moment if I thought you were a scoundrel that you would have the job." Judge spat. "What are your thoughts on Mark?"

"I assume Mr. Wallace took him." Wasn't that why Penelope had left, to rescue Mark? Beau pulled up on the reins. Judge halted beside him. "Are you thinking something different?"

"We need to consider the scenarios. Think like a marshal, not a husband and father, Beau."

His mouth flattened. Judge was right. He should be thinking with his head, not his heart. "One, Penelope went after Wallace to save Mark." He didn't want to believe she'd left on her own. He didn't want to believe that she'd left with a crooked man because he could offer her a better home. "Two, Mark followed Penelope."

Judge leaned against the pommel and looked Beau in the eye. "Three?"

Beau's eyebrows rose. "Is there a three?"

"Wallace took them both?"

Leaves rattled with the wind. Beau watched them for a moment, praying the truth would rain down. "If that were so, then why did Penelope leave a farewell note?"

"Maybe he coerced her into writing it." Judge's white mustache twitched. "He did enter the house undetected and deposit a flower in her room."

Beau should have been there. He should have stayed with her and allowed Miller to search for Jessup.

"Don't let your mind wander, Beau. Don't think I haven't thought the same. I could have protected your family better."

A slow breath eased from Beau's lungs. "No, Judge. They're mine. I should have been there to safeguard my family. It was my responsibility. Not yours."

"A responsibility I agreed to take over while you captured Jessup."

"Which I failed to do."

"And now we know why. He's had an accomplice."

"I'm not certain Jessup wasn't the accomplice. At this point, I'm not sure Jessup killed that railroad man either, even if what Calvin says about the man's horse being close by is true."

"You're thinking Wallace is the one in charge?"

"I am not certain. But I do believe he is using Jessup to get to Penelope."

"And you think he used Mark to gain her cooperation?"

His heart didn't wish to believe anything else. His mind told him he needed to consider the possibility that she had left on her own accord and that Mark was hiding in a corner like he did on occasion. "I honestly don't know, Judge. I wish I did."

Chapter Sixteen

Penelope walked down the boardwalk with her head high. She smiled at the ladies and gentlemen as she moved past them as if nothing were amiss. Yet all the while, she kept an eye out for Mr. Wallace. If he wanted her, she'd make sure he'd see her and come get her. However, she hoped to make it home first. To Beau's home. To the pistol lying in the top dresser drawer neatly tucked beneath Beau's shirts. During her flight from the Winterses', she had come up with another idea. One that could possibly keep her in Oak Grove, even if it meant being arrested by her husband.

Her stomach swam with nerves and fear. What if she froze when she saw Mr. Wallace, as she'd done in Judge's library? What if she didn't make it to the cabin on the other side of town?

The hair on her nape rose, and she glanced over her shoulder. Not ready to face her future yet, she ducked into Taylor's General Store. She smiled at Mr. Taylor as she entered. Several bolts of colorful fabric lay on a table. The bright yellow called to her, reminding her of sunshine and happiness. Reminding her of Esther.

"Hello, Mrs. Garrett, what can I do for you today?"

She was pleased the owner recalled her name. She'd met him once, before she'd been kept like a princess locked in a tower. "Hello, Mr. Taylor. May I get this?" she said handing him the fabric. "Do you have a pair of boys' suspenders and a belt?"

"Aah. A young man has trouble keeping up his britches."

The bell on Taylor's entrance jingled, causing Penelope to jump. She froze and then glanced behind her. She breathed a sigh of relief when she spied a lady and her child entering through the door.

"Is everything all right, Mrs. Garrett?" the proprietor asked her.

She pasted on a smile. "Yes, of course."

"Is there anything else?"

She picked out random gifts for each child and a particularly nice one for Beau, along with scented soaps that smelled like spices. "Do you have a sheet of paper so I may leave a note for my husband?"

Mr. Taylor's white bushy brows furrowed. "You don't wish to tell him?"

She shook her head. "It's a gift."

"I see," he said, handing her brown paper and an inkwell. "It is so nice to see a young couple in love."

The feather pen stilled in her hand. Love? Did she love Beau? She chewed on her lip for a moment. The vast emotions swirling through her heart said she did, and very much so. Did Beau love her? She didn't think so. How could he? He'd married her only to save his family from scandal. Of course, she had married him only to save her life, which was all for nothing. She hadn't expected Mr. Wallace to arrive in Oak Grove so soon, or even at all. She hadn't thought he'd find her.

"Thank you, Mr. Taylor. It is nice to be in love." She paid for her purchases. "Can you wrap these and have them delivered to the house?"

Mr. Taylor looked at her over his spectacles. "You don't want to take them with you?"

"No, sir. As I said, they are gifts. Delivery is fine." She pulled money from her reticule and then turned to leave but quickly halted when she spied a can of coffee next to sugar and flour. The cupboards had been lean before they went to stay with the Winters. Beau would need supplies when they returned. "May I apply funds to Mr. Garrett's account?"

"That is quite unusual, Mrs. Garrett, but of course. How much will you be applying?"

She pulled a few notes from her purse and handed them to Mr. Taylor. By the rise of his eyebrows, she could tell he was surprised. "For leaner times. I'm trying to be prepared."

"Yes, of course. That is always a good idea."

"Thank you, Mr. Taylor." She was grateful he didn't pry into where her funds had come from. It was no secret Beau did not earn an income as marshal and that he often took side jobs, cutting wood and doing other odds and ends for folks in Oak Grove.

She nodded to the lady and child, peered through the window of the front door and then slipped outside when she did not see Mr. Wallace. The bank caught her eye and another thought came to her. She walked across the street to the edifice and was thankful to find no patrons inside. She approached the barred window and smiled at the clerk. "Hello, I would like to deposit funds into my husband's account."

"Of course, Mrs. Garrett. Are you on the marshal's account?"

"I do not believe so. As you know, my husband has been hunting down the criminal who robbed your bank. I'm certain he hasn't had time to attend to business." Beau rarely had time to even say hello to his family.

"I understand. Our policy does not allow for deposits from those not on the accounts."

Penelope blinked. "I do not see what the problem is. I am not withdrawing funds. I'm adding to them."

"I understand, Mrs. Garrett."

Desperation gripped her. "Look, I am in a bind, and I need to leave this in my husband's account so that he may feed our children in my absence." She slapped the money onto the counter. "Now, if you do not wish to have a substantial deposit, I can take my business elsewhere."

"Of course, Mrs. Garrett. I can make a concession this time, if you are willing to state in writing that you will not hold the bank responsible if you attempt to retrieve your funds."

She refrained from rolling her eyes. It wasn't as if she would be in Oak Grove to 'retrieve her funds,' but the clerk did not know that, therefore she could not blame him. "I will do as you ask."

The banker handed her a sheet of paper and an inkwell. She'd spent more time composing notes this day than she had while living in St. Louis. She scrawled her name at the bottom and was even more grateful that she'd practiced penning her name during her travels.

"Would you like a receipt, Mrs. Garrett?"

"There is no need, sir." The receipt would remind her of Beau and the children. It would remind her of everything she'd left behind and the great deal of happiness she'd had for such a short time. Something in her chest broke, and she hiccupped on a sob. She demanded the tears keep from falling. It wouldn't do for the townsfolk of Oak Grove to see her crying only moments before she left or was arrested.

Penelope exited the bank and drew in a deep breath of air filled with dust and horse. Now that her purse was lighter, she could meet Mr. Wallace.

As she walked down the street, she drank in another breath and committed to memory the clapboard buildings lining the main thoroughfare of Oak Grove. She would miss this place with the cleaner, fresher air, and the skyline free of so many buildings and smokestacks.

"Mrs. Garrett?"

Penelope turned and eyed a young man in short pants and suspenders. "Yes."

He handed her a note and then took off running. She looked up and down the road, inspecting the shadows between the buildings. She unfolded the paper, and as she read the words, her heart clutched. It was as she had feared. Mr. Wallace had Wren and wanted her to meet him near the Belfry Monument. She tucked the note into her reticule and fought back the tears She could do that but not without arming herself first. She glanced over her shoulder and then headed toward the small shanty she'd called home.

* * *

Beau nudged Dusty and headed toward the church. As he suspected, he found Reverend Scott and the ladies at the church. Scott agreed to ride out and get the Gannons. The ladies agreed to gather a posse and have them meet Beau in an hour's time.

Beau turned on his heel to leave as Judge finished giving instructions to Reverend Scott.

"Marshal." Mrs. Wheelwright beckoned him. "Is everything well with Mrs. Garrett?"

His eyebrows dipped together. "Why do you ask?"

He and Judge had opted not to inform the church ladies that Penelope was missing, too, only Mark. They had hoped that upon finding Mark they would find Penelope and save her from another wildfire of scandal.

"I saw her walking into Taylor's General Store not too long ago. She looked pale. However, I suppose if my child was missing, I would not feel so well either."

Beau attempted to stop her rambling, but she kept going. He would have rushed out of the church if he didn't think she might have something more pertinent to say.

"Even so, I do not think I would go to Taylor's to shop unless I believed the boy had gone there, too."

"Why did you not say something earlier?" He thrust his hands onto his hips.

"I did not know it was of consequence."

"No, of course not." His jaw twitched in time with the pounding headache forming in his temple. "Judge."

His friend shook Reverend Scott's hand and followed Beau outside, where Beau told him what Mrs. Wheelwright had said.

"She was at Taylor's?" Judge questioned. "What on earth for?"

"I suppose we should find out." Beau jumped onto the saddle and raced Dusty toward the general store, not waiting for Judge to mount his own horse.

When he reached the shop, Beau burst inside. Several patrons gasped. He found Taylor helping a young man with some candy.

Beau took in a calming breath and strode across the floor. "Have you seen my wife?"

Mr. Taylor motioned to a pile of brown paper packages. "Nearly half an hour past. She purchased gifts for you and the children. I was just about to have them delivered."

"Delivered?"

"Yes, she left specific instructions to have them sent to your home."

"Am I to assume she went there?"

"I would have no way of knowing that, Mr. Garrett. Although I did happen to see her enter the bank."

Beau nearly knocked Judge over as he left the general store. "I'm heading to the bank."

Judge lengthened his stride to keep up. "I have to admit, Bobby Jean has often left me perplexed over her actions, but nothing of this sort. What is your wife about, and where is Mark?"

"That is what I intend on finding out."

He pushed through the door and found the banker behind the window.

The man's mustache twitched. "Marshal, I was about to send a note to the jail."

"A note? From my wife?"

"Not exactly." The man stammered, and Beau couldn't believe he had even considered playing match-maker between the banker and Penelope. "Well, I guess so."

"Yes or no?"

The note shook in the man's hand as Beau snatched it from him. "What is this?"

"A receipt."

Beau snapped his gaze to the banker. "For?"

"A deposit, as it says at the top there." At Beau's silence, the man continued, "In your account."

"What does this have to do with my wife?" Beau stared at the amount. It was a year's worth of income, if he kept busy with the odds-and-ends jobs he'd taken on.

"Mrs. Garrett made the deposit."

"My wife did this?"

"Yes, Marshal."

"Beau," Judge said. "We can figure this out later. Right now, we need to find Penelope."

Beau swallowed the knot in his throat and nodded. He turned to leave and then stopped. "Has anyone else been here since my wife?"

The banker shook his head.

Once they stepped into the hot sun, Beau adjusted his hat. "Where now?"

"The hotel? The saloon?"

"Does any of that make sense?"

"It does if she's looking for Mr. Wallace."

"Why?"

"She acts like a lady saying goodbye and leaving farewell gifts, Beau."

He knew this, but he didn't like it. "Mark?"

"It is my hope he is safe and hiding from his brothers."

"Mine, too."

"But if he is, then why would Penelope leave the safety of your home and venture into danger?"

"Marshal," a young man approached him. "You looking for a pretty lady with black hair?"

"I am." Beau fished a coin from his pocket and tossed it to the youth. "What do you know?"

"I was given a note by a man to give to her. Uppity sorta fella."

Beau tossed another coin at the boy.

"Didn't sit well with me once I gave it to her, so I followed her."

"And?"

"Well, she took off to a rundown shack on the edge of town. Walked in like she owned the place."

Beau glanced at Judge. "Home. She went home."

The boy shook his head. "I don't know about that. Her place don't look like she belongs there."

No, Beau supposed the lad would not think so, but she did. It was her home. Their home. "What about the man?"

"Can't rightly say, Marshal. Made my skin crawl. Didn't follow him none."

"Thank you for your help, son."

The boy grinned, black teeth and all. "Least I can do, Marshal. You rescued my sister."

"Where can I find you?"

"Not proud to say, Marshal, but you ask for Cain at the saloon. They'll know where to find me."

Judge clapped the boy on the shoulder. "I'm right proud of you, Cain."

"Thank you, sir."

Beau shook the boy's hand and then made haste to Dusty. Now that he knew his wife's location, he had hope he would find her and his son. Before Mr. Wallace did.

The house wasn't far, but the time it took to get there took too long. He felt punched to the gut when he saw a wagon tied to the hitching post out front. Had they arrived too late?

As Penelope approached the cabin, the tension left her shoulders. A sense of safety cloaked her. She entered the home and made straight for the bedroom. She tossed her reticule onto the bed, shed her jacket and gloves, then opened the drawer and slipped her hand beneath Beau's shirts until her fingers brushed against the weapon. Relief warred with nerves. Judge had taught her how to shoot, but aiming at a target was quite different than aiming at a man. Could she do what it took to protect herself and save Wren?

She slipped the gun into her pocket and left the bedroom. The sight of Mark stopped her dead in her tracks.

"What are you doing here?"

"I wanted Pa. I wanted to come home. I miss it here."

"Oh, Mark." She knelt in front of him. "Your pa is out chasing a bad guy right now."

"What if something happened to him? What if he don't come home like my real pa?"

Besieged by emotion, she gathered him in her arms

and hugged him. More so than anyone, she understood the pain and fear racking the boy. She pulled back to look him straight in the eye. "You like Judge, right, and believe what he says is true?"

Mark nodded. "Judges can't lie. That's what Matthew said."

"I believe your brother is right. Judge said your pa is the finest lawman around. The best, even. He'll catch Mr. Davis and will be home sooner than you can imagine." She only wished she'd be here when it happened. "First, we need to get you back to the Winters' home."

In haste, too. She needed Mark far from her before she met Mr. Wallace at the Belfry Monument. She couldn't risk him using this child who'd taken up residence in her heart, along with his siblings and his adopted father.

The door kicked open. A dark shadow loomed in front of her, but by the lack of height and the girth, she knew it wasn't Beau. It was Mr. Wallace!

She pushed Mark behind her. "Run!"

Her heart sank when the back door burst open to reveal Jessup Davis. Mr. Wallace in front of them. Mr. Davis behind them.

"Run, get help." She shoved Mark toward the bedroom, but Jessup snagged Mark's collar before he crossed the threshold.

"Don't you dare touch him," she cried.

"And what are you going to do about it?" Mr. Wallace asked as the back of his hand collided with her cheek.

Stars lit up Penelope's vision. She stumbled backward and collapsed onto the floor. She pressed her hand to her face to quell the throbbing and glared up at Mr. Wallace. "You're despicable."

"I've heard that before, Penelope, but if you'd heeded your father as you should, we wouldn't be here, would we?"

"Let the boy go, and I'll return to St. Louis."

"Your actions have left me without funds. You have forced me to rob a bank and lower myself to associate with guttersnipe like Mr. Davis. I will not be showing you grace or mercy, my dear." Mr. Wallace tipped his chin toward Mr. Davis. "Take him out by that useless girl. You know what to do."

"No!" Penelope jumped to her feet and darted toward Mark as she slipped the gun from her pocket. Not wanting to risk Mark's life, she aimed at Wallace and pulled the trigger. He gripped his shoulder as he howled in pain. She aimed toward Mr. Davis, hoping to get him to release Mark, but he tumbled out the back door, taking the boy with him. *No!* Distracted, she didn't see Mr. Wallace advance till she felt the sting of his hand on her cheek again. He snagged her upper arm, his fingers biting into her flesh through the fabric of her gown. He jerked her against him, and the pistol hit the floor. His foul breath forced a gag from her. "Leave him be. Let Wren and him go. They've done nothing wrong."

"That maid of yours caused me a lot of problems, Penelope. She's going to pay. As for the boy, well, let's just say what happens to him is your due penance. Be thankful I leave the rest of the children alone."

Tears filled her eyes. What had she done? She'd thought to save her life by answering Beau's mail-order-bride ad. Instead she'd risked the children. "Please, let them go."

"I'm afraid I can't do that."

If only Beau was in town and not chasing Jessup Davis in the hills. If only he'd followed the villain here. *Oh, Lord, please let it be so. For Mark's and Wren's sake.*

She heard the pounding of hooves and tried to jerk her arm from Wallace's grasp. He peeked out the curtained window and grinned. "Looks like I'll get to make you a widow, Penelope."

The toe of her shoe slammed into Mr. Wallace's leg. He stumbled and loosened his grip. She tried to scramble away, but he snagged her by her hair. "If I didn't want you to see me kill your husband, I'd knock you out cold."

"Am I to assume once our vows are said and my inheritance is in your grasp, I'll meet the same fate?"

He met her with silence and a cold, hard stare, but she wanted to know the truth. "Is that how your previous wives died, Mr. Wallace? At your hand?"

"That is none of your business, gal." He tugged her by the hair as he took another look out the window. "Now keep your trap shut or you'll be dead, too."

She had to think of something. She couldn't let him hurt Beau, or Mark, or Wren. This was all her fault. If only she'd stayed in St. Louis and walked down the aisle as she should have instead of running from certain death, none of the people she cared for would be in their current predicament.

"I'll do whatever you ask. Please."

"We've already ascertained that isn't happening, Penelope. And when we do make it back to St. Louis, you're going to play like all is fine or your father will be next."

Beau had heard the gunshot and jumped from Dusty and started for the front door when Judge grabbed his shoulder. "Don't rush this."

"That's right, Marshal," a man he assumed was Mr. Wallace sneered as he stood shadowed in the doorway behind Penelope. A gun to her head. "Don't rush this."

"Beau?" Penelope croaked, her eyes wide with fear. "Mark's in the barn with Je— Ow!"

She cried out when Wallace pulled her hair.

Beau took a step forward, but Judge held him back with a hand on his arm. He slid a glance to Judge. "He's hurting her."

"Your gal is tougher than you give her credit for. If she wasn't, she wouldn't have risked the punishment and warned you about Mark."

Beau clenched his jaw and eyed the barn.

"As long as he's away from Wallace, he's fine," Judge whispered.

"Can we be certain? Sounded like she was about to say Mark was with Jessup."

"Possible, but I have my doubts Jessup will hurt a child." Judge shook his head. "But if we move, we risk her."

Beau took off his hat and glanced toward Wallace. "What do you want?"

"Just to leave town, Marshal. No harm will come to the boy or to Wren."

Beau's eyebrow jumped. "Wren? Who is Wren?"

"My friend." Penelope winced as Wallace jerked her closer.

"I see I wasn't the only thing you kept from the marshal."

Beau's gaze flitted to Penelope, and as it did, he spied movement behind the brute holding her. Brian and Reverend Scott skirted the barn, while Miller opened the back door and Mr. Taylor climbed through the bedroom window. Several other men from the town surrounded his home.

Relief washed over him, but he tried not to show his emotions to Wallace.

"Judge Winter, how about the annulment so my wife and I can leave. As soon as it is delivered, I will release my hostages."

"I don't think I can do that, Mr. Wallace."

"And why not?"

"Let *my* wife go," Beau said between clenched teeth, letting the man know exactly whose wife Penelope was.

Wallace must not have liked what Beau had to say. He jerked Penelope backward by the hair and pointed his gun at Beau.

"Pa," Mark hollered as he ran from the barn with a bloodied lip and ropes dangling from his wrists.

Helplessness overtook Beau. Fear unlike he'd ever known, even in the midst of battle in the War Between the States, assailed him. He froze, unable to choose between throwing himself between his son and Mr. Wallace's weapon and trying to save his wife from the hands of a deranged man.

Just then, a young woman ran after Mark, coughing. Smoke billowed from the barn, separating like a drawn curtain when Brian and Reverend Scott opened the doors and dragged out an unconscious Jessup between them.

Wallace's gun shifted from Beau to Mark, and Beau's heart nearly stopped.

"No!" Penelope screamed as she slammed her elbow into Wallace's ribs. But Wallace sidestepped her, and Beau watched in horror as he dragged her into the house. The shouts and screams hastened his stride as Beau darted toward the house.

Before he could reach the porch, gunfire erupted. Beau ducked but continued on, not caring if he was shot. All that mattered was getting to his brave wife, who stumbled out the door and fell to the porch, a pool of red forming beneath her shoulder. His heart lurched. His past was repeating itself, and he had no one but himself to blame. He never should have left her alone. Never should have married her. He crouched and crept along the side of the house. He peeked through the window. Where was Wallace? Was he near Penelope and waiting to cause her further harm?

"Got him," Miller called out a moment before he stepped out the front door, tugging along a bleeding Wallace. A gunshot through his arm was the cause. Beau gritted his teeth, but he was thankful the man was alive and far from his wife. Better to have his day in court than meet his death.

"You shot him?" he asked Miller.

"No, he was already shot when I went in. Think your lady got him."

Beau knelt beside Penelope. His fingers smoothed back her hair, revealing a bump and a purpling eye. His need to hold her in his arms won over the rage trampling his veins. He pulled her onto his lap and cradled her against his chest. A red stain soaked her dress and grew larger with each ragged breath. He watched the base of her neck for a pulse. "Penelope, darling, please be okay."

Her ice-blue eyes fluttered open and focused on him. "Beau." She gasped in pain. "Beau, I'm sorry. I should have told you."

Yes, she should have. "Not now."

Her lids slid shut and fear quaked his heart.

"Penelope! Penelope, darling."

Judge's shadow encompassed them. "Let's get her to Doc."

"You know I didn't want a wife," he said, looking up at his friend. "I never should have married her."

"Beau." Judge gave him a steely eye. "Now's not the time. She needs the doctor."

"I can't move." The stillness in her limbs triggered hopelessness. Her rough, shallow breaths took him to another place, but he couldn't mark the differences. Mary Ella had betrayed him and their country. Her selfishness had seen her demise. Penelope had been selfless, risking her life to save Mark. To save him. She'd bravely taken on Wallace without thought for her safety. "She's been so brave. She tried to protect us when I'd failed to protect her."

"Marshal," Judge snapped as he knelt in front of him and pressed his handkerchief to Penelope's wound. "We have to get her to Doc."

Judge groaned as he scooped Penelope's slight body

from Beau's arms. "She don't look like much, does she?"

"She isn't much, Judge. Your bones are catching up with your white beard." Beau climbed to his feet, dusted off his britches and took his wife from Judge. He glanced toward Wallace with a narrowed gaze.

"This isn't over," Wallace spat. "If she would have obeyed her father none of this would have happened. Her inheritance should be mine. It's all her fault I had to rob that measly bank and she'll pay for those actions. And as soon as she is my wife, she'll pay for shooting me." He smirked. "If she survives."

"I don't think so, Mr. Wallace." He gazed down at his wife's pale face as he strode to the waiting buckboard. She was *his* wife. Penelope Prudence Garrett, and the mother of their children. He wasn't letting anyone take her away, not even death, if he could help it.

He climbed onto the seat.

"Pa, I'm coming." Mark jumped into the back and leaned over his shoulder. "Say she'll be all right, Pa. She can't leave us, too."

"I know, son," he said, cupping Mark's head in a hug. "I don't have that say. Only the Lord does."

"It's all my fault, isn't it? Just like when my pa died."

Beau stared at this boy. They shared the bond of blood, and now he sensed a stronger bond in the empathy he had. Beau had been so caught up in his own guilt and grief that he'd failed to realize the children might feel the same. "You're not to blame, Mark. You're just a child."

"It's 'cause I got sick that my real pa was out riding

after the doctor. It's because of me he fell off the horse. And now Penel—Ma might die, too."

Judge released the brake and slapped the reins. Penelope moaned when they jerked forward. A red blotch soaked her gown and the handkerchief he pressed to her shoulder. Tension knotted Beau's stomach. He'd seen men shot. He'd seen them die. He never expected to sit by his wife as she fought for her life. He couldn't lose her.

"Mark, only the good Lord knows when we'll take our last breaths. It wasn't your fault your pa died. We've got nothing to do with people dying unless we pull the trigger, which you didn't. Your mama gave up her life to give Luke life and she would have done it all over again, and for you and Matthew, too, because she loved you boys, and she loved your pa. You and Matthew and Luke were her gifts to him, to carry on his name and his character. Matthew looks just like him, but you carry him, too, Mark. In your quiet caring, you carry him. Now, suppose he wouldn't have gone out after the doctor. Esther and John would not have received treatment in time and their young little bodies wouldn't have been able to fight the sickness like you had. You getting ill saved your brother and sister. You didn't kill your pa. You didn't hurt Penelope either."

Mark sniffed. Tears streaked down his dirty cheeks. "Penelope wouldn't have left the judge's house if it hadn't been for me."

If that was the case, why did she meander about town instead of going right after Mark? "Son, it might seem that way, but trust me when I tell you she didn't know you were missing. Although I have no doubt Penelope would have gone after you if she'd known."

"It's not my fault, Pa?"

"No, Mark. It's not."

If it was anyone's fault, it was his for not being there to protect his family. He knew they were in danger. It's why he'd taken precautions. However, they hadn't been enough. He should have known and been more vigilant. He should have realized Jessup wasn't smart enough to rob a bank on his own. His obsession with Jessup had distracted him and made him lose focus. His desire to be home with his family and his new bride had him thinking with his heart. Not his head. "She'll be all right, Mark."

She had to be. The well-being of his family depended on it. He lifted her against his chest and held on to her. Words left unsaid clawed at his throat, urging to be voiced, but he couldn't do it. What if he spoke them and the good Lord saw fit to take her anyway? Expressing his emotions would cause only greater pain, and he didn't think he could bear that.

"Just another few moments, Penelope," he said, and then kissed her brow, uttering a silent prayer.

Chapter Seventeen

Pain ripped through Penelope's shoulder as she tried to stretch. Pungent smells assaulted her nose. Bile rose in her throat. She jerked upright and cried out in pain before collapsing back onto the pillow.

"Penelope?"

She rolled her head. Wren sat in a wing chair with her feet curled beneath her. What was Wren doing here? Were they back in her father's house? She glanced around the room and tried to gain her bearings.

"Wh-where are we?" she croaked. "Water?"

Wren rose from the chair and poured water into a cup. She helped Penelope sit up and pressed the rim to her lips. "You're at the judge's house."

"What happened?" Penelope asked after she'd taken a sip.

"I should get your husband," her friend said.

Penelope shook her head. "My husband? Beau?"

"Yes. Mr. Garrett."

"He's here?"

"Hadn't left yer side in two days, till Mr. Judge insisted he get some rest. Said Marshal wouldn't do you no good if he was grumpy as a badger when you woke."

"I see."

"He only left after I promised to fetch him soon as you did. Guess I better do just that."

"Wait," she said, trying to push up once more, but her body rebelled, and she collapsed back to the mattress again.

"The doctor gave you some medicine." Wren's hand settled on the doorknob. "I best get the marshal. I wouldn't want to go to jail for disobeying."

"He might get cranky, but I don't think he'd do that. Although he might lock you in the henhouse." Penelope attempted a smile and then patted her hand over her hair. "How do I look?"

"Like you've been shot."

Penelope gasped and glanced down at her gown. A small pink spot stained the pristine whiteness. Memories flooded her. She'd been shot by Mr. Wallace. Jessup Davis had been there, too. Another image flashed into her mind. Mark had been in the house when she'd exited the bedroom. "Mark?"

"He's been pacing the hall like a caged animal."

"He's fine?"

"Yes, Miss. Right as rain. Just fretting over you a bit much."

Penelope twisted her fingers together. "Will you send Mark in before you fetch Beau?"

Wren nodded. "You've a right fine gent, Nell. Handsome, too."

Penelope warmed at Wren's pet name for her. "Thank you, Wren."

"Much finer than Mr. Wallace."

"Wren, draw the drapes open, please."

Her friend did as bid but kept her head down as she turned to leave. "I'll be going now."

"Wait," Penelope said as she pulled herself to a sitting position. "Did Mr. Wallace hurt you?"

Wren shook her head and slipped through the door.

Before it closed, Beau rushed into the room, and fisted his hands on his hips. "You're awake?"

She pulled in a breath and was met with the smell of fresh coffee and the scented soaps she'd purchased for him. She closed her eyes, afraid to see the disappointment in his eyes. "I'm sorry, Beau. If I would have known—"

"Stop."

She looked at him. "Beau, it's my fault Mark was in danger."

"No, darling. It was Mr. Wallace's fault that Mark was in danger and that you were nearly killed." A muscle in his jaw ticked as he stared into her eyes. "I do wish you would have told me about him, then much of this could have been avoided."

A hot, wet tear rolled down her cheek. "I'm sorry."

The edge of the bed dipped beneath his weight. He gathered her hands in his and gazed into her eyes. "Do not apologize for this again. I admit I don't quite understand the workings of the female mind, and, darling, yours seems to run overtime in perplexing me, but I do not blame you for Mr. Wallace's doings."

"Thank you, Beau."

"None needed. Wren told me about Mr. Wallace's previous wives and their mysterious demises. She's a fierce protector of you, Penelope." The corner of his mouth quirked up. "I'm thankful that you had the wits and fortitude to run from that union before it was formed. And I'm right proud of you for attempting to protect yourself and shooting the scoundrel." He released her hands. The mattress sprung up as he rose. "You must know I've sent for your father."

Air left her lungs. "Beau, why?"

What did that mean? Was he sending her back to St. Louis? Did he not want her as his wife?

"He'll be here as soon as he can to fetch you." His Adam's apple bobbed.

Her heart pounded in her chest. An ache worse than her gunshot threatened to tear her asunder.

"I don't understand." Was he angry over her deception? How could he tell her he didn't blame her and then send her away?

"It's only right, Penelope." He clenched and unclenched his hands. The tears in her eyes mocked the weakness threatening his resolve. She'd married him for protection, and he'd failed her. Just as he'd failed Mary Ella. Now that Mr. Wallace was locked up where he belonged, she was no longer in danger. She was safe and she could marry a man suitable to her needs. Someone who could offer her chandeliers and candlesticks. Someone who wouldn't stand by as another man shot her.

His mind hadn't been set until he walked in and saw her with the quilt tucked around her waist. The red stain soaking her gown was like a fist to the gut. She deserved more than he could offer her. She needed a husband who could safeguard her.

"I can do better, Beau."

"You've done enough." It was all he could manage not to pull her into his arms and bury his face into her neck and beg her for forgiveness. She'd been perfect, selfless and courageous. Without fear, she'd almost sacrificed herself for the sake of Mark. For him.

He risked a glance at her and nearly gave in to the need to hold her. To lock her up and keep her by his side. He nodded, turned on his heel and gripped the doorknob.

"What about the children?"

Her question stopped him, but he did not turn. "They are resilient, Penelope. They will be fine."

He walked out, shut the door and hung his head as he leaned against the solid wall. The boys would be all right. They'd understand. He'd make sure of it, and eventually, they would laugh and smile again. He wasn't too certain about himself though.

"You all right, son?" The scent of tobacco filled the hall, and Beau knew Judge had been out in the garden, contemplating the right words to say. The garden was where Judge often went to smoke his cigar and think over the problems of Oak Grove or how to deal with an upcoming case. The fact that Beau was the center of his thoughts unnerved him a little.

Beau shuddered and drew in a breath. "I will be, Judge."

A strong, heavy hand clasped his shoulder. "Did you ask her what she wanted, or did you make a decision based on your own thoughts?"

He shrugged and looked Judge in the eye. "My

thoughts on the matter don't have much to do with it, Judge. Fact is, she almost died."

"A bullet to the shoulder didn't quite almost kill her, Beau." He shook his head. "Now, that's not saying I don't understand. If that had been Bobby Jean, I no doubt would have felt the same, purely helpless, purely foolish and full of blame."

"That about sums it up." Right along with a runaway wagon full of thoughts. He wanted her to stay, but if he loved her, and he did, he couldn't let her. He had to make her go. Penelope remaining in Oak Grove would only see her killed. And he couldn't live with himself if that happened.

"Still, a wise man would ask his wife how she felt about the matter." Judge dropped his hand to his side. "She is your wife, Beau. For better or worse, until death do you part."

That's what scared him, the death-parting-them bit. Seeing her injured. The smell of alcohol as her wound was cleansed. Her cries of distress. Falling unconscious and writhing in pain as Doctor Harden dug out the bullet. He couldn't do that again, especially the hand-wringing, pacing agony of waiting her for to open her pretty blue eyes. "I don't know, Judge. Guess we'll have to be better or worse hundreds of miles apart. She can't stay here."

He'd rather send her away and wonder how she was doing than see her shot. And as long as he was a lawman, she would be in danger.

"What about the children, Beau? Are you going to send them away, too?"

"Why would you suggest such a thing?" Beau asked.

Had his friend lost his mind? He knew what he'd gone through at the hands of those with good intentions. "I'll find them a proper nanny."

"They need a mother."

"They have one—" Beau clamped his mouth shut. "It's not fair to goad me into a losing argument, Judge." Not when he was vulnerable and ready to throw his hands up in surrender. If things were different, he'd keep her by his side until they grew old and gray, but they weren't. He was a marshal. He put bad guys in jail. And as long as there were men out there like Jessup Davis and Karl Wallace, he'd spend long days in the saddle and long nights under the stars, leaving her alone and vulnerable to whoever chose to take advantage of the situation. Just as Wallace had.

"They're in as much danger as she was, Beau. When are you going to realize Wallace wasn't your doing?"

"If I hadn't been obsessed with Jessup, Wallace wouldn't have gotten close to her."

"You don't know that, Beau."

"Everyone was vigilant, and she was careful, too."

"Until she wasn't. He used the goodness and kindness of her heart against her."

"Yes, he did."

His shoulders sagged. "I didn't want to be saddled with a wife in the first place."

"No, most men don't think they want a wife until they get one. Then they just don't know how to get along without her."

Beau wouldn't allow that to happen. He'd experienced grief. He could get on just fine minus Penelope. One foot in front of the other. "My mind is made up,

Judge. As soon as her father arrives, she's going back to St. Louis."

"That could take weeks."

"I am aware of that fact." He scratched his beard. "I'm taking the children home. Will you allow her to remain here until her father arrives?"

"I reckon so, Beau, but I don't like it, and I'll not reel Bobby Jean in if she gets it in her head to interfere again."

"I imagine she'll be sore enough to not speak to me for a time." Which was fine with him. He was itching for some alone time with the children. "With Jessup behind bars and nearly confessing to murdering the railroad man over a disagreement things seem to be tied up for now. I'm considering visiting my parents. It's about time they met their grandchildren. Miller will see to keeping the law while I'm gone."

"Running will get you nowhere. You should know that better than anyone."

"I appreciate the reminder, Judge, but the visit is past due."

"I understand. Will you at least allow your brood to say their goodbyes to Penelope before you leave?"

Beau nodded.

Judge rocked back on his heels. "You're not thinking about quitting the law, are you?"

He shook his head. If he even considered it, he wouldn't send Penelope away. He'd keep her and hover over her every waking moment. "No, I'm a lawman. I'll always be a lawman."

"Don't forget, Beau, you're a father and a husband,

too, which should take precedence over a career that doesn't pay to keep bread in your belly."

"Respect my decision, Judge. I didn't want a wife, and I still don't."

"That doesn't change the fact that you have one."

Beau grunted. "Don't you think I know that? We'll get an annulment and be done with the business. She'll go back to St. Louis to her high society life and I'll go back to my humble home." And he'd be fine, better than fine, even. She'd no longer be his responsibility and he would not be met with failure. And he would never again leave his heart vulnerable to another woman. Not as long as it was owned by Penelope, which would be until his dying breath.

Chapter Eighteen

Penelope shuffled from the door and climbed back beneath the covers. She buried her head into the pillow and sobbed. She should have stayed in St. Louis. She wouldn't know this ache ripping her apart from the inside out. A pain much worse than the gunshot in her shoulder. She should have married Mr. Wallace, then she would have never known what it was like to care for Beau and the children.

The door clicked closed, and Penelope halted her sobs as the scent of fresh-baked bread and warm coffee wafted into the room.

"Are you all right?" Bobby Jean whispered.

The sobs renewed. Her shoulders quaked.

"Oh, Penelope." The bed dipped as Bobby Jean sat, then she took her hand. "I am sorry. I have half a mind to chase after Beau and give him a good piece of my mind."

"No." Penelope rolled over and swiped the tears from her eyes. "Has he left the house?"

"I believe he has." Pity filled Bobby Jean's eyes.

"I'm only sorry that man is too hardheaded to realize his own heart. He's running scared."

Penelope eased to a sitting position. "Scared? Why would Beau be scared?"

Bobby Jean stood and smoothed her hands down her apron. "It's not my story to tell. However, you should know the full of it before you heed his wishes and leave Oak Grove when your father arrives."

"I don't know, Bobby Jean. If he wanted me to know, he would have told me."

"If you had a chance to do this again, would you?"

Penelope gulped. "The chance to never know this pain? I would not."

"The chance to know love?"

"Love? Is that what this is, this agonizing pain at the thought of never seeing him again?" The suffocating clutch in her lungs that almost prevented her breath? The fear of never seeing him smile or laugh or sense the thrill of seeing him walk in the door after days of waiting for him to come home? Never feeling his fingers tuck a loose strand of hair behind her ear or his lips take hers in a kiss? *Oh, Lord, how will I survive this?*

"I'm afraid so, Penelope."

What sane person would do this all over?

"Never would I do this again." She clutched her fist to her chest as she hiccuped on a sob. "I would have rather married a man like Mr. Wallace and risked the horrible fate he intended for me than experience this terrible emotion."

If only the ladies of her acquaintance who often bemoaned their arranged marriages understood the trouble their parents had saved them, they would be eternally grateful. She would now forever be a voice for arranged marriages. Love had no place in a woman's heart. Not among the upper classes. They were too delicate by nature to sustain such a devastating blow. She was too delicate, by far. And yet she had survived being shot.

"Unfortunately, dear, the loving comes with heartache." A pensive look flitted through Bobby Jean's eyes. Had she experienced this hurt deep in her heart? Had Judge been the cause? "I believe the pain may help us realize just how deeply our love goes."

Thinking on the exact moment she knew without hesitation that she loved Beau, only moments ago, she knew her friend might be right. She straightened her spine and locked her typical cool reserve in place. "I cannot admit my love for Beau, not to you, to him or even to myself. Doing so will destroy me, and I have fought too hard to survive."

Bobby Jean closed her eyes and nodded. "At least hear me out, Penelope. Before the war, Beau fancied a neighboring girl. They courted. Our families believed a marriage would soon be in the works. Then the war broke out and Beau joined the cause along with Judge, Reverend Scott and the Gannons. Mary Ella followed the boys and found herself enamored with the enemy."

"Why would she do such a thing?"

"She was a foolish young girl. Vulnerable and gullible. Beau paid her no attention when she sought it. You see, he's always been about duty first. It's who he is. It's how he is made. Unfortunately, duty to his country and to his town wars with his duty to the family."

Penelope laced her fingers together. "Which is why he left us here without hesitation."

Bobby Jean nodded. "Except he hesitated, and he returned often. He did not do the same with Mary Ella. And when she accused him of compromising her, he denied her claims and refused to marry her."

Penelope gasped. "Why would she do such a thing?"

"She wasn't only taken with the enemy, she was caught spying."

"Oh, no! And Beau?"

"He didn't know about it until it was too late. Several of his men were killed and Beau was nearly hung for treason. Judge vouched for him, as did the Gannon brothers. Evidence was brought forward proving Beau had no part in the matter."

"Thank the Lord," Penelope breathed.

"Yes. However, he didn't walk away unscathed. You see, Beau comes from a family much like yours. Like mine. Reputation matters more than a man's character, and Beau's father nearly disowned him when he refused to marry Mary Ella for scandal's sake. His widowed brother, in dire want of a wife, stepped in instead."

"Oh." Now she understood Beau's need to wed her and to keep scandal from touching the children. They'd already been subjected to so much. How would their annulment affect the youngsters? How would her leaving Oak Grove? "I see." She slipped from the bed and began pacing the carpet runner.

"Beau blamed himself for not protecting her. He blamed himself for not sending her home to her father when she first arrived at their camp." Bobby Jean's lips flattened. "He blamed himself for her death, even though it was due to a severe case of melancholy after the birth of Esther. And worse, he blamed himself for his brother's demise. You see, Beau may not have been disowned by his father, but his brother was in order to punish Beau, because he knew the way to hurt Beau was through Zach and the boys. When Mr. Garrett realized Zach went and married Mary Ella, he forced him from their family home and with very little funds. What monies were available were only allowed if Beau severed all communication with his brother."

"Poor Beau."

"Don't pity him any more than you wish to be pitied. Don't get me wrong, Mr. Garrett has always been a kind man and loved Beau and Zach. He was right proud of Beau for joining the war, too. Mary Ella's father was his friend, and Beau refused to argue his position when she accused him of those awful things. So when Beau refused to marry her, his father believed the worst but only because Beau kept everything bottled up inside. He was still reeling from the death of his friends and the trial and the fact that he'd been betrayed by the woman he'd thought to marry."

"I don't pity him, but now I understand why he wishes me to leave. I deceived him, just like Mary Ella."

"Up until two months ago, he's had no family. He's kept himself guarded and closed off from every female he has encountered since Mary Ella, but he let you in, Penelope. The deception has nothing to do with him wanting you gone. He wants you to leave because he feels responsible for almost getting you killed. He wants you to leave because he loves you and refuses to see anything bad happen to you. He wants you to leave because he is scared of losing you."

Penelope's brow wrinkled. "I don't understand. Isn't he losing me by sending me away?"

A smile curved Bobby Jean's mouth. "Seems silly, doesn't it? Which is why I felt you needed to know Beau's story."

"What should I do?"

Bobby Jean gripped Penelope's hand. "That is up to you, but do you love him?"

Penelope swallowed past the knot in her throat. Her friend was asking her to acknowledge the one thing she knew would destroy her if she admitted it. She bobbed her chin. "Yes. Yes, I do love him."

"Then you stay and you fight. And you prove to that hardheaded, stubborn mule that you are no simpering female to wilt beneath a lead ball in your shoulder."

"It does hurt, but it won't kill me." Penelope grinned. "I can see you have an idea, my friend. What do you have in mind?"

"How about planning that party to celebrate your marriage to Beau?"

Penelope stared out the window. She wanted to stay and win Beau's heart, and if Bobby Jean was right, she already had. However... She nibbled on her lip. What if her friend was wrong and Beau didn't want her, as he'd so adamantly told Judge? Could she handle the disappointment and the pain?

She turned to her friend and shrugged. "I don't know, Bobby Jean. I just don't know."

Halfway to Onion City, a mere thirty minutes into their journey, Beau regretted leaving Penelope. The downpour outside the coach had nothing to do with his change of mind. If it hadn't been for the other passengers and the tight time schedule, Beau would have had them turn around. He drew lazy circles on Esther's small back as she slept. John curled up beside him and slumbered, too. The three older boys alternated between lazy yawns and glares that could stop a mangy dog in its tracks.

Since the moment the conveyance jerked forward with the group of sullen-faced children, he knew he'd made a mistake. They missed her. He missed her. Gravy, he loved her. A fact he'd known for some time. Since the night of the storm when he'd held her.

However, it wasn't until this very moment that he realized that leaving her and sending her back to her father was not a great act of love on her behalf. It was cowardice. Pure and simple. He didn't think he could relive the fear of watching her fight for her life. Relive the idea of losing her. But wasn't that what he was doing by running?

By gravy, the first chance he got, they were heading back to Oak Grove. His parents and reconciliation could wait. He needed to stop Penelope from leaving Oak Grove.

He'd disappointed the children. He'd disappointed himself. By the time they arrived in Onion City and procured a conveyance back to Oak Grove, would he be too late to stop Penelope from leaving? He hoped not. He loved her. He knew that for certain now. And he knew sending her away wasn't the way to prove his love to her. It was a shame it had taken him so long to figure it out. If only he could have made up his mind before he'd packed the children and loaded them onto the coach.

Another thirty minutes would tell him how long it would be before they could go back to Oak Grove. Then he'd tell the boys his plan. He'd tell them they would chase their ma all the way to St. Louis if need be. Beau leaned his head against the upholstered seat and closed his eyes.

Murmurs from the driver and shouts from outside alerted Beau. The conveyance increased speed. Were they about to be held up? He sat up and looked out the window. Several horses chased after them.

He heard the sound of gunfire, and his arms tightened around Esther.

"Halt!" came a man's voice that sounded oddly familiar.

The coach continued, and from the window, he saw a pair of horses speed past, one with two riders colored in a flash of white. One was a female with distinctive black curls. Beau's pulse beat furiously and he pounded on the roof. "Stop," he shouted to the driver.

"What are you thinking?" a gentleman said from his corner. "You want us to get robbed?"

"That's my wife out there."

"Ma!" The boys tumbled over each other to look out the window.

"You've a wanted man inside," Penelope shouted.

Beau narrowed his eyes. What was she doing?

The wheels rolled to a stop, and as the door swung wide, the boys jumped to the ground. Beau handed Esther to the lady sitting across from them and dipped through the opening. Penelope released her hold from

Miller and swung a leg over the horse. She half fell to the muddy ground. She righted herself and appeared from around Dusty.

Beau kept his smile in check and shook his head. "What are you wearing?"

She crossed her arms and pursed her lips. "You don't like it? I did it just for you, Marshal."

"Pa's underwear!" Luke doubled over in laughter.

"And his gun belt," Matthew added.

"Is that your badge, Pa?" Mark leaned closer to make certain.

Sure was. Beau turned to the other riders. He looked from Miller to Brian.

Brian shrugged and Miller quirked his lip. "Talk to Judge. He made her marshal two nights ago."

"A female marshal?" Beau narrowed his eyes at her. "What's going on, Penelope?"

"Judge made me acting marshal. Figured it was the only way to get these men to do my bidding." She nodded toward the Gannons.

"What's this about, lady?" The driver shouted from his seat. "I've a schedule. Thought there was a wanted man on board."

She smiled up at the man. "I've no doubt, with your abilities, a few moments will cost you very little time, sir."

The man puffed out his chest and blushed from the compliment.

"This man is wanted." Penelope pointed at Beau. "And I've been given authority by Oak Grove's judge to bring him back."

"In my long underwear?" Beau asked.

She leaned forward. "Well, I am a practical woman, Marshal. I did what I thought necessary to grab your attention."

"That it has." He slid out of his coat and draped it around her shoulders. "And everyone else's." He looked at the Gannons. "I'll have your hides for letting her do this."

Miller guffawed. "As if we could stop her. She's a mite stubborn."

"I wouldn't have it any other way," Beau said. "Now, what are the charges? Why am I wanted?"

"Well, Marshal, it's like this. Seems you've stolen my heart."

His chest thumped. "What's that?"

"I love you, Beau Garrett," she said, and then glanced at the ground. "I hope you can love me, even though I can't cook or wash clothes. Even though I cause a scandal. I can't promise to be the perfect bride, but I will do whatever I can to protect our children and our home. And I will love you until my dying breath."

He reached for her and tugged her into his arms. "Oh, darling! You might not be the perfect bride by most standards, but you're my perfect wife. I love you, Penelope, and I always will."

He leaned in and kissed her, and then quickly pulled back. "Shall we go home?"

"Only if it's to our humble cabin, Beau." She grinned up at him. "I want to go home, our home."

"My pleasure, darling. My pleasure."

* * * * *

LOVE INSPIRED

Stories to uplift and inspire

Fall in love with Love Inspired—
inspirational and uplifting stories of faith
and hope. Find strength and comfort in
the bonds of friendship and community.
Revel in the warmth of possibility and the
promise of new beginnings.

Sign up for the Love Inspired newsletter
at **LoveInspired.com** to be the first
to find out about upcoming titles,
special promotions and exclusive content.

CONNECT WITH US AT:

Facebook.com/LoveInspiredBooks

Twitter.com/LoveInspiredBks

Get 4 FREE REWARDS!

We'll send you 2 FREE Books plus 2 FREE Mystery Gifts.

Love Inspired books feature uplifting stories where faith helps guide you through life's challenges and discover the promise of a new beginning.

FREE Value Over **$20**

YES! Please send me 2 FREE Love Inspired Romance novels and my 2 FREE mystery gifts (gifts are worth about $10 retail). After receiving them, if I don't wish to receive any more books, I can return the shipping statement marked "cancel." If I don't cancel, I will receive 6 brand-new novels every month and be billed just $5.24 each for the regular-print edition or $5.99 each for the larger-print edition in the U.S., or $5.74 each for the regular-print edition or $6.24 each for the larger-print edition in Canada. That's a savings of at least 13% off the cover price. It's quite a bargain! Shipping and handling is just 50¢ per book in the U.S. and $1.25 per book in Canada.* I understand that accepting the 2 free books and gifts places me under no obligation to buy anything. I can always return a shipment and cancel at any time. The free books and gifts are mine to keep no matter what I decide.

Choose one: ☐ **Love Inspired Romance**
Regular-Print
(105/305 IDN GNWC)

☐ **Love Inspired Romance**
Larger-Print
(122/322 IDN GNWC)

Name (please print)

Address _____ Apt. #

City _____ State/Province _____ Zip/Postal Code

Email: Please check this box ☐ if you would like to receive newsletters and promotional emails from Harlequin Enterprises ULC and its affiliates. You can unsubscribe anytime.

> Mail to the **Harlequin Reader Service:**
> **IN U.S.A.:** P.O. Box 1341, Buffalo, NY 14240-8531
> **IN CANADA:** P.O. Box 603, Fort Erie, Ontario L2A 5X3

Want to try 2 free books from another series! Call 1-800-873-8635 or visit www.ReaderService.com.

*Terms and prices subject to change without notice. Prices do not include sales taxes, which will be charged (if applicable) based on your state or country of residence. Canadian residents will be charged applicable taxes. Offer not valid in Quebec. This offer is limited to one order per household. Books received may not be as shown. Not valid for current subscribers to Love Inspired Romance books. All orders subject to approval. Credit or debit balances in a customer's account(s) may be offset by any other outstanding balance owed by or to the customer. Please allow 4 to 6 weeks for delivery. Offer available while quantities last.

Your Privacy—Your information is being collected by Harlequin Enterprises ULC, operating as Harlequin Reader Service. For a complete summary of the information we collect, how we use this information and to whom it is disclosed, please visit our privacy notice located at corporate.harlequin.com/privacy-notice. From time to time we may also exchange your personal information with reputable third parties. If you wish to opt out of this sharing of your personal information, please visit readerservice.com/consumerschoice or call 1-800-873-8635. **Notice to California Residents**—Under California law, you have specific rights to control and access your data. For more information on these rights and how to exercise them, visit corporate.harlequin.com/california-privacy.

LIR21R2

IF YOU ENJOYED THIS BOOK
WE THINK YOU WILL ALSO LOVE

LOVE INSPIRED

INSPIRATIONAL ROMANCE

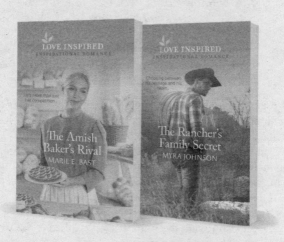

Uplifting stories of faith, forgiveness and hope.

Fall in love with stories where faith helps
guide you through life's challenges, and discover
the promise of a new beginning.

6 NEW BOOKS AVAILABLE EVERY MONTH!

SPECIAL EXCERPT FROM

LOVE INSPIRED
INSPIRATIONAL ROMANCE

He needs a housekeeper. She needs a job.
This holiday season, will they join forces—
and find true love?

Read on for a sneak preview of
Her Christmas Dilemma *by Brenda Minton.*

"We need a housekeeper because I can't chase you down every other—" Tucker suddenly remembered they had an audience. "We can talk about this at home."

Nan, spritely at seventy with short silvery hair, grinned big and inclined her head toward the other woman.

"Clara needs a job," she said.

"I don't think so," Clara shot back.

"You need something to do," Nan insisted.

"She doesn't want the job." Tucker winked at the woman and watched her cheeks turn rosy.

Flirting was an art he'd learned late in life, and he still wasn't too accomplished at it. He'd never been a ladies' man.

"No, I really don't," she answered. "I'm only here temporarily."

Should he feel relieved or let down?

"You should introduce us," he told Nan.

"Tucker Church, I'd like you to meet Clara Fisher," Nan said. "She's one of my kids."

One of Nan's foster daughters. She'd had a dozen or more over the years. He held a hand out. "Clara, nice to meet you."

It was a long moment before Clara slid her hand into his. Then she stepped back, putting space between them.

LIEXP1121

"Nice to meet you, too. But I'm afraid I'm not interested in a job." She gave his niece a genuine smile, then her gaze lifted to meet his. "I think that we probably met in school, but you were a senior and I was just a freshman."

He couldn't imagine forgetting Clara Fisher, with her dark brown eyes that held secrets and a smile that was captivating. He found himself wishing he could make her smile again.

Shay elbowed him. "She doesn't want the job," she whispered. "Can we go home now?"

"Of course she doesn't want to work for us. She's probably heard the stories about you running off two housekeepers." He gave Clara a pleading look.

"Would you take my number? In case you change your mind?"

"I won't change my mind," she insisted.

He had no right to feel disappointed. She was a stranger. And yet, he was.

"Well, we should go," he said as he walked Shay toward the door.

"I bet she can't even clean," Shay said under her breath.

He didn't disagree. But Clara looked like a woman who was trying to put herself back together. He needed someone strong who could stand up to Shay.

The woman who replaced Mrs. Jenkins couldn't have soulful brown eyes and a smile that made him want to take chances.

Don't miss
Her Christmas Dilemma *by Brenda Minton,*
available December 2021 wherever
Love Inspired books and ebooks are sold.

LoveInspired.com

IF YOU ENJOYED THIS BOOK, DON'T MISS NEW EXTENDED-LENGTH NOVELS FROM LOVE INSPIRED!

In addition to the Love Inspired books you know and love, we're excited to introduce even more uplifting stories in a longer format, with more inspiring fresh starts and page-turning thrills!

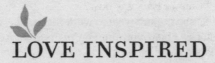

LOVE INSPIRED

Stories to uplift and inspire.

Fall in love with Love Inspired—inspirational and uplifting stories of faith and hope. Find strength and comfort in the bonds of friendship and community. Revel in the warmth of possibility, and the promise of new beginnings.

LOOK FOR THESE LOVE INSPIRED TITLES ONLINE AND IN THE BOOK DEPARTMENT OF YOUR FAVORITE RETAILER!

**With her family's legacy on the line,
a woman with everything to lose must rely
on a man hiding from his past...**

Don't miss this thrilling and uplifting page-turner from
New York Times bestselling author

LINDA GOODNIGHT

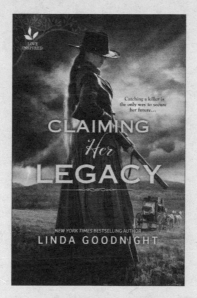

"Linda Goodnight has a true knack for writing historical Western
fiction, with characters who come off the pages with life."
—**Jodi Thomas**, *New York Times* and *USA TODAY* bestselling author

Coming soon from Love Inspired!

LOVE INSPIRED
LoveInspired.com

LI41876BPA